"I can't live like this," I said aloud, half hoping someone would answer me back, prove me wrong. But there was only silence. Teeth clenched, I pressed my palms against my eyes, trying to block out the terrible thoughts I couldn't keep at bay. They pulled me inexorably down a dark road I knew would not end well.

"I should be dead, not them," I whispered into the darkness. "It should have been me." *Maybe I should just kill myself,* I added silently, unable to say the words out loud.

"Ahem-hem. Excuse the intrusion, but that's codswallop, that is."

I yelled, and yelled loud. The voice had come from somewhere above me, and in my panicked attempt to get away I fell forward onto the floor, rolling over and scooting back against the wall like a trapped crab. Looking up, I saw…well, a ghost. I blinked rapidly, then rubbed my eyes and looked again. It was still there.

ALSO BY LYDIA SHERRER

LOVE LIES AND HOCUS POCUS UNIVERSE

The Lily Singer Adventures

Book 1: *Beginnings*

Book 2: *Revelations*

Book 3: *Allies*

Book 4: *Legends*

A Lily Singer Adventures Novella: *A Study In Mischief*

Dark Roads Trilogy

Accidental Witch

Sublime Misfit (coming soon!)

Ill-fated Hero (coming soon!)

OTHER WORKS

Hope: A Short Story

When the Gods Laughed (release Jan 2018)

ACCIDENTAL
WITCH

DARK ROADS TRILOGY BOOK ONE

LYDIA SHERRER

Chenoweth Press

DARK ROADS TRILOGY: Book 1
Accidental Witch

Copyright © **2017 by Lydia Sherrer**

Published by **Chenoweth Press 2017**
Louisville, KY, USA

Cover design by Christian Bentulan
www.coversbychristian.com

To my beloved brother, Andrew Lyle Thomas, born May 8, 1987, died Sept 25, 2005. I wish you could have been here to see me become an author. You would have laughed to read about Sebastian. I don't know how e-books work in heaven, but hopefully someday you can read this. You were in my heart the whole time I was writing it.

Love you and miss you. Always.

Your sis,

Lydia

1

"Sheesh, Mom, what's the big deal?"

"The big deal is that you are sixteen years old and we expect better behavior from you. We taught you to respect your elders. How could you do something like this?"

I winced inwardly at the disappointment in my mom's voice, but kept my face stubbornly set. "He insulted me in front of the entire class. It's not my fault our math teacher is an insufferable prick."

"Sebastian."

My dad's warning growl should have brought me to my senses, but I was in too deep to back down now. After all, the guy had insulted *me* first. "It's not like I'm saying anything new. Everyone knows Mr. Hensley is the worst teacher in our school, probably in all of Atlanta. He's only kept his job because he's banging the—"

"Sebastian!" my mom gasped in horror, but I paid more attention to the snort from my older brother in the back seat beside me. He had his nose stuck in some college textbook—as usual—but withdrew it long enough to give me what was no doubt supposed to be a look of sympathy. His permanent expression of smug superiority ruined the gesture, though. Freddie was the "golden boy" in the family and I knew he secretly enjoyed seeing me get in trouble.

If I had been smart, I would have shut my mouth then and there, just to deprive him of the pleasure. I wasn't doing anyone any good, and the look of distress on my mom's face as she twisted in her seat to meet my eyes sent a flash of guilt through me.

But I was young and stubborn, a mix that always seemed to get me into trouble. Crossing my arms, I avoided my mom's gaze, instead glaring at the back of my dad's neck. "I was only telling the truth. Isn't that what you taught me to do?"

Mom's expression hardened. "Sebastian, you will speak with respect when addressing your father. What has gotten into you? Your brother never acted like this when he was your age."

I could almost feel the grin on Freddie's face as he bent lower over his book. The look was imprinted on my memory and hung before my eyes, mocking me. I told myself to shut up, to let it go. But my mouth seemed to open of its own accord, angry words escaping in a hot torrent. "Well maybe if you weren't so busy being uptight about everything you'd notice—"

"—now see here, young man—"

"—Sebastian, honey, please—"

A horn blared, overpowering our competing voices. It was the only warning, a useless second of noise that drew our attention. But too late.

The piercing screech of tires split the air. I felt only a moment of explosive terror before everything erupted in a tumult of shattering glass and screaming metal. My body slammed forward and the seatbelt dug painfully into my chest, keeping me from flying through the windshield as the front of the car crumpled. Even so, my head whipped back and forth, hitting something with a painful crack. The world went black.

———

Beep...beep...beep.

The noise, intermittent yet persistent, was the first thing I heard. It sounded familiar, but the harder I thought about it, the more my head hurt, so I stopped.

Voices, soft but urgent, argued in the background. I tried to ignore them and sink back into blissful unconsciousness, but then I heard my name.

"Sebastian deserves to know!"

"Absolutely not. Even if he were not already in a fragile state of recovery, his father would not have wished it. It will only make the situation worse."

"How can you say that after what happened? I'm out of my mind with worry for Stephen, heaven knows what has befallen him. The boys could be next. They need to be prepared."

"It is precisely *because* of what happened that I base my decision. The boys are better protected now than they have ever been. I have taken every precaution, used every ward and spell at my disposal. The truth will help no one."

"Wards? We need the police—no, the Stewards! They'll put a stop to—"

"Don't be ridiculous, Eliza. This is a family affair. You know as well as I do that the wizard conglomerate would not lift a finger to help us. There is no proof."

"But—"

"Not another word about it. I was appointed guardian and my decision is final. You should not even be here, it is too dangerous. Besides, Stephen would want you somewhere safe. Go back to England. No wizard is foolish enough to tangle with the Dee family."

I had a hard time following the conversation. Why did my head hurt so much? I tried to raise my hand, but felt resistance as if it was attached to something. Confused, I opened my eyes and turned my head, but gasped as blinding pain shot through the base of my skull like a hundred stabbing needles. I lay there, jaw clenched, trying to ride it out and remember what had happened to put me in this state. But thinking hurt. Everything hurt.

I must have passed out, because the next thing I knew, I felt gentle fingers on my wrist, checking my pulse. This time I didn't turn my head, just cracked my eyes enough to see the paneled ceiling above. It was an uninspiring shade of tan—the color of choice in hospital rooms, it seemed, perhaps because of its calming nature. But I figured the color just made it easier to hide body fluid splatter. The thought floated aimlessly around in my head for a while before I managed to focus. What had I been doing before I passed out?

Movement at my side reminded me I wasn't alone, and I carefully shifted my eyes to see a nurse checking the monitor beside me—the source of that beeping. I opened my mouth and tried to ask a question, but only a rasp came out. It was enough to alert the nurse, though, and a smile spread across her face as she noted my conscious, if groggy, state.

"Well look who's awake! Good morning, Mr. Blackwell. Here, let me get you some water." Her voice was annoyingly perky, but the straw she held to my lips made up for it.

As soon as my throat stopped feeling like an unfortunate piece of beef jerky left out under the Saharan sun, I tried again. "What happened? Where am I?"

"You're at the North Atlanta Memorial Hospital. You were in a nasty car wreck, but your seatbelt did its job and your only major injury was a blow to the head and some whiplash. You had a concussion and you've been out for a few days, but it looks like everything is healing up just fine. We'll keep an eye on you for another twenty-four hours, and then you can go home."

Well, that explained why my head and neck hurt like the dickens. I slowly relaxed, grateful I wasn't in a full body cast. But then a thought hit me and I tensed again. "Wait, what about my family? My parents? Are they okay?" That sickening crunch of glass and metal echoed in my memory, making my stomach churn.

The nurse hesitated. "Let me go get your…relative that's here. It might be best if she explains." The woman offered me a tight smile and left.

My nausea intensified and spread, and I had to fight the urge to vomit. My relative? Who in the world? I lay, tense and shivering, mind racing even as I tried not to consider the possibilities.

"No, I will tell him, thank you." The muffled words floated through my door, wrapped up in a voice that was familiar, yet different.

A soft swish of skirts accompanied the click of a latch as someone entered my room. The door was out of my direct line of sight, so I had to wait until they entered my field of vision before I knew for sure.

Tall, slender, and austere, dressed from head to toe in black, my great-great-aunt reminded me of a Victorian head-mistress with her embarrassingly antique clothes, full skirts, and stern bearing. Her faint British accent only cemented the impression. I vaguely remembered my dad mentioning she had been born in England. Her hair, grey yet still thick and full, was pulled back in a severe bun, and with her flashing eyes and thin lips she always seemed ready to punish you for something—which in my case she usually was.

But today, she looked…diminished. It was why I hadn't recognized her voice; it was so much softer than the stern tone I was used to. The flash was gone from her eyes, replaced by dark shadows that had no end. Her usually stick-straight back was bent and her lined face was white. So very white.

"W—where's Mom and Dad?" I asked. My chest felt painfully tight. "Where's Freddie?" I might have disliked him, but he was still my brother, and in that moment all I wanted was to see his stupid face, smug expression and all.

My aunt sank slowly onto the end of my bed. I'd never seen her look so old. I mean, I knew she was old—the two "greats" in her title weren't there for show—but she'd always come across as capable of anything, as if her age was just a fashion statement rather than a handicap. The fact that she was a wizard made her all the more intimidating. It was part of our family's dark secret, and the reason my parents had kept their distance all these years. But now, here she was.

"Sebastian…"

She was acting strangely, and her hesitation fed the creeping realization in my heart that made my chest so tight it was hard to breath. Everything felt numb. "Just say it," I croaked. My whole body was trembling.

She hesitated. "Your parents…the crash…they died instantly."

"No," I whispered, eyes staring desperately, my whole body paralyzed with horror and disbelief. I heard the groaning scrape, felt the seatbelt cut into me, and saw the briefest flash of the back of my dad's head, half-turned to scold me, as everything crumpled. The vision snapped me out of my paralysis and my lungs finally expanded in a giant gulp of air. "No! Bring them back! You're—you're a wizard, you can fix it. You can do something!"

"Magic cannot bring back the dead," she said quietly, her face filled with pain.

"NOOO!" I tried to get up, to punch someone, to destroy something. To destroy myself. It was *my fault*. My petty arguing had distracted them. They'd died because of me, but I had survived.

"Sebastian!" My aunt's sharp word cut through the torrent of agony as her bony hand pushed down on my chest. If I'd had the strength to resist her, I would have. But pain pounded in my head, making me dizzy, so I fell back onto the bed. Instead of tearing the hospital room to pieces, my own insides were torn to shreds. I could feel myself breaking apart, bit by bit, as cold reality barreled around inside me like a wrecking ball. Tears pricked the corners of my eyes and made wet trails down the sides of my face. Whether they were tears of rage or grief, or simply the storm inside leaking out, I had no idea.

"Frederick survived. He has similar injuries, but should make a full recovery." Her tone was gentle, but I felt no relief, only emptiness. All his survival did was spare me that much more guilt, and at this point it barely made a difference.

The touch of her cool, dry skin as she took my hand drew me briefly out of myself. Her hesitant squeeze surprised me. I'd never seen her show affection before, not even to Golden Boy Freddie. Approval, maybe, but not affection. I should have been comforted by the effort, but instead it made me angry, and I refused to meet her eyes. I didn't want her—I wanted my mother. I wanted to be a child again as mom tucked me in, brushing a stray lock of hair from my face before bending over to kiss my forehead. I wanted to hear her say she loved me, and that everything was going to be okay. I wanted it so badly my whole body ached as my heart slowly tore in two.

I would never hear her voice again.

No, I didn't want my great-great-aunt, a woman so strict she insisted we call her "Aunt Barrington"—who ever heard of calling their aunt by her last name? Pulling my hand back, I shrank from her touch. An endless pit of guilt and grief yawned before me and I instinctively pushed everything away, every feeling, every thought.

"Get out." My own voice echoed in my ears, as dead as a corpse swinging from the gallows.

My aunt sat motionless for a long time. When I didn't move or speak, she eventually rose, her face barely visible in the corner of my eye. I thought I caught a glint of moisture on her cheek, but I wouldn't let myself look.

Finally, without a word or even a sigh, she turned and left.

2

The funeral was a blur. At least that's how I tried to remember it, because anything else was too painful. The spring weather was surprisingly obliging and poured down rain throughout the whole thing. I was grateful. It gave me something to concentrate on so I could block out the murmured words of condolence and pity. As an added bonus, it cut down on the number of attendees. It had been three days since I'd gotten out of the hospital, and I still hadn't spoken a word. I didn't want to see anyone, talk to anyone, acknowledge anyone. I wanted to stop existing.

I wanted to die.

Dad would have shaken his head in disappointment, but Mom would have understood. Maybe not approved, but understood. It was a weird way of remembering them, and I didn't understand it, but it got me through the funeral.

Freddie was subdued, yet played his part well as the oldest "responsible" child. He thanked people for their words and spoke a few himself over the fresh dirt long since turned to mud everywhere but under our little canopy. I envied the black veil Aunt Barrington hid behind. All I had was a blank stare to shield me as the people who had known my parents murmured their sad farewells, then filed away through the rows of dripping headstones.

After the funeral Aunt Barrington took us back to her house. She lived in North Druid Hills, farther south and east of where I grew up, but still in North Atlanta. I had been twelve the last time I'd visited her house. It was a number I remembered vividly because it was how many times she'd made me scrub the kitchen floor after she caught me stealing her tea scones. It could have been worse. She'd originally threatened to curse my tongue to taste only spinach for the rest of my life, so I suppose I got off light.

The house itself was some sort of historic building. I'd once heard my mom call it Queen Anne-style as she cooed over its intricate wood trim, wraparound porch, and cute little tower on one side. I thought it looked positively antique and screamed "old lady house," but at this point I didn't care where I went. My aunt could have dropped me in a field in the middle of nowhere for all I cared. At least then I wouldn't have to talk to anybody.

Freddie—a sophomore in college—had been home on spring break when…when it happened, so he would be returning to school in a few days. Aunt Barrington had asked whether it was wise to go back so soon, but Freddie was adamant. He didn't want to miss a single day of class. Part of me knew it was his way of coping, to throw himself into work and forget. But part of me called him an unfeeling, self-righteous bastard. He hadn't spoken to me, hadn't even looked at me, since we got out of the hospital. But I couldn't blame him. He knew what I'd done.

Me? As far as I was concerned I could sit in a corner and stare at the wall until I rotted. I didn't care about school, not even about the upcoming soccer season that was usually my time to shine. None of my "friends" would miss me, I was sure. Not a single one had shown up to the funeral, which was almost a blessing. I couldn't face them. I felt like a walking shell.

Dinner that night was as silent as the graveyard we'd left my parents in, minus the pattering of the rain. I ate until I couldn't stand the feel of tasteless ash in my mouth anymore. Halfway through my plate I got up and left, feet automatically taking me down the hall and up the stairs to the second bedroom on the left.

Ignoring the bag of clothes and toiletry items someone had brought from my house, I collapsed on the bed and stared listlessly at the dim ceiling. I'd barely slept since that awful moment when I'd realized my life was over, and I had no interest in the painkillers they'd given me. My pain was my punishment, justly deserved.

Alone with my dark thoughts, I escaped into memory, finding solace in a time when things were still…normal. I rarely saw my aunt growing up—on account of her being a wizard—but occasionally Mom and Dad would take mysterious trips and leave me and Freddie with her. It always made me mad. I'd wanted to stay at my friends' houses, and didn't understand why we had to put up with my grouch of an aunt since we usually avoided her. What made it even more odd was that Dad himself had been born a wizard, but he'd had renounced the use of magic and lived like it didn't exist. He tried to raise us as normally as possible, except, of course, for semi-annual lectures on the danger of getting mixed up with "all that nonsense." I'd long since learned that asking questions about magic got me nowhere when it came to Dad.

Not that knowing more would have done me any good. I was a "mundane," a normal human who couldn't do a lick of magic. The gene, or whatever it was, hadn't passed to me. Golden Boy Freddie, on the other hand, not only had it— and so was favored by Aunt Barrington—but was also perfectly content to ignore it, which had made him Dad's favorite as well. I'd always been unhealthily curious about magic, but since I couldn't use it, I'd focused my attention on what I was good at: sports and being popular. Both were arts that took study and practice, and both were more fun than things like math. It wasn't that I was terrible at math or any of my other school subjects. They were just boring.

Dad used to lecture me all the time about how important a good education was. Once he went so far as to complain that I'd have made a terrible wizard with my "undisciplined" study habits. Mom would sometimes tut-tut at my grades, but then she'd take me out to her garden and teach me the names of all of her herbs and flowers, along with their useful qualities. I'll admit, I was more interested in the ones that could be distilled into poison, but as a whole they beat math homework hands down. At least knowing about plants was useful. Dad was the scholar of the family and he'd always been disappointed I didn't love books more than air and food. Mom, on the other hand, had gotten me. She'd understood that knowledge was only as useful as what you did with it, no matter if you were a mundane *or* a wizard.

For a brief moment, I could see her face in front of me, smiling and shaking her head at some mischief I'd gotten up to. But then, like the sun being hidden by scuttling clouds, the vision faded and cold reality washed over me.

They were…no. I couldn't say it. Couldn't even think it.

Darkness crept in as evening progressed and light faded from the patch of ceiling I was staring at, trying to keep my mind blank. I dreaded the night. During the day, I was distracted by things around me, by people trying to care and me ignoring them. But in the darkness of my room, there was nothing between me and that gaping pit. It made me want to rage at the heavens, or curl up in a ball and cry until there was nothing left in me. Instead I just lay there, trapped by torment in my head. I longed for the dawn yet hated the sight of it because it meant I had to live another day without them.

———

DAYS PASSED. Freddie went back to college. As my legal guardian, Aunt Barrington decided I would move in permanently with her, so she arranged for my things to be brought over since I couldn't stand to set foot in my old house. I especially couldn't stand to see Mom's garden, no doubt full of sprouting weeds without her calloused but gentle hands there to pick them out. My things didn't matter, though. All my possessions were meaningless without the people I loved there to share them with me. I even started to miss Freddie's sarcastic remarks, which said a lot.

Along with boxes of useless stuff, my aunt gave me a long list of house rules, including, but not limited to: no running, no yelling, no loud music, no friends over, no touching the antiques—which was basically everything in her house—and, most importantly, no trespassing in the library. After she laid down the law, my aunt explained in rather cryptic language that her house was "protected" and that I shouldn't go in and out willy-nilly. There were no house keys. If for some reason I needed to get in when she wasn't there, I was to go to the front door and touch the doorknob, and the door would unlock for me. She refused to elaborate on how all this worked. I knew it was magic, but she seemed as reluctant as my dad to even mention the word in front of me.

Once the ground rules had been set, Aunt Barrington generally left me to my own devices. She stayed downstairs and did whatever it was wizards did when they weren't pretending to be normal. I knew she had a mundane job— she was a librarian or archivist, something with books—but she must have taken time off after the funeral, because for days she never left the house. On occasion there were visitors, usually older men and women who all looked as austere and old-fashioned as my aunt, though there was one middle-aged woman who came by several times. She always seemed to know when I was staring at her down the hall stairs because she would turn and give me a piercing look before disappearing with Aunt Barrington into the library.

Except for meals and the occasional restless foray, I stayed in my room. One afternoon, though, the agony of unending silence sparked an idea, and I ventured downstairs in search of my aunt. At home, my brother and I had shared a game console. I didn't know where it was, but it hadn't been brought over with the rest of my things. I thought if I could get it, I could lose myself in mindless video games.

Treading hesitantly down the hall stairs, I stuck my head into the kitchen, the dining room, and finally the parlor. All empty. The sunroom at the back of the house—full of potted plants and brightly lit on sunny days—was dark and empty. Finally, dragging my feet, I headed for Aunt Barrington's library. It was the only room on the first floor that had no windows, and the door was always closed. I'd only caught glimpses inside once or twice when I was a boy, seeing nothing but the corner of a tall bookshelf. The one time I'd tried the doorknob—when curiosity had overcome my common sense—I'd found it locked. As soon as I'd touched it my aunt had appeared behind me, as though she had some sort of alarm against the pawing hands of young boys. I was pretty good at talking my way out of things when the need arose, but the sight of her beady eyes and grim mouth had tied my tongue in knots. I considered myself lucky to have gotten off with just an ear boxing and a warning: if I ever so much as touched the doorknob of her library again, my hands would shrivel into twigs and stay that way until I learned not to snoop.

I'd avoided her library ever since. Even now, standing in front of the door, I eyed the doorknob warily, opting instead to knock gently on the wood.

There was absolute silence until the door opened abruptly with a whoosh. I jumped back in surprise, resisting the urge to wilt under my aunt's glare of impatience. She peered at me through the gap she'd made, blocking most of my view with her body. Strange whirring, rustling, and clicking sounds came from the room behind her, and I marveled that I hadn't heard a peep until the door was open.

"What do you want, Sebastian? I am very busy at present."

"Well, I was wondering," I began, but the sight of a book casually floating past the opening above my aunt's head struck me momentarily dumb.

"Yes? What were you wondering?" Her sharp question snapped me out of my shock.

"Uhhh...yeah, um. I was wondering where my game console was? From my, um, house?" I wondered if she even knew what a game console looked like.

Aunt Barrington's eyebrows drew together. "It was taken away with the rest of your parents' things to be sold."

"What? But it was mine!" Disappointment stabbed through me.

"As a matter of fact, it was not. You were simply allowed to use it. Being your guardian and the executor of your parents' will, I decided it was not a healthy addition to this household. While some mundane technology is...useful, this was one thing you most certainly could do without." Seeming to think the conversation over, she began to close the door.

"But what am I supposed to do all day?"

The door halted, then reopened a few inches. "I take it you are ready to return to school, then?"

I tensed and drew back, shaking my head. The mere thought of facing the world, facing life, made me nauseous. I wasn't Freddie. I needed to escape reality, to escape the constant knowledge of what I'd done and lost.

With a sigh and a not-unkind expression, my aunt opened the door a little wider and stepped out, closing it firmly behind her.

"Very well, then. Since you obviously require a task to keep your idle hands occupied, it is time you began earning your keep."

"What? But, all I wanted was—"

"Idle hands are the devil's workshop," she said, ignoring my protest, and began describing a frighteningly long list of chores, from washing the dishes to sweeping the floors, dusting the furniture, and ironing the linens. I didn't even know how to use an iron.

"But why don't you enchant things to do all those chores for you?" I asked. "Isn't the purpose of magic to make life easier?" According to my dad, magic was a dangerous liability to be avoided at all costs, but I'd never really believed him. Maybe at last my aunt would teach me about magic.

My aunt arched a brow. "I see you are not familiar with Goethe's *The Sorcerer's Apprentice*. As a mundane, you have no need, nor reason, to consider magic. Yet, since the subject has arisen, it would be irresponsible of me to not disabuse you of your childish misconception. Magic is both powerful and highly dangerous and should never be used for frivolous things that our own two hands can do perfectly well on their own. Manual labor is healthy for the mind and body. Now, if you would kindly cease your prattling, I have a very delicate spell I am working on." With that, she turned and reentered her library, closing the door behind her with a snap.

I stared glumly at it, wondering what the point of being a wizard was if you couldn't have self-cleaning dishes. It sounded terribly boring. But I *had* been looking for something mindless to do that would stop me from dwelling on… other things. And if this kept her from bringing up the subject of school again, it would be easier to go along than to argue. I was too drained, too empty of feeling to care about anything for very long, not even my annoyance at having to do chores.

Unfortunately, my plan only half worked. While the chores did fill my endless days with less tortuous moments of mind-numbing activity, it didn't ease the pain, and nights were just as sleepless. The chores also failed to stop my aunt from bringing up school. I took to simply not responding. I figured she wasn't strong enough to pick me up and carry me to the car, and there was nothing she could threaten me with. If she cursed me, I would deserve it. Unfortunately for my sense of guilt, Aunt Barrington seemed determined to be as patient as she was capable of being and never threatened me with so much as a jinx. For some reason it made me angry, but that was a nice change from empty, so I welcomed the resentment.

Things came to a head one night when we were at the dinner table. I'd gotten to the point where my disgust toward food won out over my instinctive will to survive. I dropped my fork on the table and got up, intending to head upstairs and lie on my bed, staring at the ceiling until I passed out from weariness or the sun rose again.

"Sebastian, I have informed the school principal that you will be returning to class tomorrow."

I stopped. No subtle prodding this time. I guess she'd gotten tired of waiting and had reverted to her normal, no-nonsense self.

"The teachers have been notified," she continued, "and

will have catch-up material ready for you in addition to your regular homework."

I didn't look at her.

"They will be lenient, at first, I am sure. But the semester is already well on its way, and you will have to work hard to finish with satisfactory grades."

Moving my leaden feet, I started toward the stairs, still silent.

"Sebastian!"

Her sharp voice made me pause. I wanted to ignore her, but I'd been taught to obey authority. Just because I flouted it on occasion when it came to prigs and idiots didn't mean I had no respect for it. My aunt was neither a prig nor an idiot, and her tone brooked no refusal.

Slowly, I turned, fixing my listless gaze on a leg of the dining room table.

"You will pack your school things tonight. You will retire at a decent hour and rise in time to prepare your own break-fast before I drive you to school. I am not your maid, nor your mother—"

"You're right you're not my mom!" I yelled, suddenly furious. I didn't know if it was her bossy tone or the mention of my mother, but I snapped. "I don't *have* a mom anymore! You think I'm going to just skip off to school like nothing happened? Well, you're crazy! I hate you and I hate this house! I should be dead. It should have been *me*! It was my— my—" I choked, unable to get the words out. I couldn't face what I'd done.

My ears rang, my head throbbed, and I suddenly felt as weak and flimsy as tissue paper. Staggering, I grabbed at my recently vacated chair and collapsed into it, slumping down in defeat. It was as if all my energy, my anger, my very life force, had blown out in one furious gust, and I was empty again.

Eyes on the floor, I heard my aunt shift, the long skirts she always wore scraping faintly against the legs of the table. "Whether or not you like me, or this house, is irrelevant." Her tone was firm, but lacked the bite of anger I'd expected. "This is your current situation, and it will remain so until you come of age. Your parents left you in my care, and they would have wanted you to finish your education."

I made a derisive sound.

"Your *mother*, rest her soul," Aunt Barrington continued, her voice a tad harder, "would have wanted you to at least graduate high school. She sacrificed a great deal for you and your brother, and I pray you do not sully her memory by continuing in this petulant manner."

Eyes jerking upward, I glared at her, ready to start yelling again. She must have seen past the stubborn rebellion in my eyes, though, because instead of scolding me, her gaze softened. "I miss them as well, Sebastian. And before you protest that your pain is unique and no one could possibly comprehend it, you should know that my mother died when I was only a young girl. Our father..." She paused, lips thin and jaw tight, then sighed. "Our father was stern and not used to showing affection. He raised us as best he could, but was by no means a loving man."

Her expression softened again, and for the first time since the car crash I actually felt something besides blinding pain, rage, and guilt. I didn't know what it was, but it gave me pause long enough to listen to what she was saying.

"Death touches us all, but it is not ultimate. Should the whole world simply lie down and die? Give up the fight? If not, then why should you? Your parents would want you to *live*. The least you can do is honor their memory."

She fell silent, and we sat together in the darkening room. I didn't say anything for a long time as I let her words sink in. It was hard. Everything hurt so much, physically, emotionally, mentally. I didn't want to live. I didn't want to face life without them. Maybe other people could go on, people who hadn't killed their own parents, accident or not. I wasn't sure I could. But looking up at my aunt's face, lined and weathered, yet strong, I decided it would be less trouble to go to school tomorrow than argue.

I would go for one day, and one day only. It was all I could imagine coping with. Beyond that, everything hurt too much to think about.

"Okay," I finally said, and slowly stood. My aunt didn't stop me this time, and I dragged myself out to the hall and up the stairs. As soon as I collapsed on my bed, intending to stare at the ceiling and steel myself for tomorrow, I was overcome by a wave of weariness. My eyelids slid shut like trap doors and I slept, really slept, for the first time in days. Unsurprisingly, my school things did not get packed.

3

Despite my usual inability to get anywhere on time, by some miracle—or perhaps wizardry—my aunt had us at the doors of Brookhaven Academy a good five minutes before the bell rang. Normally I would have ridden the bus, since it was one of those nice private schools that could afford them. But I didn't live in Brookhaven anymore, and Aunt Barrington had yet to fill out the paperwork to get her house added to the bus route. I hoped she did it soon, because I'd never been so glad to get out of a car before. Let's just say that my aunt wasn't one for small talk.

It was rather ironic, then, that after only five steps toward the school's front doors I wanted nothing more than to get back in that car and beg her to take me home...well, back to her house. It only took those few steps for people to notice me, and, inevitably, to start pointing and whispering.

"Oh my gosh, look. It's him."

"What happened?"

"Parents died. Car crash or something."

"Dang. That sucks."

Again, and again, the same exclamations and morbid curiosity, the same half-pitying, half-distasteful looks. And always, the same inevitable conclusion: orphan.

I felt sick.

Before everything happened, I used to swagger around school like I owned the place, head held high while I flashed my handsome smile. Any other incident I'd have laughed at and brushed off. But this...this was different. It wasn't people's opinions that bothered me, it was the terrible, crushing pain of that gigantic hole inside. And every side-long look, every whisper, made it worse. The thought of spending a whole day being reminded that my parents were dead and that I was an orphan—I couldn't take it. But as I slowed and looked over my shoulder, I saw that Aunt Barrington's ancient Buick had already disappeared down the street.

Shoulders hunched and eyes on the ground, I turned and walked quickly up the front steps and through the entryway, hoping to disappear into my first class as soon as possible. But when I finally reached the door to my US History room and slipped in, what I found was ten times worse.

Normally, I would time my arrival carefully: just late enough to be the last one in and have everyone's attention as I swaggered nonchalantly to my seat, but not late enough that the teacher bothered writing me up. Now, as I slid through the door just before the bell rang, every eye in the room locked on to me with unnerving intensity. Excited whispers rustled through the class like dead leaves blown by a winter wind. I was momentarily frozen in place, pinned down by their callous scrutiny.

"Welcome back, Sebastian. We're...sorry for your loss." The soft words of Mrs. Kimball, the history teacher, broke the spell.

Even as grief washed through me I had to fight down a

flash of anger, resisting the urge to yell at the whole class to shut up and stop whispering about my parents like they were the latest hot news in a gossip magazine. Hands clenching and unclenching on the straps of my backpack, I forced myself to look at the ground and walk to the back of the room where I picked the most isolated seat possible and slumped into it.

I didn't hear a word the teacher said during class. I just withdrew into a blank shell and tried to ignore the curious faces stealing glances at me over their shoulders. Some of them may have even been my "friends." I didn't want to know, didn't want to acknowledge or talk to them. I just wanted to be left alone.

Second and third period were more of the same, though I had at least learned my lesson and hurried from class to class, slipping in and hiding at the back before everyone else arrived. Nobody spoke to me, save for a few murmured platitudes that made me wince and think of my parents' funeral.

Only once did I hear a friendly voice. Cory, as lanky as me but with a shock of straw-blond hair, called out my name in the hall between second and third period. He was one of my soccer teammates, and probably the only person in school I would consider a real friend and not just a groupie. But I ignored the call and ducked around a corner, hoping he wouldn't follow. If he did, I knew he would say something, would try to be kind and understanding. But no matter what anyone said, all it did was hurt more.

Class was bad, but I knew lunch would be worse. I considered taking refuge in the library to get some peace and quiet, but I hadn't had time for breakfast that morning, so by now my stomach was tight and aching.

Dredging up energy, I forced myself to think, carefully strategizing the most direct yet unobtrusive path to the cafeteria line. The plan I came up with was good. It might even have worked, if my soccer team hadn't been waiting to ambush me. They must have been keeping an eye out, because as soon as I came through the door one of them shouted my name and they all crowded around me.

"Hey, man. It's good to, uh, see you back." Derek, our goalie, took the lead in what was obviously going to be an awkward conversation.

I shrugged, not looking directly at any of them.

"Yeah, you're just in time!" Cory enthused. "Remember, our first game is this weekend and, no offense to Finn or anything, but we need you. Bad."

At Cory's comment, Finn shot the gangly kid a glare, and if things had been normal, I would have rolled my eyes. My friend's mouth was going to get him killed someday.

Finn, a forward like me, must have been picked to fill my place as striker. The striker's job was to be the central forward player and lead goal scorer—and, by default, the most popular player on the team. Finn had held the spot until two years ago when I came along and "stole" his position when I was just a wet-behind-the-ears freshman. He'd never forgiven me for it.

At this point he could have the position for all I cared. I couldn't stand the thought of playing soccer anymore. I would never again hear my mom yelling my name from the stands, or need to explain the scoring system to my dad, who always forgot it even though he went to every game. The thought made my gut tighten and I wondered if I'd even be able to eat lunch.

For the briefest moment I tried, I really did try, to care. I tried to *want* to go back to my old life when all that mattered was winning games, being popular, and staying out of trouble. Okay, not that last one, but at least avoiding suspension.

The effort was pointless. My attempt at caring was flattened by the vast weight of loss that swept everything else away.

A sudden crashing sound made me flinch, transforming in my mind to car metal screeching, crumpling, collapsing… but no, it was just a student across the cafeteria who had dropped his lunch tray.

Caught in the silent stare of my teammates, all I could do was shrug. I couldn't even look at them, tell them 'no' like a man, and walk away. They would want to know why, and there were no words to describe the utter despair I felt inside. I was letting them down, and the shame of it only added to the mountain of guilt slowly suffocating me.

"Come on, man. What's going on? We need you." Josh, one of the midfielders, punched me good-naturedly in the arm. I jerked back, remembering the tremendous force of the crash that had flung me about like a rag doll.

"Hey! Lay off," Cory growled and shouldered Josh away, as if sensing my discomfort.

The silence returned and I knew I had to say something to get them to leave. "I…can't," was all I managed to get out.

"What?"

"No way!"

"Come on!"

My teammates shuffled in agitation as Derek spoke up, trying to restore calm. "I'm sure Seb just meant he needs a couple weeks to get back into practice. We've been training hard, we'll be fine our first game. It can't be easy getting back to normal after…" He trailed off.

There was a moment of tortuous silence before Finn saved me, of all people. Though he probably spoke up more to cement his place as the new top dog than because he wanted to spare me further pain. "Come on, guys. Let's give him some space. We'll be fine this weekend. I'll make sure of it."

One by one they turned away, some more quickly than others, and returned to their seats. The soccer team's groupies that usually surrounded me stayed glued to their chairs, whispering to my teammates as they sat. I kept my eyes down, avoiding their looks—whether scornful or sympathetic, I didn't want to know. Soccer wasn't the most popular sport in the school, but we were way cooler than the track and field geeks and out-ranked the usually popular lacrosse team by our sheer volume of wins for the school. The football team, of course, considered themselves the greatest thing since sliced bread, but because fall was their season and spring was ours, we managed to pretend they didn't exist.

When the shuffle of feet had finally quieted I looked up to find Cory still standing there, looking concerned.

"You sure you're okay, Seb?" He took a step closer.

I shook my head, whether in answer to his question or a desperate plea for him to leave, I didn't know.

"Here, let's go get some food. I'll sit with you," he said, voice cheery as he attempted to sling an arm around my shoulder.

I shrugged him off, backing up. "Leave me alone, Cory. I…I need to be alone."

He deflated, looking hurt, but nodded. "Alright. Just yell if you need me, okay?"

Though I gave no response, he seemed not to need one as he offered a half-hearted grin and turned to rejoin his teammates.

Blessedly alone once more, I kept my head down as I navigated the edge of the room, heading toward the lunch line. Anyone who noticed me got out of the way, and by this point I was getting better at blocking out the whispers. I tried not to think about anything but lunch. If I could just get some food and sit down somewhere quiet—

Feet entered my field of vision, giving me just enough

warning to stop before bouncing off the chest of Bryan, Brookhaven Academy's star quarterback. He and I were about the same height, but he had a good hundred pounds on me, and not all of it muscle. His less-than-perfect physique didn't stop him from winning games, just put a dent in his following of female admirers. The cheerleaders tended to gravitate toward the other, more trim team members. Maybe that was why he was so surly all the time.

"Well, well, well. If it isn't Sebby, back from the dead," he sneered.

One of his three thick-necked teammates chortled. "Yeah, we thought you'd died."

"Shut up, idiot," Bryan snarled, obviously wanting to be the sole focus of my attention.

I glared into the quarterback's meaty face, hate flaring as my fists clenched of their own accord. Bryan was a bully, pure and simple, and the fact that our soccer team had beaten the football team in number of wins the last two years running meant there was no love lost between us.

"Shut up and get out of my way," I growled, having no patience for this mouth-breather and his cronies. They guffawed, as if I'd tried to say something funny, and failed.

"What? Can't take a friendly little joke? Gonna run home crying to your mommy?" Bryan paused, a malicious smile spreading across his face. "Oh, wait. I forgot. She's dead."

I lunged, not even conscious of my own rage-filled movement until I'd landed a solid blow to Bryan's jaw that whipped his head around. Before I could follow up, his teammates were on me, and the fight was in full swing. It didn't matter that I'd made the critical error of starting a fight without backup, or that I would probably be suspended. All I wanted to do was pound Bryan's face to a bloody pulp.

I don't remember the words I shouted, but I'm sure they alone would have gotten me a week's detention. I don't remember how many times I was punched or how many blows I dealt in return. I barely recall the circle of students around us, yelling encouragements and placing impromptu bets. But I most certainly remember the hot goth chick decked out in a studded leather jacket and spiked boots that emerged from the crowd to give Bryan a swift and devastating kick to the groin. I stared in shock and awe as Bryan's massive bulk dropped like a rock and he curled into a fetal position, moaning in agony. His cronies, busy holding my arms behind my back so he could punch me unhindered, were as shocked as I was. Their hesitation gave the goth chick time for a second go at her downed opponent, and the crack of Bryan's nose breaking was music to my ears. I only got to enjoy it for a second, though, before teachers arrived and the crowd of students scrambled to make themselves scarce.

Bryan was carted off to the school nurse, but I, despite my black eye, bleeding lip, and tender ribs, was marched away to await the principal's wrath along with the goth girl and Bryan's cronies. Phone calls were made, words were had, and I was threatened with suspension. Ironically, it was the happiest I'd been all day. If I got suspended, I wouldn't have to come back to school and face all the painful reminders of what I'd lost. A small part of me felt ashamed, the part that knew my mom would be disappointed. But I locked it away, refusing to even think about her face after that flash of pure agony Bryan's words had caused. For the first time in days, weeks even, I had something to think about besides what had happened, and I relished the feeling, stoking the anger that kept my guilt and pain at bay.

Through it all, I couldn't help sneaking peeks over at the girl who'd come to my rescue—not that I'd needed rescuing, of course. She ignored everyone, including me, and didn't seem angry or worried. In fact, she looked bored, alternating between picking at her black nails and staring at the ceiling with an expression of utter disdain. I recognized her as one of the juniors, though I'd never met her in person—I'd gotten the impression she avoided all human beings on principle. I didn't even know her name. Everyone just called her the goth girl.

I tried not to be curious. She meant nothing to me and was probably just one among Bryan's many enemies. The fact that she'd had the balls to strike while the iron was hot, so to speak, was intriguing, but I pushed it from my mind. I was probably going to be suspended anyway, and I'd never see her again. No big deal.

My aunt finally arrived to collect me, lips pressed together and face white with rage. She said nothing, however, and I dragged myself after her, shoulders slumped as I drew back into a blank shell and prepared for the inevitable tirade. It would suck, but at least I'd be away from all the curious stares.

It didn't come in the car. It didn't come once we arrived at the house. Without being told, I made a bee-line for my room. Aunt Barrington let me disappear upstairs without comment. Her restraint surprised me, but I pushed it away with everything else so I could collapse on my bed and stare blankly at the ceiling, finally able to relax.

A while later, someone knocked on my door and, when I didn't bother answering, came inside. Eyes closed, I desperately told myself it was my mother, come to talk to me after I'd caused some sort of ruckus at school. She would always sit down on the bedcovers with a long-suffering sigh and, instead of scolding me or asking why, she'd tell me a story. Usually it involved her own adventurous youth living in inner-city Atlanta or the summer trips her family used to take to her grandparents' farm. Sometimes she'd talk about her college days and holding down two jobs just to afford tuition. But she'd always get me laughing at some ridiculous situation she or her friends had gotten into and, impossibly, gotten out of again. Only after I was smiling and had rolled over to look into her sweet, beautiful face, would she grow serious and ask me what had happened. Somehow, no matter I'd done, she would manage to tie my situation back into her own story and show me how my actions had hurt other people. Other people were always her primary concern, not herself. Again and again she would tell me to "be kind, even when the world punishes you for it." After our talks, I would always feel sorry and promise to do better. I wanted to be like her, to be kind to people, even though my low tolerance for stupidity made it difficult.

I heard the rustle of skirts brushing against wood and the creak of an antique chair. My happy memory vanished like a candle snuffed out by a gust of wind. There was a long silence before Aunt Barrington finally spoke.

"I have tutored many students in my long life, but never have I raised a child. When I was a girl, students who fought in school were caned by their teachers, though such a punishment would doubtless be wasted on you."

I didn't reply, too drained to care.

"Very well. Tell me what happened."

I still didn't speak, but this time because I couldn't believe my ears. Was she asking me for my side of the story?

"Come now, Sebastian. While a rank troublemaker you most certainly are, I have never known you to be physically violent. I assume you had a reason for attacking that boy. I wish to know what it was."

Stunned into obedience—my aunt had always been a "punish first, ask questions later" kind of disciplinarian—I told her what Bryan had said.

Her lips tightened and her eyes flashed at my description. The reaction made me fantasize for a moment about her turning Bryan into a slimy, hideous, wart-covered toad. More realistically, his parents would be getting an earful later that evening, but it never hurt to dream big.

At the end of my story, she sighed. "Would that children these days were taught the basics of manners and human decency. While someone else's rudeness does not legitimize your violent response, in light of the situation, the principal and I have decided it would not be in your best interests to suspend you. On my recommendation, however, he agreed you may benefit from time in a less...crowded environment. You will, therefore, spend your lunch period in detention for the next week, in addition to after-school detention—"

"What?" I sat up suddenly, horrified at the thought of spending even more time at school when I'd assumed I had escaped it altogether.

"Counseling was considered," she continued, ignoring my interruption, "but for the present, I believe time and a little space will do the most good. Professional counseling will most certainly enter the picture, however, should any such incident reoccur." She gave me a steely-eyed look and I fell back on my bed, eyes squeezed shut, groaning.

There was no point trying to explain how it felt, how having to listen to "I'm sorry for your loss" all day was like losing my parents a hundred times over again. Maybe she'd gone through similar loss when her mother died, but at least she hadn't *caused* her mother's death. I couldn't, I literally *could not,* bear another day like that.

My aunt's chair creaked as she stood up. In the following silence, I could feel her staring at me. I didn't move.

"Fire tests gold as suffering tests brave men. What is done cannot be undone. Therefore, a wise man would persevere, knowing that suffering produces endurance, and endurance, character, and character, hope." With that she turned and left, closing the door behind her.

4
<hr>

I lay in the darkening room for a long time, wrestling with despair and confusion. Her words rankled me. Was I brave? I didn't like to think I was a coward, but maybe I was. I wanted to dismiss her little speech as the empty words of an old fool. Who was she to talk? A cranky old woman, alone in an empty, boring house. I didn't need her stupid "wisdom." But without it, what did I have left? My parents were dead. Worse, it was my fault. My brother cared little for me, a feeling he knew I returned. School was empty, and my future held nothing but years and years of loneliness and pain. My life was over. Why should I persevere? What hope was there?

Darkness fell, and I fell with it, sinking into a restless sleep. I saw my mother and called out to her, but she only smiled and turned away, disappearing into the mist with a soft word: Wait. What did she mean? Wait for what? Then I saw my father, but he looked strange. He was taller and younger, as if I was seeing him through the eyes of a little boy. I sat on his knee and he told me a story, one of Aesop's fables. I remembered how he used to love those old tales, but

I couldn't recall ever hearing the one he shared with me now. It was about a king who had a dream that his son would be killed by a lion. So he locked the boy up safely in a palace full of beautiful pictures of animals to keep him company. But the prince grew to hate his gilded cage and tried to use a branch of thorns to tear up the picture of a lion that he blamed for his captivity. He hurt himself on the thorns and the wound grew infected and the prince died. As my father faded, I could hear him say, "Goodness, what a silly lot we are."

The dream changed again and now I could see both of them, but they were so far away. I yelled their names over and over, running toward them, but they only grew smaller. Just before they disappeared from sight, they both turned and pointed up.

I woke in a cold sweat, my limbs tangled in the sheets and my throat raw. Tears of grief and frustration leaked from my eyes as I struggled upright, throwing off the sheets and sitting on the side of the bed, head in my hands. My chest ached like I'd been stabbed through the heart with cold steel. But that wasn't what hurt the most. Mentally, emotionally, it felt like I'd been ripped in half right down the middle. Half of me was gone, dead forever, and the other half was flailing around gasping desperately for air.

"I can't live like this," I said aloud, half hoping someone would answer me and tell me I was wrong. But there was only silence. Teeth clenched, I pressed my palms against my eyes, trying to block out the terrible thoughts I couldn't keep away. They pulled me inexorably down a dark road I knew would not end well.

"I should be dead, not them," I whispered into the darkness. "It should have been me." *Maybe I should just kill myself,* I added silently, unable to say the words out loud.

"Ahem-hem. Excuse the intrusion, but that's codswallop, that is."

I yelled, and yelled loud. The voice had come from somewhere above me, and in my panicked attempt to get away I fell forward onto the floor, rolling over and scooting back against the wall like a trapped crab. Looking up, I saw...well, a ghost. I blinked rapidly, then rubbed my eyes and looked again. It was still there.

We stared at each other for a long moment and my fear began to fade, turning to curiosity. Growing up in a wizard family meant I knew more about the supernatural than most. That is, I knew the "supernatural" was mostly a load of crap that people made up for profit, for entertainment, or for their own misguided delusions. Ghosts, though—they were real. I didn't know much about them except that genuine sightings were rare, and that those who allowed themselves to be seen did so for a reason.

"W—what do you want?" I asked, slowly rising from the floor. My heart had calmed from its jackhammer pounding to a much more respectable thump in my chest.

"Well, you not dying would be an excellent start, young chap. Believe me, it's not all it's cracked up to be."

I gave a startled laugh that ended in a nervous hiccup. The ghost appeared to be that of an old man, wearing house shoes and some kind of bathrobe—or was that a dressing gown? He had a truly magnificent mustache which curled up at the tips, and a bushy beard that was just this side of untidy. The impressive amount of hair on his face, however, was in comical contrast to the few wisps of fluff left on his head. For a brief moment, my old self surfaced and I opened my mouth to make a joke. Then I remembered I was talking to a ghost.

"Um, okay. So...I'm still alive. Now what?"

"Well, that would be up to you. Tea and biscuits are an

excellent choice, one of my personal favorites. But in your situation, sleep is most likely the best course of action. As I recall, you have school in the morning." The ghost's British accent reminded me strongly of my aunt. Who was this guy?

I sat, stunned and unsure how to take his odd response. Or the whole situation in general. Oblivious to my confusion, the ghost floated down from his hover around the ceiling to sit on my bed, crossing one leg over the other as he dug around in the dressing gown's pocket for something. Of course, he couldn't really dig into it, just stick his incorporeal hand through the spot where his pocket was and wiggle it about in a vague gesture of rummaging. Then he pulled the hand out, appearing to hold something I couldn't see, and rooted in another pocket with the other hand. Now holding two invisible items, he put one down and gestured with the other as if opening a box and plucking out something within between his thumb and forefinger. Setting the "box" down, he lifted the other object and mimed stuffing a pipe. Finally, he appeared to light said pipe—invisible or imaginary, I couldn't tell which—and brought it to his lips for a good, long draw.

Noticing my stare, he shrugged. "An old habit. I can't smoke anymore, of course, but there's nothing wrong with my imagination. It is comforting to remember life's little pleasures, at times."

I shook my head, wondering if I was still dreaming. "What the heck is going on?" I murmured. The question was meant for myself, but the ghost thought otherwise.

"Technically speaking, you're having a conversation with a constrained spirit who—"

"No, no. I meant, who are you and why are you here?"

"Ah! That is simple enough. I am Peter Blackwell, your great-great-grandfather. But for heaven's sake, do *not* call me pappy, or pawpaw, or greatpa, or any such nonsense. Peter will suffice. And as for why I am here, well, that should be obvious. I'm here because you called."

I stared at him, completely nonplussed. Besides my aunt, I'd never met anyone on my dad's side of the family. "Uh… you're my great-great-grandfather?"

"Indeed. Not much family resemblance, I'll admit. But then I've looked better," he said, mouth twisting wryly as he gestured at his ghostly form.

"Okaay…so…what do you mean I called?" I asked, thinking of my dream and trying to remember if I'd said anything to anyone but my parents. But even though barely a few minutes had passed, the images of my mother and father were already slipping away.

"Well, not called, exactly. I can, ahem, sense, you might say, when my descendants are in a tight spot. Since I'm still around, it seems a shame not to make myself useful."

"And why *are* you still around?" I asked. General lore about ghosts said that they were the disturbed spirits of those that died with something left unresolved. Of course, general lore was about as accurate as a compass next to a magnet, but I figured the lore had to have come from somewhere.

"That is none of your business, young whippersnapper," Peter huffed.

My curiosity was sparked, but at that particular moment the seed of an idea sprouted in my mind, and why he was here became less important than what he could do. "Never mind that for now," I said, leaning forward, my whole body tingling with excitement. "What about my parents? Have you seen them? Did they send a message?"

"Ah. Well. Not exactly." The old ghost looked uncomfortable. "I haven't gone *on*, you see. Nothing returns after passing through the veil. No words, no messages, and no spirits."

Disappointment exploded in my chest and I gasped at

the unexpected pain of it. For one brief moment, I'd thought I would see my parents again. Struggling against despair, I pressed him. "Are you sure? They might not have gone on, right? They could still be here? Could you call for them? Find them for me, please?"

"I *am* sorry, lad," the ghost said very softly, putting down his imaginary pipe. "They are gone. To something much better than this, I'm sure, bless their souls. Thomas was a bit rough around the edges, but he had a good heart, and poor, sweet Alison..." He fell silent, completely unaware of the tumult he'd sparked inside me—grief, guilt, despair, and... hope. Stubborn, stupid hope, refusing to be crushed.

"But surely there's something you can do?" I asked, desperate. He shook his head, eyes on his hands. I flailed, grasping at anything I could think of. "Tell me about the other side, then. Where are they? Are they alright? Are they happy? Do they know—" my voice broke, but I cleared it and forged on, "—do they know how I'm doing?"

But he simply sat there, shaking his head until my words petered out. His gaze met mine, and for a moment, I saw my own fathomless pain mirrored in his eyes. Heaving a great sigh, he shook his head a final time. "I already told you, boy. Nothing comes back through the veil. It is a one-way road. A good thing, I should think. Those that pass it deserve some peace and quiet, after all. And if we knew for sure what lay beyond, we'd have no use for faith, now would we? No, better not to know..."

I shivered, wanting to curl up in a ball and wither away into nothingness. If I passed through that veil, would I see them again? "So, what's the point?"

"Of what, my lad?"

"Of anything!" I burst out, wondering why this stupid ghost had even bothered me if he couldn't fix a single thing.

"Why, everything, of course!" He seemed shocked at my

question. "Life is the point. It is a gift that many would die for. What do you have against it?"

"My parents are dead, that's what," I hissed at him, fists clenched. I would have thrown myself on my bed if he hadn't been sitting on it. Instead I just stood there, quivering from the tumult of emotions inside with no way to let them out.

"And a great and terrible tragedy it is," Peter said softly, his wrinkled face seeming to cave in. "Come here, Sebastian my boy. Sit." He gestured to the bed beside him in a fatherly sort of way.

I didn't want to. I wanted to scream and rage and destroy things. It wasn't fair! They shouldn't have had to suffer for my mistake. But my feet moved of their own accord and I slumped down onto the bed, feeling a chill on my arm where it almost touched Peter's ghostly form. He refrained from putting an arm around me, perhaps aware of his effect on the living.

"No one can deny that a terrible thing has happened. Tragedy does not discriminate. It comes to the old and young, the happy and unhappy, the evil and the righteous just the same. It is, you might say, a symptom of our imperfect reality. Our saving grace, the reason humanity survives, is a curious phenomenon. While tragedy crushes some, others it strengthens, and through that strength, life goes on."

I sat, drained once again of all feeling, and tried to care. Aunt Barrington had said something like that as well, something about being brave. But why bother? Why not be crushed and let it end?

Be kind, even when the world punishes you for it.

I could hear her words so vividly, as if she were right there beside me. Would it be kind to give up? To end my own life? It would be easier, certainly, maybe even deserved. But kind? Would anybody even care? Aunt Barrington might, a little. She usually acted like I was a nuisance, but recently had been strangely kind, so I wasn't sure. Golden Boy probably wouldn't even notice. Cory would be bummed, but my soccer team had good ol' Finn to lead them to victory. So who was I supposed to be kind to: myself, or everyone else?

I groaned, rubbing my eyes again as if I could find answers behind my eyelids. All I found were more questions, though, so I finally fell back on my bed, empty and worn out.

"A tired mind does not wise decisions make," Peter intoned, rising into the air. "Get some rest, and we shall see what answers the dawn brings."

Not bothering to reply, I crawled under the covers and shut my eyes, hoping the darkness waiting for me would be empty of dreams.

Thankfully, it was.

5

When I woke up the sun was shining and the birds were twittering like they had no concept of how rude it was to be cheerful that early in the morning. I'd always been a night owl, and school mornings were the bane of my existence. Hiding under my pillow, I thought dark and murderous things about whoever had decided seven-thirty a.m. was a good time to start school. It was several minutes before I even remembered what had happened the night before. I sat up abruptly, looking around, but the ghost was nowhere in sight. It crossed my mind that I might have had a dream within a dream, and the ghost was just some coping mechanism within my subconscious.

"Good morning!"

I jerked in surprise, banging my elbow on the headboard as the very real—if rather pale in the sunlight—ghost materialized through the wall beside me. "Ouch! Jeez, what are you trying to do, scare me to death?" I grumbled, rubbing my smarting elbow. "Ever heard of knocking?"

Peter gave me a long look, one eyebrow raised quizzically as he wiggled his incorporeal fingers.

I flushed. "Okay, whatever. At least come through the door next time, will you?"

"Apologies, young man. Distances are a bit...different when you have no body or gait by which to measure them. I had not intended to appear quite so, ahem, dramatically."

"Well, feel free to *disappear* as dramatically as you want. I need to get ready for school and I don't want some creepy dead guy in the shower with me."

Seemingly unfazed by my black mood, Peter clapped his hands together in delight. "Excellent! Feeling better, then, are you?"

"No," I growled, "I just don't want to spend all day stuck in my room with an annoying figment of my imagination." Despite the pale shape before me and the slight chill raising goosebumps on my arms, I was stubbornly determined to remain skeptical. After all, I could be hallucinating. Or maybe the trauma of the past few weeks had finally broken me and I was going insane. Either way, I didn't feel like dwelling on my family secret just then. Magic hadn't saved my parents, and so far my encounter with the supernatural was just plain irritating. Maybe if I convinced myself Peter wasn't real, he'd go away.

"Oh, never fear, I'm not locationally limited. Some ghosts are, of course, but I am quite mobile." Looking solemn, Peter patted my shoulder with a ghostly hand, sending shivers down my spine. "I'm here for you, lad. Near or far, high or low, you can count on me."

I groaned.

———

THE FIRST THING I learned about ghosts that day was—news flash—they were annoying. You couldn't make them go away since they had no body to push out the door. You couldn't even threaten to break their teeth if they spoke another word. The only time Peter stopped nattering on was when I went down to breakfast with Aunt Barrington.

That's when I learned a second thing about ghosts: just because they faded out of sight didn't mean they were gone. The first time I heard Peter's disembodied voice whisper in my ear, I jumped so hard I managed to spill my glass of milk all over the floor. My aunt gave me a look that would have curdled the milk currently soaking into her very valuable antique Persian rug. But before I could decide between apologizing and running for my life, she spoke a phrase in some strange language and the milk disappeared, just like that. I barely heard her admonition to "be more careful," as I wondered nervously whether she had some wizard-y sixth sense that could spot Peter. But all she did was go back to her poached eggs and tea.

It took me until the car ride to school to stop jerking in surprise every time my new "companion" spoke in my ear, his voice sounding like it was coming from a tiny earbud that only I could hear. By then, I would have gladly run to school on my own two legs if it meant getting away from him. He commented on everything I did, droning on about how things had been in his youth. I refused to admit I was curious, and definitely didn't voice any of the dozen questions I had about ghosts, my family history, or magic in general.

By the time we approached Brookhaven's front drive, I'd realized why I was so ticked off: the stupid ghost had managed to distract me from wallowing in guilt and misery all morning. Occupied as I was with ignoring him, I hadn't had time to dread going to school, pout about detention, or feel sick to my stomach knowing the looks I was going to get, especially after my spectacular fight the day before.

As soon as Aunt Barrington's wheels stopped turning, I

was out of the car and halfway to the school's doors, hoping my irritating shadow would stay behind.

I counted to ten and, hearing no voice, began to relax. Which, of course, was the same moment I noticed a group of girls, one with neon green highlights, whispering with their heads together as they gave me sidelong looks. I raised my hand self-consciously to touch my impressive black eye, wondering what story people were telling about the fight. Disturbed orphan went crazy and attacked star quarterback? The sick feeling in my stomach returned and I slowed, legs feeling like pillars of lead.

"Goodness, what malady has stricken that young lady?" Peter's whisper was back, almost comical in its alarmed concern. "Is she in need of a hospital? Never have I seen such a sickly color of hair except in those laid upon their death bed."

I snorted, surprising myself as much as the girls still whispering behind their hands. They fell silent, blushing. The one with the green hair sniffed, turning her back as if offended that I'd had the audacity to bring attention to her gossiping.

"I think the only malady she needs to worry about is her face getting stuck like that," I whispered back, feeling the hint of a grin lift one side of my lips.

I'd laughed. And made a joke. What was wrong with me?

My momentary mirth was snuffed out and I started forward, long legs eating up the distance between me and the door as I stormed into the school. Guilt and confusion roiled inside me. How could I laugh when my parents were dead? What in the world was I supposed to be feeling—or doing, for that matter? My heart told me to lock myself in a dark room and let sorrow consume me. But my mind wondered if Aunt Barrington and Peter were right, if my parents would have wanted me to live out my life as best I could.

My abrupt change of pace must have left Peter behind, or

else he recognized my foul mood and wisely decided to keep silent. I didn't hear his voice as I stalked through the halls, students giving me a wide berth at the sight of my bruised face and murderous scowl. I didn't care anymore. Let them whisper. They were like vultures, feeding on the spectacle of my misfortune.

I couldn't decide if class that day was better, or worse. The sick feeling in my stomach was gone, replaced with sullen irritation at everyone and everything. I made a half-hearted attempt to listen to my teachers, though only because it got Peter to shut up, not wanting to "hinder my education." Of course, then he would whisper corrections as I scrawled notes from the board, pointing out my misspellings. Apparently, he didn't understand the concept of shorthand. Or of chronic 'I don't give a crap.'

Despite his irritating habits, I found myself grudgingly grateful for his company—not that I had any intention of telling him so. He provided a focus for my annoyance, and anger seemed to do better for me than paralyzing grief. With his invisible presence by my side, I was no longer dreading every look, word, and interaction I had.

The only time I wished he would go away was during detention after school. In contrast to lunch detention—a blessed reprieve from the gossipmongers in the cafeteria, not to mention Bryan's angry teammates—after school detention was pure torture. I was given a blank sheet of paper and instructed to write an essay on what had prompted my behavior, why it was wrong, and what steps I would take to "make wiser choices" in the future. I stared at the paper, grinding my teeth at the memory of Bryan's comment, and trying not to think about what people were calling me.

Crazy.

Violent.

Orphan.

I had to endure Peter's attempts at helpful essay prompts, unable to tell him to shut up in the dead quiet of the detention room. The only thing that kept me sane for that seemingly endless hour was daydreaming about goth girl. I wondered why she'd jumped into the fight, what grudge she had against Bryan. I wondered what her background was, who her parents were, what kind of music she liked, and if I was ever going to see her again. She obviously wasn't in detention, so perhaps she'd been suspended, maybe even expelled. Or maybe Bryan's thugs had gotten ahold of her. It wasn't a pleasant thought.

Though I hadn't responded to him, Cory had caught up with me in the hall between fifth and sixth period and told me that Bryan had needed to go to the hospital for reconstructive surgery on his nose. My friend had been gleeful about it, of course, and I couldn't deny a certain savage pleasure the news brought me. It was a fitting punishment after what he'd said. I tried not to think about it too much, though. Whenever I did, I could see my mom's face, no less beautiful for the sad expression on it, the same one she had always worn whenever she was disappointed in me.

When the detention teacher stood and told us we could leave it was like being released from purgatory. I left my paper on the desk, blank except for a rather creative expletive. Someone had mocked my dead mother. There was no way I was going to apologize for my "unwise decision." Bryan had gotten what he'd deserved.

I exited the school with a sigh of relief, my mood lifting slightly at the thought of escaping to the quiet solitude of my room.

"Hey! You with the shiner," a voice yelled behind me.

I spun, still jumpy from a day spent looking over my shoulder, expecting Bryan's thugs to attempt a revenge pounding. But it was only goth girl, of all people, leaning up against the concrete wall in an alcove to the side of the doors, apparently waiting for me.

She must have mistaken my surprise for confusion, because she yelled at me again. "Yeah, you, Einstein. C'mere."

Looking over my shoulder, I didn't see my aunt's car parked in the school driveway, so I walked forward cautiously, half expecting a violent outburst after what I'd seen her do to Bryan.

"Good heavens, Sebastian, do not approach! She is surely afflicted with the Black Death, or some other equally terrible sickness of the skin. Simply look at her pallor and the dark rot about her eyes and lips!"

I had to hide a grin, but Peter's hissing comment reminded me that I needed to do something about my nosey shadow. I held up a finger to goth girl and took off my backpack, stooping and pretending to rummage in it as I held a whispered conversation.

"You really need to brush up on modern fashion, Peter. That's makeup, not a disease. And I think you've done enough harm for today. Bug off, will you? I don't know how much more of your mutterings I can take." What I didn't say, of course, was that the last thing I wanted to do was have a conversation with a hot girl in front of him. He was like a little brother—a very old-fashioned little brother—that your parents made you bring along when you went to hang out with your friends. Only worse, because I couldn't park him in front of some arcade game and disappear.

"Are you certain you'll be all right? The way she slouches, she is clearly weakened from fever and sickness. Perhaps not the Black Death. I suppose that *is* far-fetched. But think of all the other possibilities. Consumption, typhoid, cholera, even scarlet fever!"

"Seriously, Peter. Go away. She's not sick. Those diseases

don't even exist anymore. I'll see you back at the house. Or, better yet, I'll see you in a few weeks. Or never. You're a pain in the butt," I muttered, a bit harsher than necessary, perhaps, but if it made him leave…

"Humph, if you insist," came the disgruntled whisper. Then nothing.

I stood up, slinging my backpack across one shoulder and wondering if the ghost had actually left or had just fallen silent and was now spying on me. Either way, there was nothing I could do about it, and goth girl was looking impatient. I headed over, chin up and shoulders back, trying to act like this was all perfectly normal, despite my rapidly beating heart. What would she think if she knew I'd been daydreaming about her not minutes before?

Stopping a few feet away, I cocked an eyebrow, doing my best to give her a cool look. Swagger was three-fourths attitude, one-fourth body language, and while I had plenty of practice with both, I wasn't really in the mood. But it was against my principles to pass up a chance to impress a good-looking girl.

Goth girl eyed me up and down, taking in my tall, lean form, slightly curly dark hair, and brown eyes. As was only natural, I returned the favor, admiring the sculpted curves of her body clad all in black. Rivets, buckles, and fishnets adorned her in fine punk goth style, or at least as much of a punk goth style as the school would allow. They had no required uniform, and a relatively loose dress code, but I was pretty sure her strategically ripped t-shirt and low-riding pants were not within regulations. But then, she wasn't "at" school, technically. The spiked boots she wore looked even more lethal than the ones she'd kicked Bryan with. Her studded leather jacket hung from one hand while the other lifted a cigarette to her lips. She took a draw, watching me with a calculating expression as I examined her.

I stepped a bit closer and leaned against the concrete, forcing her to look up to hold my eyes. She wasn't exactly short—about five six if I had to guess—but most people had to look up to meet my eyes since I'd hit my growth spurt a few years ago.

"That's an impressive black eye you got, kid."

I shrugged, assessing her words to figure out how to respond. She'd called me a kid, possibly because she was intimidated by my height and felt the need to stress her advantage in age, even if it was only a year. At the same time, she'd called my black eye impressive, so she obviously wanted to talk about the fight, but not to mock me. I thought furiously, trying to craft a sufficiently charming and witty response.

"Not as impressive as your boots. I wish you'd been wearing them yesterday." I cocked my head, not quite smirking, but letting a hint of it show through.

She grinned.

Bingo.

I was good at reading people. It was one of the few things I was actually proud of, and I used it liberally without remorse. After all, I wasn't hurting anyone, just charming them. Life was generally easier when people liked you, or at least thought they did. Social situations were my element, and I enjoyed manipulating those around me to serve my purposes. At least I had before…before everything happened. Now, remembering how hard I normally worked to impress my "friends," it seemed stupid. Yeah, I used to be the social king of my own little empire, but look how fast it had crumbled as soon as something bad happened.

The thought wiped the smirk right off my face, and I leaned more heavily against the wall, tired and no longer bothering to hide it.

She watched me with interest as she took one last draw

on her cigarette, then dropped the butt and ground it into the concrete. "You look like shit."

Her deadpan observation coaxed a chuckle from me. "I feel like shit."

And I did. Tired, drained, and with a splitting headache coming on. I was sure the bags under my eyes made me look positively goth myself, no makeup needed.

Pushing herself off the wall, she sidled past, so close that she almost brushed me with her hip and shoulder. "Come with me," was all she said as she sauntered off toward the sidewalk.

I turned and watched her go, momentarily mesmerized by the sway of her hips before I shook my head and tried to focus. I knew Aunt Barrington would be arriving any second to pick me up. She would kill me if I just disappeared without an explanation. But at the moment, I didn't really care. The more important question was, what in the world was going on? What did goth girl want? Was I going to play it safe and crawl back into my cave of sorrow? Or was I brave enough to take a chance and live a little. I half expected to hear Peter's voice enumerating the dangers of going off with strangers, but there was only silence. He must have really disappeared, and I wondered if I'd hurt his feelings.

On impulse, I made my decision, and was striding, almost running, after goth girl before I could change my mind. At this point, my life couldn't get worse, and I had no desire to live out the rest of it like a zombie. I'd felt more alive in the past five minutes than I had in weeks. That had to count for something, right?

6

-----

oth girl led me around the back of the school to the parking lot for teachers and older students who drove themselves. I had been about to get my own permit when…well, it was safe to say I wouldn't feel comfortable driving again any time soon.

Expecting to see some shiny Mustang or sleek Charger, we instead stopped in front of a dull, dented wreck that might have once been olive green. Now it was a patchwork of brown rust spots.

"What in the world is *that*?" In my astonishment, I must have sounded a bit more disdainful than I'd intended, because she bristled.

"*That* is my car, asshole. Where I live, even halfway-decent-looking cars get jacked."

"Oh, er…" Backpedaling, I tried to repair the damage. "Well, it looks very, um, sturdy." I winced inwardly, not just at my words, but at the screeching creak of hinges as she hauled open the driver's door.

"It's a 1969 Chevy Nova, and it'll still be running after you're six feet under. Now shut up and get in."

I wondered if she intended to put *me* six feet under. My cynical side pointed out that it would save me a life full of pain. But as I hauled open my own door and slung my backpack into the back seat, I was surprised to realize that maybe, just maybe, I didn't want to die after all. I didn't really want to *live* either, though, so where did that leave me? My fingers trembled as I fastened my seatbelt, the faded bruises on my chest aching. But I pushed the memories away, determined not to let them ruin things.

She started the car—it took a few tries, but when it roared to life, it *roared*—and soon we were headed out of the parking lot and down the street. She drove at a leisurely pace, and I wondered if she was actually that responsible or if the car simply wouldn't go faster. I looked out the back window as we pulled away, half expecting to see my aunt's car appear out of nowhere. But the school driveway was empty. Pushing it from my mind, I tried to lean back and enjoy the ride. It was difficult, considering how much the car rattled as it moved along, jolting painfully over every bump and dip in the road. I doubted goth girl's claim about its longevity, but wisely kept my opinions to myself.

"So…where we going?" I finally asked over the rumble of the engine, unable to restrain my curiosity.

"You'll see," was all I got in return.

Determined not to be nervous—she didn't seem like the axe-murdering type—I sat back and watched the trees, stores, and houses pass by, everything bathed in late-afternoon light. We were headed south, out of the nicer neighborhoods of North Atlanta and into the poorer suburbs of the southern half, closer to the airport. I grew more nervous the farther we went, acutely aware of the increasing distance between myself and my home turf. I had no cell phone. The one my parents had given me had been broken in the accident. But even as I considered it, I realized I'd rather get myself out of any trouble I encountered than call someone, much less Aunt Barrington.

We'd left the school just as rush hour was beginning, so it took quite a while to get wherever goth girl was taking us. Eventually, we reached neighborhoods with fewer trees and lots of scruffy, uncut grass around the sidewalks. More than a few buildings on either side were boarded up, and graffiti decorated many a wall and fence.

Goth girl slowed as we approached what had probably been a department store long ago. The large brick building was boarded up, with yellow caution tape over its entrances and its walls festooned with a kaleidoscope of street art. I noticed one of the corners seemed to be leaning out farther than a normal wall should, but didn't say anything as we parked in the alley behind the building and got out.

She led me through a patch of weeds, already surprisingly tall for this early in the season. They would be growing over our heads by the summer. At the back of the building, cleverly hidden behind some rusted metal sheets, she revealed a hole in the wall and bent down to duck through. I followed, eyes adjusting quickly to the dimness as she led me along a dusty hall littered with bits of rubble and up a set of stairs. The scattered pockets of graffiti inside looked old, as if no one had come around to add to them in a long time.

Our final destination, I discovered with more than a little trepidation, was the roof. But goth girl moved with the casual confidence of someone who knew the ground she walked upon, so I tried to put visions of collapsing buildings out of my mind. Once on the roof she headed for a cluster of chimneys, and I saw that a space around them had been swept clean. There were several old blankets strewn about, as if this were a frequent escape that had been tidied up to make it more welcoming.

Goth girl sank down on one of the blankets, back against

a brick chimney as she reclined in their long shadow. She pulled a cigarette from her pocket and lit it, taking a long, slow drag. Not knowing what else to do, I dropped down beside her, leaning back wearily and looking up at the evening sky. I felt a nudge at my side and glanced over to see her offering me the cigarette, eyebrow raised. I eyed it, considering. I'd never smoked before, mostly because I knew it was unhealthy, expensive, and addictive, and therefore on my list of "unwise life choices" AKA "dumb things not to fall for," along with doing drugs, getting wasted, and getting someone pregnant. I wondered, though, if a few pulls on it would numb the nagging pain in my chest. Everything else I'd done that evening was stupid, so I decided I might as well be consistent.

Accepting the cigarette, I held it between thumb and forefinger and took a cautious pull. I knew not to inhale the smoke all at once, but apparently even proper inhalation technique didn't prepare virgin lungs for the acrid burn. I tried to hold it in, but my body took over and I coughed violently, spluttering and gasping around the smoke in my mouth and lungs.

Goth girl laughed, taking back the cigarette I shoved in her direction. "It's an acquired taste, I guess," she said, then took a draw herself, lifting her head to blow the smoke out in a perfect stream above us.

"I'll—I'll pass—thanks," I managed around my coughs, deciding I preferred my nagging chest pain over lungs burnt to a husk.

"Suit yourself."

"Those things are—are pretty unhealthy, you know." I coughed once more and looked around, wishing I had a bottle of water.

Goth girl rolled her eyes. "Thanks, *Mom*. I'm so glad you told me, otherwise I never would've guessed. It's not like it's almost the twenty-first century. Clearly we still have no clue about the long-term health risks of smoking."

"Whatever. Just trying to help." I crossed my arms, realizing I sounded like Peter, and decided not to offer any more advice.

She shrugged. "Sometimes life sucks so bad that all you care about is coping now, not surviving later. And sometimes…sometimes you do something bad to avoid something worse." Her voice turned dark and she fell silent.

Subdued, I stared at the cloudless sky. A part of me itched to question her, but it wasn't a very big part. Mostly I was just…sad.

The sun moved slowly toward the horizon as she finished her cigarette, then put it out by grinding it against the chimney beside her, leaving a smudge of ash on the brick.

"I'm sorry about your parents," she finally said, her voice quiet.

I didn't respond. Though I tried to appreciate her concern, I wished she hadn't brought it up. The reminder was like a punch in the gut as the pain came roaring back. My eyes burned, but no tears came to give me relief. Desperate for a distraction, I asked the first question in my head. "Why did you attack Bryan?"

She shrugged. "He's a bully and a bastard. Isn't that reason enough?"

I gave her a skeptical look. "Maybe. But you seemed like you had a score to settle. I haven't seen you beat up any of the other bullies at school, so why pick on Bryan?"

I knew I'd read her right when she sighed and looked away. Her fingers twitched, as if wanting a cigarette between them, but she didn't move to take the pack out of her pocket. "He tried to grope me once. Seemed to think he was entitled to something. I didn't get a chance to thrash him properly then, so…" She shrugged again. "Plus, I really, really don't like bullies. I'd heard what happened to your parents and…" she stopped. Maybe she'd felt me flinch, or just noticed my pain-filled eyes. Whatever the reason, she changed topics. "I'm Meg. Meg Garcia."

Surprised, I gave her a sidelong look, eyes lingering on her pale skin and wondering if she was adopted.

She snorted, a wry twist to her mouth. "Racist."

"What?" I protested, "I'm just surprised, that's all."

"Uh-huh. Then you'll be even more 'surprised' to know my dad died in a drug bust."

My eyes widened and I tried not to stare, quashing the immediate impulse to ask what had happened. My curiosity was replaced by anger at myself for having such a callous thought right after she'd told me her father was dead. I was no better than my so-called friends at school.

Though I'd not said a word, Meg seemed to read my mind. She gave a derisive laugh, "Don't fool yourself. Right now, you're wondering if my dad was a drug dealer, and that's about as racist as you can get."

I looked away, face hot. The idea had, indeed, crossed my mind.

"For your information, he was a cop. He was killed in the line of duty taking down a drug ring. I was twelve. Mom never got over it and lost her job, started drinking…and using. His pension paid the bills for a while, but then we lost the house. Had to move south." She gestured at the surrounding rooftops shining in the evening sun. "Only good thing Mom ever did was put some money away in a trust for school. Said she'd be damned if I didn't get a good education, though it didn't seem to do her any good. She has a masters in business but still ended up white trash." Meg glared at the horizon, then sighed long and deep. "At least it was less money for her to spend on drugs. The only thing I have left of my dad now is his name."

Silence descended to our rooftop, broken occasionally by a passing car below. I stared at the sky, unable to look at her. I'd never realized the world could contain so much sadness. Before, I'd always been happy and well cared for, so I assumed everyone else was too. Later, when it had all changed, I'd felt like I was the only person in the world who knew what pain felt like. But now...

"I'm...sorry," I said, voice hoarse. It was all I had to offer. In that moment, I realized what everyone else must have felt like, the helplessness of watching me suffer, unable to do anything but give that tiny bit of empathy. That acknowledgement of my pain. I would always hate hearing it, but now, at least, I wouldn't hate people for saying it.

Meg let out a long sigh, yet remained hunched, shoulders tense. I dared a glance, and thought her face looked oddly troubled, almost guilty. But I must have imagined it, because when she looked up at me her face seemed to burn with an inner fire and her normally dark eyes now glinted with red.

I drew back and blinked hard, startled by her intensity. When I looked again, though, everything was back to normal. Her deep brown eyes held mine, searching for something.

"Do you ever wonder..." she trailed off, then started again. "Do you ever wonder if there's a way...a way to get them back? My dad? Your parents?"

My heart leapt at the mere thought, then constricted as Peter's words echoed in my mind. *Nothing returns after passing through the veil.* I shook my head sadly.

"But why not? The world is full of strange things. Maybe there's something out there, something you don't know about." Meg's words were low and quick, as if she didn't want anyone else to hear them, though there was no one there besides us. "If there *was* a way to get them back, even the possibility, would you really let it pass by? Wouldn't you at least want to try?"

Silence rang between us as I tried to wrap my mind around what she was saying. It was difficult to think past the pounding in my chest. In fact, my whole body was on edge, adrenaline pumping through me once I let myself consider, just for a second, my parents alive again. How desperately I wanted to apologize, to hug them and beg for their forgiveness. I would be good. I'd never get in trouble at school again. I'd get straight As and graduate valedictorian if only I could have them back. I would do anything. *Anything.*

It wasn't a preposterous idea, if I ignored Peter's statement. My family came from a line of wizards, after all. Ghosts existed, and probably other magical beings as well. I knew nothing about magic except how dangerous it was, thanks to my dad. But if it was dangerous, that meant it could do powerful things. I remembered my anguished plea to my aunt in the hospital. She claimed magic could not raise the dead. But what if it could? What if there was something out there she didn't know about? I'd been so wrapped up in my grief for the last few weeks that I hadn't even considered the possibility. How could I have been so stupid?

"Do you—" I swallowed, barely able to form words around my desperate, fragile hope. "Do you mean—do you know—" I couldn't finish the sentence, so I simply waited, holding my breath.

Meg looked thoughtful. "Maybe."

I scowled. But before I could question her further, she shifted, rising with fluid grace and offering me a hand.

"Come on, kid. I'd better get you home before someone calls the police."

Crossing my arms, I glared at her. "My name is Sebastian, and I'm not going anywhere until you explain what you meant."

I thought I was being clever, putting my foot down. Fired up as I was, I was sure I could out-stubborn her, even if it took all night.

Meg shrugged. "Suit yourself." With that, she turned and left, disappearing down the decrepit stairs with a squeak of boards and rustle of debris.

I stayed put, sure she would come back once it was plain I wasn't following her. My confidence slowly deflated as the seconds ticked by and I heard no returning footsteps. Finally, there was a crunch of glass underfoot, and I felt a surge of triumph. I noticed rather belatedly that it had sounded too far away to be coming from the stairs. Another crunch, and I realized I was hearing her traverse the ground floor hall, littered with broken beer bottles left by long-ago partyers.

It wasn't until I heard the rustle of weeds below that I began to re-think my position. But no, surely she wouldn't...

The sound of an engine roaring to life sent me scrambling to my feet and I pelted down the rickety stairs. Hoping I didn't trip and impale myself on something, I navigated the dark interior of the building at top speed and managed to duck out of the hole in the brick wall just in time to run yelling after her swiftly departing vehicle.

It slowed, then halted.

Breathing heavy and trembling with adrenaline, I made my way to the passenger door, heaving it open with a grunt and dropping into the seat without a word.

Meg casually rolled her window down, letting in the crisp spring air, then pulled out of the alleyway and headed north. The evening glowed with the setting sun, so there was plenty of light for me to see the smirk on her face.

Thoroughly annoyed, but impressed in spite of myself, I hunkered down to consider her words and, more importantly, figure out what I was going to tell Aunt Barrington to keep her from turning me into a newt.

7

Meg dropped me off a couple blocks away from Aunt Barrington's house. No sense tying the hangman's noose myself, after all. I was just turning from the sidewalk up the steps that led to her house when a tut-tutting noise in my ear made me jump what felt like a foot in the air. I spun around, looking for the source.

"It seems the prodigal son has returned. You're in a right bit of trouble, you are."

I sagged against a nearby tree and tried to catch my breath. "Peter, you worthless turd, don't *do* that to me! I almost had a heart attack."

The faint outlines of the ghost stiffened in the semi-dark and he drew himself up, attempting a regal look despite his dressing gown and slippers. "Harrumph. Beg pardon, *sir*, but how exactly *do* you suggest I go about announcing myself?"

"I don't know. Say something in a normal voice instead of wheezing in my ear like a dying duck? It's not like anyone's around to hear you." I resumed my progress toward the house, moving a bit less energetically now that I was thinking about what awaited me. "So…how mad is she?"

"Absolutely livid."

"Great," I groaned, running a hand through my hair so it stood up in untidy bunches.

"Where *did* you wander off to? I thought it polite to give you some space with the young lady, but when I came back to check on you, you had vanished. That was quite unwise. Anything could have happened!"

"Yeah, yeah. Whatever." Quickening my pace, I took the front steps two at a time, wanting to get things over with as quickly as possible. I was already going to get an earful from my aunt, no point sticking around for another lecture from Peter. I reached for the front door, but it opened before I could grasp the knob, revealing Aunt Barrington herself, tall and imposing as a granite statue. At the sight, my stomach dropped to my toes and I ducked my head.

"Where have you been?" Her voice was flat and deceptively calm, but I could feel the anger rolling off of her in icy waves.

I coughed. "I've been with, um, a friend. They waited for me after school."

Silence.

"I've been really…well, you know…and uh, didn't think you'd mind if I spent some time with…someone." Playing the sympathy card was a bit underhanded, but technically true. From a certain point of view. Plus, it was my only chance to avoid whatever Really Bad Thing my aunt had in mind for me. I dared a peek at her from under my eyelids and tried not to flinch when she caught my gaze and held it with a will of iron.

More silence.

Nervous, I shifted from foot to foot, trying to think of what else I should say. "Sorry I didn't call," I mumbled. "My cell phone was…well it hasn't worked since…you know." The fascinating distraction of Meg Garcia's presence was wearing off, and I could feel the depressing darkness seeping back in.

Finally, Aunt Barrington sighed, the lines on her face deeper than normal. "Your actions have caused a great deal of grief for both the school and myself. We were concerned you might have...well, suffice it to say that I had yet *another* discussion with the principal. Your behavior has not improved your situation."

I shrugged and looked back at my shoes, not really caring what the school thought.

"Sebastian!" Her voice cracked like a whip, and my head came up of its own accord. I could see the thin, hard line of her lips and the glint of her eyes in the dim light.

"If you still hold any affection for your parents, I highly suggest you consider how they would react to your behavior. I am neither your mother nor your father, but I *am* your legal guardian and responsible for your welfare. I will not tolerate such reckless behavior. I understand that you...that we all are going through a difficult time. Regardless, you are almost an adult and perfectly capable of behaving like one. I will see to it that you have a working mobile phone and in the future you *will* inform me of your whereabouts. Or else."

She didn't elaborate on what "else" was, but I didn't dwell on it. Anger had flared inside me at her implication that I didn't care about my parents—anger at her, but also at myself. Anger, confusion, and guilt.

Of course I cared. I cared so much I felt like it was tearing me apart, minute by minute. I knew they wouldn't have approved of me going off with a stranger, and yeah, it probably hadn't been smart. But nothing bad had happened, and the fact was, they weren't there to care anymore. I had to deal with my life as it was, not as I wished it would be. Things would never be the same, but maybe, just maybe...I tried not to think about what Meg had implied. I couldn't get my hopes up. But if I ever wanted a chance to fix things, getting in trouble with my aunt would only make it harder. So instead of yelling at her and storming off like I wanted to do, I shrugged and muttered, "Sure."

She stared at me for a moment more, perhaps deciding whether I needed punishment after all. But finally, she stepped aside and said, "Dinner is on the table. You had best wash that brick dust off your hands before you sit down."

Shrinking a few more inches under that knowing stare, I slunk past her and headed for the bathroom. How had she known I'd been around bricks? Had Peter told her where I was? But Peter hadn't known himself...unless he'd followed me and only pretended he hadn't? No, he seemed too self-righteous to be that devious.

I got through dinner and another sleepless night by picturing Meg and repeating her words over and over again. *Maybe there's something out there, something you don't know about...maybe.*

Of course, being related to wizards, I was more informed about the 'somethings' out there than most mundanes —'somethings' like a certain ghost whose dry post-dinner lecture I studiously ignored. So, was Meg a wizard? Did she have some sort of spell that could resurrect my parents? A spell that even my aunt didn't know about? I had no idea, but for the first time in weeks I felt something other than guilt and desperate grief. If there was even the faintest possibility I could fix my mistake and put things back to normal, I would do anything to make that happen. It was the only way I could live with myself.

Meg knew something, and I was going to find out what it was.

———

THE NEXT DAY, detention flew by as I considered different ways to wheedle the information I wanted out of Meg. I'd hardly noticed my surroundings all day—not Cory's irrepressible chatter, not everyone's stares and whispers, not even the teacher's lecture about appropriate language and her threat of more detention if I didn't complete the assigned essay. I could sit there the entire day for all I cared. It was a quiet place to think where no one was ogling me.

Peter was suspiciously quiet. I whispered his name a few times throughout the day, but he never answered. I didn't know if he'd stayed home, still offended by my insults the day before, or if he was silently stalking me. I tried not to worry about it.

As soon as detention let out, I raced to the school entrance and out the door, eyes searching intently for any glimpse of Meg. There was no sign of her at the front, so I went around to the parking lot and spotted her dented Chevy in a far corner. At first, I thought it was empty. But when I got closer and rounded it, I found her sitting in its shade, back pressed against the passenger door, smoking a cigarette.

I paused, my plans and schemes momentarily forgotten at the sight of her. She wasn't what you'd call beautiful. Not the kind of beautiful that poets wrote songs about. But she had an unmistakable allure, one that demanded your attention and wouldn't take no for an answer. Today, she wore a black skirt over torn fishnets with a loose crop shirt that—while lacking strategically placed tears—still managed to hint at all the important curves…

"Took you long enough," Meg drawled between puffs of smoke. "Thought I was gonna grow old and die before you figured out where I was."

I shook my head, realizing I'd been staring, and tried not to shift uncomfortably at the thought of where my mind had been straying. I needed to focus. Still silent, I sank down on the warm asphalt, setting my backpack beside me and leaning against the rear tire. Should I ask her about last night straight out? Or try to be subtle?

She answered the question for me. "You up for another adventure?"

My pulse quickened and I was already scrambling to my feet before I remembered Aunt Barrington's warning. I sank back to the ground. "Yeah, but not today. I live with my aunt now and she's...testy. She got really mad yesterday when I disappeared without saying anything. But she said she'd get me a cell phone soon. After that we can, er, have an adventure."

A flicker of annoyance crossed Meg's face. "That crone who's been dropping you off? Who cares what she thinks. Are you gonna let some old lady push you around?"

"I don't let anyone push me around," I said coldly, "but if you've got nothing better to do than insult my family, I'll find someone else to talk to." I pushed myself up again, surprised at my own words. I wasn't sure where the emotion had come from, but despite everything, no one was allowed to insult my aunt but me.

We locked eyes for a moment, and I gave as good as I got, knowing I had to gain some kind of respect or she'd never tell me anything. I thought I saw that strange red light in her eyes again, but it was gone so fast I must have imagined it. Her eyes were clearly a rich brown, so dark they sometimes looked black.

With a huff of air through her nose, Meg looked away. "Whatever. Forget it. Now sit down, jeez. I'm gonna need a neck brace if I have to keep looking up at you."

I snorted, but complied, deciding to get straight to the point. "Tell me what you meant last night, about there being things out there that I don't know about. How do you know

I don't know about them?" I raised an eyebrow, giving her what I hoped was a mysterious look.

Meg shrugged. "Most people go around with both eyes closed pretending they know everything. I usually assume people are idiots until they prove me wrong. The jury's still out on you." She grinned, to which I rolled my eyes, not taking the bait.

"I don't really care what you think of me, I just want to know if there's any way...any possibility..." I couldn't say it out loud, it sounded too ludicrous.

"Hang with me, kid, and you'll find out more than you ever wanted to know, believe me," Meg said, letting out a half laugh that turned into a cough. Once she'd gotten her breath back, she looked at her cigarette, mouth twisting down. With a sigh, she ground it out on the asphalt, then heaved herself up. "Shouldn't you be getting back to the school? Your auntie will be looking for you."

I gave her a token glare, just to show I wasn't taking orders, then heaved myself up as well.

Meg reached for me and I pulled back, not sure what she wanted.

"Give me your hand, dumbo."

Hesitant, I held it out.

Pulling a pen from her shoulder bag, she wrote a number on my palm. "Call me when you're a free man. Until then, try to keep from getting pounded to a pulp. I won't be back in school till next week and Bryan's goons are probably plotting your demise as we speak."

"I'll keep an eye out, thanks," I promised, unable to hold back a grin. It wasn't every day a hot girl wrote her phone number on my hand. I told myself to shut it and focus on the important part: getting information. But the smile didn't go away. It seemed to amuse her, because she grinned back.

"See you around, squirt." With a flip of her hair, she

turned and moved to the front of her car, hauling open the driver's door with a loud creak and getting in.

Her epitaphs were getting real old, real fast. But I consoled myself that she said them with wry amusement rather than scorn. Just then, the vision of a stern, thin-lipped face interrupted my thoughts, and with a nervous twinge in my stomach I got moving toward the school. I walked backwards, though, so I could keep the Chevy in sight as long as possible as it pulled out of the parking lot and headed down the street.

"Getting into more trouble, then, are we?"

I only jumped an inch or two this time—an improvement, considering—but I still glared as Peter's wispy form materialized beside me, barely visible in the bright sunshine. The sneak had been eavesdropping.

I glanced around, nervous, but there was no one else in sight. "It's none of your business," I hissed and turned, jogging back toward the school and hoping ghosts couldn't move faster than a walk.

My hopes were dashed as Peter appeared in front of me, floating along without any visible effort as he gave me a worried look. "See here, young man. That girl is trouble on two legs! You can't possibly be considering—"

"I'll consider whatever I want. Now shove off!" I managed to say it without panting, despite my pace. It was nice to know that after a month off the soccer field, my body hadn't gone all soft on me.

"But, Sebastian, be sensible. What she implies is impossible, and if it is indeed more than her own childish fantasy, she could be aligned with some decidedly dangerous forces. Think of your parents!"

"I *am* thinking of them!" I stopped, my breathing quickening, though not because I'd just run from the parking lot to the school. Looking around again, I stepped into the shadow of a tree next to the school building. The last thing I needed was for someone to spot me arguing with what looked like the thin air, since anyone sharp-eyed enough to spot Peter's faint outline would probably assume they were seeing things. "Look, Peter, I appreciate you talking to me, before, when I was…in a bad way. But I'm fine now, and I have things to do. I don't need you around messing it all up. So just go away, will you?"

"But you most certainly are *not* all right. You seek to meddle with the powers of life and death—a futile quest, I assure you, and one that could damn your very soul! I regret that my presence has only driven you from despair to madness, not acceptance, as I had intended. Your parents are *gone*. They are never coming back. Until you are at peace with that fact, you will never heal."

We glared at each other for a long moment. I pushed away the twinge of doubt I felt at his words, determined to move forward. It was my only chance.

"You're wrong," I finally said, voice low.

"I most certainly am not!" Peter huffed.

"Have you ever been beyond the veil?" I challenged.

"Well…not precisely…that is—"

I stabbed the air in triumph. "Ha! Then how do you know there's no coming back? You don't. No one does, really, and so I'm not giving up. I'll never give up."

"But, see here—"

"Just shut up, will you!" I said it louder than I'd meant, and the sound bounced off the school and echoed across the parking lot. Startled, I lowered my voice. "Will you cut the lecturing crap? I don't need a babysitter. I need a friend. And since you obviously don't know how to be anything but a busybody, you might as well just disappear back to where you came from."

Peter's face fell and he seemed to wilt, his incorporeal

form dimming, becoming almost invisible in the shade of the tree. I felt a pang, and opened my mouth to apologize, but then forced it closed again. I was no fool. I already knew the path I'd chosen was one of danger, maybe even death. But if I couldn't fix my mistake, then perhaps death was better than this living hell.

I turned away and stepped toward the sidewalk.

"W—wait." His voice quavered.

About to leave the shade of the tree, I stopped and looked back. Peter's face—white and misty—was set, and his eyes…they seemed almost real. His round pupils were not empty, but filled with a swirling darkness that spoke of endless pain. I couldn't look away.

"Wait," he repeated, then seemed to gather himself. "I can be a friend. I'll admit, at my age I have forgotten much of what it feels like to be young and…alive. But I let my family down once before, and it doomed us. I—I do not want to do so again."

Moving hesitantly, I came back. For the first time I felt an awe at his presence that, before this, I had been too wrapped up in my own grief to notice. I wondered what he meant by doom, but felt now would be a bad time to ask. So instead I said, "Are you for real?"

"Well, as real as a ghost can be, I suppose." He sniffed, twitching his pale mustache.

"No, I mean, are you serious? You really want to try and be my friend?" I felt half hopeful, half incredulous. How could a who-knew-how-old, pompous dead guy be my friend? At the same time, having a ghost on my side could have definite benefits.

Peter nodded solemnly. "Dead serious, lad…no pun intended, of course."

A chuckle escaped my lips, and I shook my head. "Look, if you're serious, there are some ground rules we need to get clear first. The most important one is: you keep your friend's secrets. No matter what."

"Well I...that seems...in this particular situation, that is...a bit hasty?"

I gave him a stern look. "It doesn't matter. You can't be my friend if I can't trust you."

"But what if—"

"You can't have it both ways, Peter. Either you're my nanny or my friend. You can't be both, so choose."

"...Very well. Friend it is."

"You won't tell my aunt what I'm doing?"

"No."

"You swear?"

The ghost heaved a deep sigh. "On my honor as a gentleman, you have my word."

"Good." I crossed my arms, aware that my time was short and I needed to get back before Aunt Barrington threw a fit. "The next rule is, friends never steal each others' girls."

"I beg your pardon?"

"Okay, so obviously you can't 'steal' anything. What I mean is, friends don't sabotage each other's, er...efforts," I finished lamely, aware that my face was growing red.

"I see."

"Never mind. The point is, friends have each others' backs."

"I...have your back? That's odd, I thought I had mine..." He looked over his shoulder as if trying to examine his own backside.

"No, I mean we *watch* each others' backs."

"Oh! Very well, if you insist, but...is there something wrong with it?" Now he attempted to circle around behind me.

I clutched my head, wondering if this was more trouble than it was worth. "Holy cow, what century are you from? It means we help each other out, idiot. You know, like two guys in a fight? They watch each other's back so they don't get jumped from behind."

"Ah! Now I see. But do you expect that we will encounter many altercations? I'm not corporeal, you see, so I might not be of much assistance—"

I sighed, giving up. "Just do the best you can, okay?"

"I shall. On my honor, I shall!"

"Good…well…we'd better get going. Aunt B is probably looking for me by now and I don't want to get in trouble again."

"An excellent plan…friend."

I rolled my eyes. "Just call me Seb."

"Seb it is. Lead on!"

Shaking my head, I turned and jogged the rest of the way around the school building, feeling cautiously optimistic despite the ache in my chest that I suspected would never completely go away. I had a plan, and I had a friend…sort of. I wasn't sure how that whole thing was going to work out, but maybe Peter would surprise me.

8

My week didn't get any better, but at least it didn't get worse, either. After some cajoling from Peter —who pointed out that Aunt Barrington would be unlikely to let me out of the house, much less buy me a cell phone, if I was failing class—I finally started paying attention in school and turning in assignments. Every second I spent adding sums or answering stupid essay questions was torture. I couldn't get the image of my parents, dead and rotting under the ground, out of my head. They haunted my waking and my dreaming, and all I wanted was to get on with it. But I knew I would never succeed if I didn't play things right.

The first step was to get a cell phone and regain some semblance of my aunt's trust so I could come and go freely. It was tedious, pretending to care, but it got things done faster than ignoring her authority, and I wasn't ready to run away. It was a tempting option, because then I could focus fully on my mission without pointless distractions. But there were too many risks. Despite the information Meg had promised me, I doubted I could depend on her for food and shelter.

So I went to school, did my classwork, and finished detention without complaint. I even tried to smile—or at least not frown—when people spoke to me. I didn't feel like a dead man inside anymore, but I certainly wasn't alive. My heart and mind burned with purpose, fueled by a spark of improbable hope. Yet there was no joy or comfort in it.

Peter, to my amazement, kept his promise. He was surprisingly good company for a dead guy. Despite his quirky ways and old-fashioned manner of speaking, he had a wickedly dry sense of humor and, unlike most adults, wasn't a total bore. With his humor and faint accent, I wondered if my family, the Blackwells, had originally been from England. That would explain a lot about my aunt. The similarities between her and Peter were striking—except for the sense of humor, of course. He managed to keep my spirits up even though I resisted his attempts at levity. Eventually, I realized it helped pass the time and kept me from wearing myself down with worry.

By the end of the week we were whispering together about various classmates and their terrible fashion choices— the lack of trousers and ties was scandalous, Peter informed me—while I rated the hotness level of girls. Though initially hesitant to talk about women, Peter warmed to the topic and told me all about how different girls were back when he was young. He especially lamented their lack of ball-gowns, but I pointed out that at least now it was easier to see their legs. That set him off mumbling about ungentlemanly behavior, so I rolled my eyes and let it drop.

Personally, I went for faces over legs. Despite the efforts of the cheerleading team, I knew better than to value looks above personality. I'd witnessed enough of their drama to know that I should admire such beautiful disasters from a far. A nice face, though, that was hard to stay away from. You could find out a lot about somebody from their eyes, the tilt of their brow, and the curve of their lips, not to mention their laugh lines. I always looked for laugh lines. My mom said they were the mark of a good person. Unfortunately, I had yet to meet a girl whose face I liked who would also put up with me, popular or not.

When the weekend finally came, I breathed a sigh of relief. I had a whole two days to recover before facing the world again. Plus, I'd persuaded Aunt Barrington to take me to get a cell phone. I'd tried for it earlier during the week, but she'd said she had quite enough to deal with at work without trying to wrap her head around "mundane technology." Apparently, there were a lot of girls where she worked because she complained all week about the "lack of manners taught to young women these days." I was surprised someone as old as my aunt was still working full-time, but I vaguely remembered my father mentioning that wizards lived longer than most mundanes. Even so, she *had* said she was looking for a replacement, she just couldn't find anyone who met her high standards. I was sure she'd be working till the day she dropped, with standards like hers.

Putting my aunt's work woes out of mind, I focused on my mission. As soon as we got back to the house from our shopping trip I rushed up to my room and called the number Meg had given me. Gripping my new phone in one sweaty palm, I wiped my other on my pant leg as I listened to the line ring. Peter was busy playing a game of darts, as he often did to occupy himself. He used darts that I could neither see, nor hear, so I figured they were just as imaginary as his pipe.

"Hel—hella—lo?" The voice that answered the phone did not sound like Meg's, though the words were so slurred I wasn't sure I'd have recognize it either way.

"Um, hi? My name is Sebastian. I'm one of Meg's friends from school. Is she around?"

"MEEEG!"

I winced and held the phone away from my ear as the person on the other line yelled right next to their phone's mouthpiece.

"Sh—she's comin'."

"Er, thanks." I waited with bated breath. Finally, I heard footsteps and Meg's soft voice telling whoever had answered the phone to go lie down.

"Hello?"

"Hey, Meg, it's Seb."

"Oh, hey."

There was silence, and I resisted the urge to ask who the other person was. Her mother, perhaps? Meg didn't seem in a rush to volunteer the information, so I decided not to poke around.

"Um, I got a cell phone."

"I couldn't tell."

I felt a tug on the corner of my lips. Meg was as prickly as a porcupine, but I was quickly growing fond of her sarcasm. "Well, I did. So, can we go on this adventure you mentioned?"

There was silence for a moment. "No," Meg finally said, voice low. "Not today. It's…not a good time."

"Tomorrow, then?"

"Yeah, tomorrow night. How late can you get away with?"

I thought about that. "With school being the next day, probably not past ten."

"Well, ask for eleven. Tell her it's my birthday or something. Say whatever you have to."

"Okay." I noticed Peter, while not looking at me, had drifted over in my direction as nonchalantly as a ghost playing an imaginary game of darts could.

"We'll meet where I dropped you off the other night. Be there at eight."

"Got it," I said, and hung up. "You know, you don't have to eavesdrop." My words made Peter's mustache twitch as he turned toward me with affected surprise.

"What's that, my boy? Me? Eavesdrop?"

I rolled my eyes. "We're friends, remember? You keep my secrets, I keep yours. At least, that's how it's supposed to work." I eyed him. He still wouldn't tell me why he was here, what unfinished business kept him from passing on, or how he had "failed" the family. He clammed up at the mere mention of it and, if pushed, would vanish, returning extremely glum hours later. So, I'd stopped prodding him.

Looking at his painfully curious expression, I sighed. "If you have a question, ask it."

"Ah, well. In that case...what is the plan?"

"She's picking me up at eight tomorrow night."

"And?"

"I dunno." I shrugged. "She's not exactly a chatty person. I assume she'll tell us what we're doing once she sees us."

"Hmm." Peter, looking contemplative, twirled his mustache around a finger, or at least tried. His mustache wasn't quite long enough, but I got the impression it had been at one time, because it was a gesture he seemed to unconsciously default to on a regular basis. "I do not like it," he finally declared. "She could be up to anything, and we have no guarantee it is with your best interests at heart."

I snorted and waved away his concern, throwing myself back on my bed to stare at the ceiling. "Of course she doesn't have my best interests at heart. Who do you think she is, the Red Cross? I think she wants an ally, or at least a tool, and maybe a friend. Anyway, I'm not an idiot. She wants something. Our job is to find out what it is, and hopefully get what we want in the process."

"If you say so. I still have a bad feeling about this."

"You're dead. You don't get feelings anymore."

"Well! I never—that is quite unfair, you—"

I sat up, laughing. "Calm down, grandpa. You'll lose your teeth if you let your mouth hang open like that."

Peter stared at me for a moment more, then, catching on, closed his mouth and crossed his arms, lips pressed together in a very Aunt Barrington-like way. "That was not amusing, young man."

"Yes, it was." I grinned and lay back down, still chuckling.

"Then I suppose rudeness is another rule between friends? You must annoy each other at every opportunity?" His indignation was palpable.

"Definitely."

"Hmph. Scandalous, if you ask me."

"You're catching on."

"Harrumph!"

"You'll get over it."

He did, and soon got his own back when he reminded me of the mountain of catch-up work I had to do for school. I tried to blow it off, but I knew if I wanted to stay in my aunt's good graces, at least for now, I needed passing grades. Peter softened the blow by offering to help with my American History essay, and promised that, if we got everything done, he would give me a tip on convincing strict, old women like Aunt Barrington to let me stay out late at night.

Maybe having a ghost for a friend wasn't so bad after all.

9

Peter's tip wasn't very fun, even if it did get the job done. Finishing all my assignments in one day made my brain feel like a puddle of mush, but it gave me the leverage I needed. With proof of my studiousness in hand, I told my aunt that a friend needed help with their homework and had asked me to come over. Why so late? They worked part time and could only study at night. My aunt looked surprised, and possibly suspicious, if her eyebrows were anything to go by, but I got my permission. Peter, it seemed, was smarter than he looked, and I decided to pay more attention to him in the future. Not that I'd be taking his advice or anything—what self-respecting teenager would? But maybe he wasn't as clueless as I'd assumed.

We arrived at the meeting place five minutes early, then sat around watching the sunset for over half an hour before Meg finally graced us with her presence. Peter had promised to keep quiet if I let him tag along, but he couldn't seem to resist a few muttered comments about the character flaws of tardy people. I ignored him and climbed into Meg's car, shutting the passenger door with a firm pull—the only way to get it to stay.

"Took you long enough."

She gave me the finger.

"Touchy," I muttered, deciding to let the silence settle and simply enjoy the breeze on my face. We were headed south again, but not by the same route she'd taken last time.

After a while, my curiosity got the better of me. "So, where we going?"

"You'll see."

"Seriously, Meg, you gotta start telling me stuff. I'm not your pet dog."

"Well, maybe you should be."

I could see her teeth as she grinned in the dimness.

"You wish. Now, where are we going?"

"You'll see."

I heaved a sigh. Clearly I wasn't going to win this. Then again, I couldn't keep following her around like a blind beggar either. I needed her to trust me. Maybe I could take a leaf out of Peter's book.

"You know, whatever it is you're trying to do, I make a better friend than a tool."

"I dunno, you look like pretty good tool material to me." There was that grin again, but it flashed for only a moment before her face grew oddly grave.

I gritted my teeth and took an educated guess. "Yeah, but if you ever want to see your dad again, you're going to need a friend to watch your back."

Silence.

"You're not as dumb as you look," she finally said.

"And you're not as shallow as you pretend."

"Dang, there goes my cold-hearted-bitch card. And I fought so hard for that thing."

I laughed. I couldn't help it. "Don't worry, I'm sure you'll get it back Monday morning at school. But for now, let's cut the crap, okay? There's more to both of us than meets the eye, so enough with the games. We've got more important things to do."

"Jeez, you're no fun," Meg joked, but her voice lacked the same teasing note. She quieted, staring at the road ahead with a somber expression.

I waited. Sometimes silence was as powerful as words. Minutes passed.

"Do you believe in the supernatural?"

Her question caught me off guard, and I gave a cautious response. "Yeah. A bit." The understatement of a lifetime. Judging by the soft chuckle in my ear, Peter agreed, and I had to hold back a grin at the vision of him trying to twirl his not-quite-long-enough-mustache around his finger.

"Good, because the last guy I tried to show this stuff to peed his pants and ran off screaming."

"Really?" This sounded interesting.

Meg snorted. "No. I've never told anyone before. Not a soul…" she trailed off, quiet voice almost lost in the wind blowing past our open windows.

"Well, I've got a few dark secrets of my own, so you're in good company."

"Yeah? They're probably not as dark as mine."

"You'd be surprised," I muttered, remembering the screech of crumpling metal. The seatbelt felt tight against my chest, and I shifted uncomfortably.

"Probably not. I've walked darker roads than you could ever imagine, not even in your dreams."

I glanced over and saw the pain in her eyes, lit intermittently by each passing streetlight.

"Tell me."

"I—it's a long story. The details aren't important. The point is, it all started when my dad died. That's when everything went to shit. But I've been searching for a couple years now and I think—I think I might have found a way to get him back. To get your parents back, too…if you want."

"Go on." My heart started thumping, racing in my chest.

"Have you ever met a witch before? A real one, I mean."

There was a surprised hiss in my ear, and I barely managed to not twitch in response. I mentally willed Peter to keep his trap shut and hoped he had enough sense not to make a fuss.

This wasn't right. I had expected her to say wizard, not witch. What was she talking about? My brows drew together, and I took a chance. "You mean wizard, right? You know it's a genetic thing, not gender based."

"No, dumbass, I mean witch."

Well, that was just peachy. If my father had been adamant about the dangers of wizard magic, he'd been absolutely fanatical about the evils of witches. I'd asked him once, on one of the rare occasions he'd actually brought up the subject of magic. I'd assumed wizards and witches were the same kind of person, just different genders. Boy, was I wrong. Wizards, like my father and Aunt Barrington, were born with the innate ability to use magic. Witches, on the other hand, were mundanes like me who "acquired" magic by other means. The way my father had said, "acquired," you'd have thought witches were sacrificing their first-born children to the devil. Maybe they were, I had no idea. But it looked like I was about to find out.

"So…you're a witch?"

"Yeah. Scared yet?"

I gave her a sidelong look, and this time I was sure I saw a red tint in her eyes, almost a glow. But then the car in front of us sped up and I realized the glow had just been the reflection of its taillights. Or had it?

I shook my head. "I don't think there's anything left in

this world that would scare me. Not after...what's already happened."

Meg chuckled grimly. "I doubt that."

Frowning, I stared at the road ahead of us. Ghosts? Witches? What was next? Delivery owls and talking hats? I considered telling her my family background, but then thought better of it. If wizards hated witches as much as my father's attitude had implied, maybe the feeling was mutual. This was too important to let anything mess it up. So I kept quiet.

Meg didn't offer up any more information, perhaps assuming I needed time to process her "big revelation." I took the time to try and remember everything I'd ever heard about witches. It wasn't much. I wanted to ask Peter, but couldn't carry on a conversation with him in front of Meg, not even a whispered one.

Unfortunately, by the time Meg turned off the main roads and started driving through backstreets and alleys I still hadn't come up with anything useful, so I turned my attention to our surroundings. The drive had taken over thirty minutes, which meant we were far into South Atlanta.

When she finally stopped the car and shifted into park, it was fully dark out. Getting out cautiously, I surveyed the street. I was pretty sure we were in one of those neighborhoods where mugging was the norm. Meg had parked down the street from an old strip mall. When we'd passed in front of it, half the stores looked vacant, with a ubiquitous nail spa on one end and tanning salon on the other. Both were closed at this time of night.

"Come on," Meg said, voice low, almost a whisper.

"What are we doing?" I hissed back, not liking the situation one bit.

"*You're* not doing anything, just keeping watch. *I'm*

looking for something we'll need if we ever want to see our parents again. Are you in, or not?"

"No, we are most certainly not!" Peter's voice hissed in my ear. "This is exceedingly foolish. Anything could happen!"

I hesitated, though not because of Peter's frantic whisper. It was a remembered echo of my mother's voice that weighed on my conscience. But she was gone. If I could just hear her voice again for real, I didn't care what kind of trouble I got into.

So, I nodded.

Meg motioned, and I followed. We crept down the street and turned into the alley behind the strip mall. I wasn't sure why we were sneaking. There was no one in sight, and the one lonely street light within sight was flickering on and off, doing little to push back the shadows between us and the rest of the alleyway.

We reached a metal door, the back entrance to one of the stores. It had no handle, or even a keyhole, so I was skeptical how Meg thought she was going to open it.

"Keep watch," she whispered at me, grabbing my shoulders and spinning me around to face the alleyway. I dutifully scanned our surroundings and, seeing nothing, peeked over my shoulder. Meg was in front of the door, face close to where the doorknob would have been. Then she started whispering. I strained my ears, trying to catch her words, but I couldn't decipher what she was saying. It sounded like she wasn't even speaking English. That made sense, I supposed. On the very few occasions I'd seen Aunt Barrington use magic she'd spoken a strange language as well. But in Meg's case, I was puzzled where she was getting her powers. If she wasn't a wizard, she couldn't use magic directly. What creature or force was she calling upon?

Completely forgetting the alleyway, I watched, fascinated, as Meg chanted some sort of incantation. Then her tone changed and she spoke in short bursts, as if giving orders. Suddenly, the metal door shifted, inching outward. Meg grabbed the edge with her fingers, straining to grip the smooth metal as she pulled outward. As soon as a crack appeared, she slipped her fingers inside and pulled the door all the way open. I noticed a soft red glow inside that faded as soon as Meg got a good hold on the door. Remembering I was supposed to be keeping watch, I turned away before she could notice me staring.

"Come on," Meg whispered behind me, and I turned to see her faint outline in the doorway, beckoning me inside. As I entered, the street lamp flickered on and I could read the name plate on the white-washed wall beside the door. It said, "New You Counseling Center."

Once inside I crept down a hall, passing a few office doors as I followed Meg in the near-complete blackness. The only light was a red glow from the exit sign above the door we'd come through. Was that the light I'd seen as Meg had opened the door?

My partner in crime had stopped halfway down the hall where she now crouched in front of another door. Just as I caught up with her I heard a lock click. She opened the door with one hand while the other reached inside her jacket pocket to produce a penlight. Its white glow illuminated a utility closet with cleaning supplies and an electric panel on the wall. I was about to ask what in the world we were doing when Meg shifted a box of toilet paper to reveal a square outline in the floor. At first I was confused, but then I spotted the hinges on the far edge. A trap door...with no handle.

Meg spoke another word, louder this time, as if she were less worried about being overheard. It most definitely wasn't English. It sounded harsh and guttural, and not at all pleasant. The trap door shifted, and I was sure I saw a red glow this time. But I blinked and it was gone, leaving me more confused than ever.

"This is where you come in," Meg whispered, breaking into my confused thoughts.

"What?"

"I'm going down there. You need to get back to the alley door and keep watch. If you see or hear anyone coming, get your butt over here and warn me."

"Er, okay. But what are you doing? What's down there?"

"Save your curiosity for when we aren't breaking and entering, will you?"

I shot her a glare, then retreated, though I couldn't pass up a look over my shoulder as I left the closet. Meg was disappearing through the trap door, and there was definitely a red glow now. I rubbed my eyes, but by then Meg had gone, closing the trap door behind her. I glared at it, wondering how she expected me to warn her through a closed door. But perhaps she'd done it on purpose so I couldn't follow—which, of course, was exactly what I'd considered doing.

Grumbling, I returned to the back entrance and inched it open enough to see out. Fortunately, it faced the entrance of the alley, so I could easily spot anyone coming in that way. Other than that, I would just have to listen carefully and hope any nighttime visitors were much worse at creeping than I was.

"This is not good, not good at all."

"Seriously, Peter?" I hissed, clutching my chest. I was sure I'd just had a mini heart attack.

"Yes, this is very serious. Very serious indeed!" He sounded genuinely concerned.

"Shh! Someone's going to hear you. Just calm down and explain, will you? Quietly."

Peter's voice lowered again and I listened to him carefully, trying to keep my senses alert to any movement outside and pay attention to the ghost's words at the same time.

"She is a *witch*. Did your father teach you nothing?"

"He taught me plenty. Whether any of it was worth listening to, though, I have no idea."

"What ever do you mean?"

"He was a wizard who was anti-magic. If that doesn't sound like a seriously confused person, I don't know what would."

"Ah, yes, that..." Peter paused, and I glanced at his wispy form, glowing faintly in the darkness. If I hadn't known better, I would have sworn I saw regret, even guilt, in his eyes. But it vanished, and he continued. "He had his reasons, I can assure you. But that is not the point. Witches are not *natural*. Had they been meant to use magic, they would have been born with it. If a trained wizard who is *trying* to be careful can wreak havoc, then an untrained mundane dabbling in the supernatural is infinitely worse!"

"But why?" I asked. "Are we mundanes somehow morally inferior?"

"Well, not exactly—that is, I might say less prepared. Wizards are taught from a very young age the responsibility that comes with their gifts. But that doesn't even begin to address the real issue."

"And that is?"

"Allegiance." He whispered it in the sort of spooky voice adults use to scare children at Halloween. Which was ironic, coming from a ghost.

I didn't immediately reply, taking a moment to listen to the silence and make sure I wasn't missing someone sneaking up on us. Finally, I took the bait. "Okay, what's that supposed to mean?"

"Something given, something gained. That is the witches'

way," Peter intoned, still trying to sound spooky. He only succeeded in making me roll my eyes. Ghosts. So dramatic.

"Yeah, so what?"

"Do you not see?" Peter whispered. "Magic is a wizard's birthright. We owe no allegiance unless it be to our very creator. But witches, they must trade and bargain for their abilities, putting themselves at the behest of powers and principalities they do not understand. It is a perilous risk, and no witch remains unchanged. They create ties that bind, for good or ill. Most often for ill, I shouldn't wonder."

A chill ran down my spine at his words. What had Meg gotten herself into? What had *I* gotten myself into? But no, it didn't matter. I tried to focus, to remember the goal. That empty ache in my chest reminded me that whatever the price was, it would be worth it. Right?

"I think you're worrying about nothing. Meg seems nice enough. Everything will be fine," I insisted, trying to reassure him.

"Fine? Fine?! How can—"

"Shh!" I cut off his rapidly rising voice with a frantic gesture. Headlights had passed the alley's entrance and I waited, wanting to make sure the sound of the engine disappeared into the distance. It faded, and I relaxed, letting out a breath. But a few moments later I noticed a glow appear on the wall. Light was filtering into the hallway as if coming from the front of the building. Carefully, I let the back door click shut, then raced on tiptoe past the utility closet to where the hallway turned left. Peering around the corner, I saw another small hall which opened up into a waiting room with a reception area. Through the room's large glass windows I saw bright headlights flicker off and a door light come on as a man stepped out of a dark-colored van.

10

"Not good," I whispered, hurrying back to the utility closet. There was no point waiting around to watch the man unlock the front door. Why would anyone park directly in front of a building they didn't intended to enter? The rattle of keys confirmed my suspicion and I skidded into the utility room, dropping to my knees and digging frantically at the edge of the trap door. It didn't budge. I dared not make a noise, either to call or knock on the wood, in case the person up front heard me.

"Peter? Peter!" My desperate whisper was barely a breath, one I hoped Peter could hear.

"Oh dear, what is it?"

At the sound of his voice I almost sagged in relief. "Go warn Meg. Hurry!"

I had the oddest sensation, as if I could feel him leave. Perhaps I was becoming attuned to his presence, the way you can sense that someone is with you in a dark room. There was no whoosh or dramatic flicker of lights, just…an emptiness. Whatever it was, I had no time to dwell on it. He was back a moment later, whispering just as frantically into my ear.

"She's coming. Let us vacate the premises post haste!"

I paused to listen and make sure our nighttime visitor hadn't yet entered the hallway. The sound of an opening door told me they were only just into the building. I bolted for the back entrance, taking a second to check that the coast was clear in the alleyway before slipping out, then catching the door as it closed behind me. Holding it open just a crack, I peered through and waited with tense muscles pumped full of adrenaline.

"Come on, Meg. Come on!" I muttered, as if that would make her go faster. But no one emerged from the utility closet. I could hear heavy footsteps approaching. She wasn't going to make it.

A figure appeared in the hallway coming from the reception area. I could only just see his face in the red glow of the exit sign—he hadn't bothered turning on any lights, for some reason. The man's movements were unhurried, but even so it would only take him a few more steps to reach the utility closet. That had to be where he was going. Why else show up at a closed office this late at night? I doubted he was there to do paperwork.

I had to act, fast. I wracked my brain, thinking desperately. Then it hit me. "Peter, quick! Distract him!"

"How?" The ghost's voice was barely a squeak.

"I don't know. Just do something. Hurry!"

The man had stopped in front of the utility closet. His hand reached for the doorknob.

"Excuse me, good sir. Are you closed for the evening?" The muffled sound of an elderly voice filtered in from the front of the building.

The man's hand, already on the doorknob, paused, and his head turned, cocked in confusion.

"Hello? Is there anyone there?" the elderly voice called out again.

Letting go of the knob, the man turned and headed back toward the waiting room. As soon as he rounded the corner and disappeared, I saw the utility closet crack open.

"Mayday! Mayday! Evacuate!" Peter's panicked command hissed in my ear.

Throwing caution to the winds, I opened the back-door wide, motioning frantically for Meg to make a break for it. She did, moving surprisingly silently for someone in boots as clunky as hers. As soon as she was through, I pushed the door closed, slowing its motion at the last second so it would click shut quietly instead of slamming.

We didn't wait around to see what happened next, but bolted down the street toward Meg's car. I winced at the screech of hinges as we opened the doors and the roar of the engine, amplified in the still night air. But no one came running down the road after us and we sped safely off into the night. It wasn't until four blocks later, and several ignored stop signs, that I finally relaxed back into the seat and allowed myself to breathe.

We'd gotten away.

"What the *hell* was that?" I demanded, turning to Meg. I was furious. Furious and full of adrenaline still pumping through my body.

"I could be asking you the same thing!" she said, eyes wide in the reflected glow of the streetlights.

"What do you mean? You're the one who led us into that. We almost got caught! Did you know that man was going to come? Was this some kind of sick test?"

"No! Of course not. Don't be an idiot."

"Then what was it?"

"My mom's boyfriend."

"W—what?" Now I was really confused.

"That man. That was Roger, my mom's boyfriend. He owns the clinic. I didn't think he'd come by tonight. They just had a—I mean, he was there yesterday, so I assumed things would be quiet tonight."

"Okay, seriously, what's going on? Were you just trying to steal his stash of prescription drugs or something? Are you pulling my leg with all this supernatural crap?"

"No! Jeez, you really are being an idiot."

"I think I'm asking very reasonable questions, considering the situation."

"Well, just calm down, will you? We weren't caught, okay? Thanks to you. What happened back there? What was that voice I heard?"

"You're not the only one with...friends," I growled, glaring at the dashboard with my arms crossed. I wasn't feeling particularly generous, considering the scarcity of information coming from her. She could just sit there and wonder for all I cared.

We drove in silence, which was fine by me. I wanted to put as much distance between us and that clinic as possible. With each passing mile, the effects of the adrenaline faded and I went from pumped to exhausted.

After a good ten minutes, Meg pulled off the main road and into a brightly lit gas station. She parked the car, then turned toward me.

"I'll tell if you'll tell," she challenged.

"You first," I countered. I was still angry.

Her eyes narrowed, but finally she sighed and blew out a puff of air. "What do you know about witches?"

"More than you might think."

Meg snorted. "Alright, Mr. Know-it-all, ever study demonology?"

I hesitated. "Not really, no."

"Good. Don't. It's a stupid thing to do, unless..." She

stopped, now looking right at me, and there was no mistaking the red tint to the whites of her eyes. "...Unless you have nothing left to lose."

Her words were simultaneously a warning and a dark caress. I shivered. A cold lump had formed in the pit of my stomach, but I ignored it, clenching my hands into fists. "I have nothing left."

Peter muttered a protest in my ear—"I beg your pardon. What am I, a lawn ornament?"—but I ignored him.

"Good," Meg continued, not privy to Peter's annoying peanut gallery comments. "Listen up. The only way to get our parents back is to make a deal with death. Of course, who knows who, or what, death is. But there's a demon known as the Prince of Decay who might be able to help us. For a price, of course."

"Jumping Jehoshaphat!" I ignored Peter's exclamation, already in the process of voicing my own objections

"Whoa, whoa! Wait a minute. Stop right there." I held up my hands. "First of all, how do you even know this demon exists? Second, how do you know he'd honor his bargain? If he's a demon, I'm sure he would have no problem lying through his teeth and backstabbing us as soon as he got what he wanted. Third, I don't know about you, but this seems like a really bad idea. Like, bringing-a-gun-to-school kind of bad idea. It doesn't seem...right. How could a demon have the power to bring back the dead? My parents aren't in...they didn't go to..." My throat closed up and I couldn't finish the sentence. The mere thought of such a thing, of such a place, set my heart racing with fear for my mom and dad.

"Oh, believe me, he has the power," Meg said, eyes glowing even more brightly. "I'll show you."

Her voice changed, and she spoke in that guttural language I'd heard her whisper before. It sounded vile, bringing to mind dead, creeping things. Suddenly, on the seat between us, a creature appeared. I jerked back in shock, scrambling away and pressing myself against the car door.

The creature was small, barely ten inches tall, and roughly humanoid. It almost looked like some sort of pixie or fairy, but twisted from its natural form. The face was elongated with piercing red eyes and tiny, sharp, red teeth. Delicate gossamer wings sprouted from its back, but the membranes were torn and appeared to be rotting in places, pieces hanging off and flapping in the motion of its brief flutters, like a wasp threatening to take flight. Its lithe form was covered in rough scales, black with tints of red. But the scales didn't seem to be a part of its body. There were a few places where they were missing and I could see smooth skin beneath. The scales reminded me of some sort of parasitic or fungal growth that had taken over its host. Whatever it was, it gave off a red glow, faint like Peter, but unmistakable in the dimness.

"What…is that?" I whispered. Peter must have been shocked into silence, because no more cries of protest rang in my ear.

"A lesser demon," Meg replied with a shrug, her eyes dimmer, but still tinted with red. "They're harmless enough, and useful for getting things done."

"How are you…how do you control it?" I couldn't imagine the creature helping Meg out of the kindness of its own heart. It was currently glaring up at me from where it crouched on the seat, teeth glistening.

"I know his name, so he has to obey me. That's how demons work, at least the lesser ones. Greater demons are similar, but they're powerful enough that they can refuse your command if you don't have a strong enough will or don't know the right binding symbols. Some are so strong you can only bargain with them, not control them. Rathla'un, tell him what you told me." Her last words were directed at the creature. The thing flinched at the sound of its name, but groveled even lower and began to speak, voice soft and sibilant.

"There is one, mistressss, a great one. Prince of Decay. All dead, all dying thingss, are his domain. Veeery strong, he is. Yes, yes. Can bring back those who are dust. Make dust into man again. Yesss. He will give you what you desire."

"And what price would he require?" I asked, clenching my trembling hands. My brain still hadn't accepted what was in front of my eyes. But I hadn't started down this road to run screaming at the first sign of danger.

"That, only the Prince knowsss. Not this lowly slave. Oh no."

I glared at the creature. "That's very convenient. How do we know this little creep isn't lying? He could be telling us a pile of made-up garbage for all we know."

Meg shook her head. "I control him. I have his name. He can't lie to me."

"Humph, we can only hope," I muttered. "So what happens if we call upon this...this Prince and he ends up asking for something we don't have or can't get. Then what?"

The little thing remained silent, tiny black lids opening and closing over its glowing red eyes.

"Enough, Rathla'un. Go."

And just like that, the creature was gone, leaving the faintest swirl of dark mist in its wake that quickly dissipated. The only trace left was a faint smell of rotten eggs.

I looked up at Meg, heart still beating hard, but slowly returning to normal. Her eyes were bright. And white. They were white again.

"That's why we went to the clinic tonight. I was looking for a book that Roger has, the Book of Names. It has the true names of all the demons in it, with a list of the spells needed to control them."

"All?" I asked, suspicious. I noticed that neither she, nor the demon, had answered my previous question. But I let it go for now. "Call me naive, but knowing the state of humanity there are probably far too many demons out there to all be named in a single book."

Meg shrugged. "Okay, maybe not all. But lots."

"And you've seen this book yourself?" I pressed, still skeptical.

"Well…no. But I know he has it."

I crossed my arms. "How?"

"Cassius. He's Roger's son. Or step-son. I don't really know which."

"Sounds to me like this Cassius guy might be leading you on." My brows drew together and I held Meg's gaze as she glared at me.

"He isn't."

"How do you know?"

"Because he wants the book just as much as I do. Roger keeps it to himself and won't let anyone in our group touch it. He teaches us little things, little names, but we know there's more in the book." Her eyes glinted with red again, and I resisted the urge to draw back. I was seeing a pattern here.

I wasn't much of a reader, but I didn't have to be to guess how stories ended when people made deals with the devil. I'd promised myself I'd do anything to get my parents back, but that had been before I was face-to-face with a *real demon*. Intellectually accepting the possibility of their existence was one thing. But actually having one in front of me was entirely different. I was shaken. Scared, even. But should I listen to my fear? Or push it aside?

"Has it ever occurred to you that he might be right?" I

asked weakly, my fearful and more sensible side prompting me. "That maybe there are forces too powerful and dangerous to toy with?"

Meg looked away, the red glint gone. In the glow of the gas station's lights I could see the lines around her forehead and mouth deepen as her stubborn scowl softened into weariness. She gave a resigned sigh. "Yes. But I have to try. I can't—I can't live this way anymore. Our lives were fine when we had Dad. Since he died, everyone and everything I've ever loved has fallen to pieces."

"You still have your mom, at least," I pointed out, trying not to sound bitter.

Meg turned back toward me, expression hardening even as her eyes glistened with moisture. "My mom is so high most of the time I can't even get her to eat. And when she's not high, she's drunk. She used to be regional manager for a big department store before Dad died. Now…" Meg's jaw clenched. I could see her facial muscles twitch as she fought her emotions.

"It got so bad we sent my little brother away to live with our grandparents—I hardly ever get to see him anymore. The only reason I didn't go too is because my mom would probably drown in her own vomit if I wasn't there to look after her. I've tried to find a rehab program, but we can't afford a facility and she won't go to the free sessions. I—I think she wants to die." Head hanging, her last words were only a whisper, but they sent shivers down my spine.

There was silence, and when she looked up her eyes were as hard as shards of flint. "No, Sebastian, I don't have my mom anymore. She died with my dad and left a shell to torture me. But if I can get him back, maybe we can be a family again. I don't care what's right or wrong or if I damn my soul to hell, as long as I have my family."

My heart echoed her despair and I wanted to clutch my

chest as the pain grew. Did I care about right and wrong? I thought I did, even if I saw some things more as guidelines than actual rules. My parents had cared, often too much. They were good people, and my mom…no, I couldn't think about her. Just the memory of her face made me feel like I couldn't breathe.

Be kind.

But where was there room for kindness, or truth, or morality in the middle of such pain? I didn't know how to cope. This wasn't some cute story with a neatly packaged problem and a tidy ending where the good guys won and the bad guys got what was coming to them. This was real life. It was messy and complicated, with no good answers and no happy ending. The only thing I could do was push onward, clinging to the desperate hope that, somehow, I could bring my parents back and fix everything I'd ruined. And if I lost my own soul in the process? Well, lawyers and politicians seemed to get along fine without theirs, so I was sure I'd learn to cope.

"Sebastian, lad, do not—"

"How do we find this Book of Names?" I said into the silence, cutting off Peter's whispered plea. I knew what he was going to say, and I didn't want to hear it. He could either stay or leave. Either way, I was *not* going to give up.

"We need a distraction," Meg said. She'd gotten her emotions under control and was once again hiding behind a mask of confident boredom. "Our group meets twice a month in the secret basement of the clinic to learn and prac-tice. We met yesterday, so we won't gather again for two weeks. I'll introduce you as a new member, and Roger will do an initiation. While he's distracted, I'll sneak away and grab the book."

I gave her an incredulous look. "That sounds like the

dumbest plan since the Spanish Armada tried to invade England."

Meg rolled her eyes. "Look at you, paying attention in history class. I never took you for a nerd."

"Hey, just because I listen doesn't mean I care." I did, actually. Military history and politics were some of the few things I found interesting in school since they were all about strategy, charm, and manipulation. Things I was good at, in other words. But I wasn't going to tell Meg that. "Let's get back to the point, okay? Why not wait for another evening and sneak into this secret basement thingy again?"

"Because the book's not there. I checked. It isn't anywhere in that place, which means he keeps it at home whenever we're not meeting. And believe me, there is no way in hell we'd have a chance snatching it there. He'd catch us, and he'd kill us."

I blanched. "Like, for real kill us?"

Meg shrugged. "Probably. He doesn't take shit from anyone. I don't know why he's interested in my mom. Probably just to...just to..." Her eye twitched and her jaw locked. It was clenched so hard I thought I'd hear it crack. In that moment I felt something strange, something other than pain. It prompted me to reach out and touch her hand, hesitant, yet gentle. She avoided my eyes, but didn't move her hand away.

"I've tried to get him to leave us alone, but he says he wants to help her. He *does* do addiction therapy at his clinic, but I haven't seen any change in Mom since they met. Maybe he just wants someone to control."

"Does he—" I swallowed, but knew I had to ask the question, knew I had to help. Mom would have wanted me to. "Does he...hurt you?"

Meg glared at me, pride in her eyes, but also fear. Finally, she snorted and shook her head, pulling her hand back and crossing her arms. "He doesn't touch me. But he doesn't need to. He can hurt me just fine from a distance."

My heart constricted, but not with the wracking grief that now felt normal. It was a new feeling, a soft tug, one part pity and one part protectiveness. It surprised me, and I tried to keep it from showing on my face by hurriedly changing the topic. "So why do you learn, what did you call it—demonology—from him?"

"Because Cassius says it'll give me power. Power to protect myself, and Mom. But I know the scraps Roger teaches us aren't enough. He would never let us learn anything that could rival his power. And if he ever caught us looking at his book…" She fell silent, a shiver passing through her body. I resisted the urge to touch her hand again.

"Okay, we can't get it at his house. So why is trying to sneak a look *while he's there in the room* a good idea?" I asked.

"My thoughts exactly," hissed Peter in triumph, as if I'd just confirmed the fatal flaw in Meg's plan. Unfortunately, he forgot himself in his eagerness and was a bit too loud. I coughed to cover the sound.

Meg gave me an odd look, but continued slowly. "Because he'll be preoccupied with you. He wouldn't use the book for something as simple as an initiation. I only need a few minutes to find the right page. I can take a picture of it. Quick and easy. He'll never know."

"Won't he notice you sneaking off, though? Not that I've done many demonic rituals or anything, but based on my brother's description of frat parties, initiations usually involve everyone."

"Cassius will cover for me, and we'll all share whatever I find."

"What's in it for Cassius?" I squinted at her, that protective feeling back again at the mention of her "friend's" name.

Meg shrugged a bit too casually. "He just wants to help, I guess."

My mouth thinned into a line. Something smelled fishy. I needed to keep my wits about me where her so-called friend was concerned. "Alright. Say we pull this off. Then what?"

"The page with the Prince's true name on it will have all the information we need to summon him. Then we can bargain and get our parents back."

I didn't point out that we still had no idea what he might ask for, though at that point it hardly mattered. We had nothing left to lose. Whatever it was, we'd find a way to get it.

I did realize, however, that I had a lot of studying to do. I wasn't overly fond of books, but I also wasn't stupid enough to think I could wing a demonic summoning ritual. Whatever information was out there, I would find it. I needed better answers than what Meg was giving me.

"Your turn." Meg jerked her chin at me, eyebrow raised.

My brow creased. "Wha—oh...that." I scratched the back of my neck. "Well, I'm not really sure. Do you believe in ghosts?"

"Not if I can't see them."

"Doesn't sound like you'd make a very good witch then." I smirked at her.

"It's called not being superstitious, dummy," she said. Despite her words, there was the hint of a crooked smile on her face. "There's a crap ton of garbage out there that humanity has made up over thousands of years. Any witch with half a brain knows not to believe what you can't see, and only half of what you can."

I shrugged. "Good point. Well, I can't promise you'll be able to see him, but...Peter? Come on, you might as well show yourself."

"No!"

The sound was barely a whisper. All the same, it was quite firm, not to mention displeased.

"Come on, you old curmudgeon. She won't bite—er, will you?" I asked Meg, trying hard not to grin. I shouldn't have been making jokes at a time like this. But somehow, it made things easier. I was so broken already, making light of death and demons and possible damnation seemed like the least of my worries.

Meg grinned wickedly, apparently of the same mind. "Only if he asks nicely."

I heard an outraged splutter in my ear. "No! Absolutely not! She is a *witch*. I refuse to consort with such—such—denizens of darkness!" His hissed reply was full of such right-eous indignation that I couldn't help but roll my eyes.

"You realize, Peter, that *I'm* a witch, right? Aren't witches anyone not a wizard who meddles in magic? Well here I am, meddling. It's your fault, you know. You're the one who appeared to me and got my hopes up."

"I—not—preposterous." He'd forgotten to whisper this time and Meg looked back and forth between me and the disembodied voice coming from somewhere over my shoulder.

"I'm right and you know it, so quit whining and show yourself."

Peter fell silent, and I felt a flash of panic. Was he going to leave? I'd meant the comment about myself as a joke, though it would soon be true enough. Did he hate witches so much that he would leave, just like that, after he'd promised to be my friend? I'd assumed I couldn't hurt any more than I already did, but the thought of being utterly alone again made me open my mouth to call him back, despite my pride and the critical look Meg was giving me.

"Friends don't abandon each other just because they

disagree." A wobble threatened to creep into my voice, but I cleared my throat and went on, refusing to show weakness. "You might not like my choices, but would you rather stay and help me through them or leave and regret it when you could have saved me?" Okay, so maybe I was pushing his buttons, but it was still true.

I waited, listening, sure Meg could hear my heart thumping away in my chest, as loud as a bass speaker on full blast. Come on, I begged silently. *Come on.*

An explosive sigh made me start, and I swear I felt the wind of it, despite the fact that Peter was incorporeal. "Very well, then, you scalawag. But I shall *not* be assisting in any demonic rituals. Do you understand? Yes, young lady, I'm talking to you too!" As Peter said, "young lady," he'd appeared in all his glory right in front of her, waving a finger mere inches from her nose.

Meg let out a yelp and jerked back. "Yeah, sure, whatever! Jeez, calm down, old man. What are you wearing? A dress?"

"I beg your pardon!" He drew himself up, clutching his robe more tightly around him. "This is a *dressing gown*, I'll have you know. A perfectly respectable piece of evening wear when one is alone in one's own domicile."

"So, it's—it's an—evening gown?" Meg asked again between snorts of laughter.

Peter glared at her. "Young people these days, they have no respect, none at all! In my day—"

"In your day everyone was a perfect little angel, right? We know, Peter, so can you just give it a rest?" I pleaded.

"Whippersnappers!" And with that, he was gone.

Meg looked around, craning her neck. "Where'd he go?" she asked casually, but I could see her nostrils were flared and just a bit more white was showing around her eyes than normal.

I shrugged. "Darned if I know. He's probably hanging around somewhere nearby having a sulk."

"I heard that." Peter's voice drifted in from outside the car. It sounded like he was sitting—or hovering—on the hood of the vehicle.

A crooked grin lifted one side of Meg's mouth. "He's a feisty one. Where'd you find him?"

The memory of that night—had it only been a week ago?—surfaced and I hunched my shoulders, as if that would protect me from the pain of it all. "I didn't. He came to me, said something about protecting the family. Supposedly he's my great-great-grandfather."

"Sick," she said, looking out the windshield. But there was nothing to see.

"Look, can we go home? I mean, can you drop me off? I...I think it's getting close to when I need to get back." Actually, it wasn't even ten, but I suddenly felt weary beyond belief. Everything that had happened that night, all the revelations, the feelings, both the pleasantly new and the horribly familiar ones, had worn me down. I needed to be alone.

"Yeah. Sure." Her voice was surprisingly tender, but I barely noticed, too tired to care. I just leaned my head against the window and watched the lights pass as we drove through the center of the city, heading north.

11
———

The next two weeks were pure torture, but I forced myself through them. The only thing that kept me from losing my mind was the thought of my parents, alive and safe. Well, that and Meg Garcia. She was back at school Monday morning, decked out in even more provocative attire than before, as if she were daring the school to suspend her again. But spring was passing by and finals were approaching, so perhaps the teachers had decided to buckle down and just ignore it, knowing they would soon be rid of us all.

Me? I didn't complain one bit, though I had to work harder than normal to keep from staring. Man, did she have some nice hips. I tried not to think about them too much—my mom had taught me to respect girls, after all—but it was hard not to. Especially when she wore those platform boots. They made the way she walked particularly... erm...distracting.

We'd started hanging out together. We hadn't agreed to it, it just happened. She and I seemed to show up at the same time and place, and neither of us made any effort to avoid the other—okay, so maybe I sought her out, but the point was she didn't avoid me. And no, I didn't go looking for her just because she was cute. I had a lot of questions that needed answering, and Aunt Barrington wouldn't have let us meet up after school during the week, not with homework to be done. Plus, Bryan had returned to school, and the murderous looks he shot me promised future retribution. With Meg around, he didn't seem inclined to try anything. Yet. Not that I was afraid of him, I just wasn't stupid. None of my moves, no matter how slick, would save me from the football team's entire offensive line coming after me at once.

Cory was still hanging around like a loyal hound. A silent, vulnerable part of me was grateful, but I pushed it away. Why wouldn't he take a hint and get lost? I wasn't normal anymore, or popular. I wasn't even on the soccer team. I was a self-proclaimed outcast and didn't want or need anyone's pity. Plus, Meg and I couldn't exactly discuss our plans with him around. I managed to avoid him most of the time, but my cold shoulder didn't seem to deter him. Whenever he spotted me in the hall he'd walk beside me, filling me in on the team's progress—I tried not to care, but hated hearing that they were doing fine without me—and chatting about other inane things like girls and the latest prank he'd pulled on the PE teacher. Things I used to care about.

Now, all I wanted was to get a moment's peace with Meg in some corner so we could talk about demonology. If I was going to do something stupid, I was determined to at least do a good job of it. It would be rather ironic if I sacrificed everything just to fail in the end.

Unfortunately, Meg didn't want to talk about it at school, so instead I was forced to get to know her better. It was a real hardship, let me tell you—completely and totally agonizing.

Did I mention how attractive her face was? Her jaw was too square and her eyebrows too thick to be "fashionably" pretty. But the more I looked at her, the more I realized fashion standards should go throw themselves out a window, because I was endlessly fascinated. Underneath all the makeup, the black eyeshadow, and lipstick, her cheekbones were strong but elegant, her chin stubborn, her eyes large and lips full. It took some close observation, but I finally figured out that she wore something on her face to make her skin appear paler than normal. Makeup wasn't my strong suit, so I had no idea what it was called. Since the rest of her was covered in black, it was hard to spot the golden tinge of her skin. I wondered if Meg's goth getup was just a way of obscuring the part of herself that reminded her of her dad. I had no idea, but I would have liked to see her without it. Just her, as herself. I didn't tell her that, of course. I liked having all my teeth straight and undamaged, thank you very much.

As fascinating as I found her face, what really captivated me was her eyes. Well, and what she hid behind them. She put on a good front—almost perfect, in fact. That wall of bored sarcasm was all the world was meant to see. But every now and then, when things were quiet, I'd catch her staring at nothing and that's when the pain would show: leaking out through her eyes, the tension in her face, the way she hunched her shoulders. I ached to make it go away, but knew I was in no position to help. She could probably see the same pain in me when I wasn't focused on keeping up my own wall. It was better not to dwell on those moments. Instead, we pretended everything was normal, joking about the absurdity of crop shorts and trying to guess how many brain cells all of the football players had put together. I said a couple hundred. She guessed ten. We both laughed.

Meg had a wicked sense of humor, one I tried not to fall

in love with too thoroughly. It was nice to have someone to verbally spar with. Meg seemed to enjoy it, too. She started to relax more and, when no one else was around, would drop her omnipresent scowl. When she laughed at my snarky jokes and scathing comments, the sound was rich and genuine. Sometimes I'd stop and feel guilty, remembering the lessons in courtesy, respect, and kindness my parents had tried to instill in me. But I wasn't like my parents. I was all sharp angles and a quick tongue. And with the raw pain inside grating at every word and thought, my tongue seemed sharper than normal.

Peter didn't show back up until the middle of the week, and I could tell by his cold greeting that I was in for a long and probably boring lecture on the evils of witches and their ways. Meg only asked about him once, to which I replied that he was sulking. I could tell she was interested, but her casual "oh" told me she didn't want to *seem* interested. So instead of pointing that out, I listened to her plans to introduce me to Cassius. He would have to vouch for me to Roger, so I had to make a good impression. Meg seemed to think he'd take to me right away, but something in her voice sounded overly optimistic. Personally, my male instincts told me we'd loathe each other on sight and spend most of our time trying to crush the other underfoot, all the while pretending to be the best of friends. That was usually how it went in situations like this, though the added element of demonic rituals would certainly make things interesting.

———

As soon as I got home on Thursday, Peter pounced. At least he'd waited until I'd headed up the stairs before he started in on me. I managed to ignore him all the way through dropping my backpack on the floor, changing into more comfortable clothes, and pulling out my math homework—which I detested. At that point, my resolve crumbled and I decided I'd rather have an uncomfortable confrontation with the ghost of my great-great-grandfather than do advanced algebra.

"—and furthermore…are you even listening to me, young man?"

"What? Yeah, of course I am."

"Well, then surely you see that—"

"I have a question, actually," I said, cutting him off.

"Oh? And what is that?"

"Have you ever met a real witch and taken the time to get to know them? Or is all this just stuff you've heard?" I hadn't really been listening, but I assumed none of what he'd said was complimentary to witches.

"Why, yes. Of course. Let me see, there was the one… hmm, no, well perhaps…hmm…" He was silent for a long moment and I could tell he was wracking his brain. I wondered if memories faded after you died. Not that Peter's power of recall would have been that great in life anyway. He looked like he'd been at least eighty or ninety when he died. Though, since wizards lived so long, that probably meant he'd been past a hundred and thirty. My dad had been older than my mom, but he'd looked more than a decade younger.

"Ah! That's it. There was a man once, back during Victoria's time when I was still a young man. Quite the sensation in the papers he was. Jack the Reaper or Jack the Rapier, I can't quite recall…in any case, he was going around killing women. Ghastly thing to do, of course. Well, my father and several other wizards looked into it, suspicious as they were of any ritual murders, and they were most certain the perpetrator was a witch. They found evidence of demonic presence—sulfur and the like—but were never able to track down the culprit. A sad situation indeed. The police never had a chance, not against a witch."

"Okaaaay…is that all?" I asked, seriously not believing my ears.

"Heavens no. There was the time…let me see…yes, well, no. Hmm…ah yes. In the fifties, or thereabouts, I helped an old friend recover an artifact that had been stolen. When we finally tracked it down, we found quite the treasure trove. This thief had been busy, and not just stealing enchanted artifacts, but fine art and expensive jewelry, too. The whole place stank of sulfur and we found a stash of demonic wards as well."

"Okay. So far we have a suspected serial killer who you *think* was a witch and a kleptomaniac with demonic wards. Does that about sum it up?"

"I suppose so, yes. Do you see, now, why you should stay far, far away from that girl?"

"No."

"But—"

"Peter, the world is full of horrible people. Murderers, rapists, liars, bullies, thieves—you can hardly go a day without hearing about some new wacko or piece of filth. Just because one, maybe two of them, in all your long life, happened to also use demonology to hurt people, doesn't mean all witches are evil, murdering thieves. For all you know, they were terrible people long before they stumbled across magic."

"That's not what I meant, young man—"

"Then what did you mean?" I asked, throwing up my hands.

"What I meant to imply was that the very worst of mundanes have found ways to use magic, whether borrowed or stolen, to do great and terrible harm. Such a thing should warn us against the use of magic by the uninitiated."

"That is a load of crap."

"I beg your pardon?" Peter gave me such a look of right-eous indignation that I had to laugh, despite how exasperated I was.

"Some of the most horrible genocides ever committed by man were done using guns. Does that mean we should outlaw guns as evil and gun owners as devil worshippers?"

"Of course not, but that is hardly a sufficient comparison to the use of magic."

"Why not? No," I held up a hand, "don't tell me, because it's beside the point. Are there really no wizards, not even one, in the history of the world who have done worse things than 'Jack the Rapier' and your witch thief? No one?"

Peter stared at me, openmouthed and speechless. I gave him a good long minute, but he didn't reply.

"I thought so," I said quietly. There was no triumph in my victory. I knew that even if I'd shut him up about his prejudice against witches, that didn't mean he was wrong about the dangers of using demonic magic. Whether the creatures were some misunderstood species of reptile, or actually fallen angels, it didn't matter. In all the stories—all of them—they were bad. Meg and I were playing with fire. I hardly needed Peter to warn me I'd get burned. The question was, could I recover, or would it mutilate me beyond recognition? I didn't know, but it was a risk I'd chosen to take, and nothing Peter could say would change my mind.

I looked up and caught him staring at me with a sad expression, almost pitying, as if he could read my mind.

"Just because I have not personally known many witches, lad, does not mean I am ignorant of their ways. Witches and wizards have been at odds through millennia untold. For as long as the lust for power has burned in the hearts of mankind, man has sought to acquire it by any means neces-sary. No, perhaps not every single witch has spent their time communing with devils. But those who seek power must always pay a price. And the price for the power you seek, I fear, will haunt you for eternity, and harm many people beyond yourself in times and ways that you cannot foresee."

He hovered closer, staring at my face until I had to look away. When he spoke again his voice was soft and pleading. "Do not take this path, Sebastian, son of the Blackwells. Even were it possible, Alison and Thomas would not want to gain their own lives at the expense of yours. No parent would."

"What about me?" I asked hotly. "Aren't I allowed to want them back? I'll be fine, Peter, I'm serious. Meg is smart and so am I. I'll do thorough research and practice hard. I'll *make* this work. I have to."

"No, lad, you do *not*. Be loyal to the life you've been given. Do not try to grasp for the one that has already passed away. All things happen for a reason. Just because we do not understand that reason does not give us the right to reject it. Who are you to say who lives and who dies?"

I clenched my teeth, wishing I could cover my ears without using my hands, since that would look pretty childish. "Give it a rest, Peter, it's too late. I've made my choice. Now, are you going to help me do this in the safest, least damaging way possible? Or are you going to keep nagging me until I kill myself just to get you to shut up?"

It may have been a trick of the light, but I could have sworn I saw a shining pearl of ghostly liquid slide down his white cheek before disappearing into his beard. "Oh, Sebastian…" He sighed. "Do you know of your namesake?"

The sudden change of topic threw me off. "No. What are you talking about?"

"My son," Peter said. "Sebastian Lyle Blackwell. He was headstrong, just like you. Never did listen to me, but I loved him all the same. He, too, was determined to…accomplish something. Something which ought to have been left well enough alone. He has been dead many years now. No father should have to bury his son, but that is the way of things, at times. I grieved, yet still had my life to live and a duty to fulfill. My life was not mine to throw away in pursuit of a past that could never be recovered, nor a future that was never meant to be. But you must find your own way, and I will not leave you to walk this dark path alone."

My throat felt thick. I swallowed, not knowing what to say. I didn't want to think about his words, because if I did, I would falter. But his loyalty meant more to me than I had any idea how to express.

I wasn't alone.

That fact alone gave me hope that things would work out, whatever happened. There was no real reason for such a notion, but I'd long since learned that feelings weren't logical.

My algebra homework didn't get done. Instead, Peter told me what he knew about witches. They were less solitary than wizards, he said, but their alliances, when made, tended to be factious, since their group dynamics were based on power play rather than family lines and loyalty. Wizards didn't trust witches, nor witches, wizards. It simply wasn't done. Neither side had much in the way of formal organization, and they were usually content to ignore each other. That was, until witches started making trouble. They were always trying to steal magical artifacts, according to Peter, and occasionally caused such a ruckus that it affected mundanes. It was always up to wizards to put a stop to it and smooth things over so that mundanes could continue on in blissful ignorance.

Interestingly, Peter said it was a wizard who first invented the idea of the witch hunt. Back before even the Dark Ages, they started recruiting mundanes with misdirection and half-truths to help get rid of witches whose demonic activity was wreaking havoc on the countryside. Of course, as time went on such hunts backfired on wizards as the general attitude toward magic users soured.

Over the centuries both wizards and witches manipulated mundanes to try and attack the other. The most famous example was World War I, though of course during World War II the Third Reich's obsession with the occult was no secret. While it was generally agreed upon among wizards not to interfere in mundane politics, witches had no such qualms. Not that there wasn't the rogue wizard here and there, Peter admitted. But in general wizards preferred to live quiet, peaceful lives among mundane, while witches were always stirring up trouble.

I tried to keep Peter's bias in mind as I listened to all his stories. He was a wizard, after all, and history was written by the victors. At the very least his stories gave me better perspective for his attitude toward Meg. I had to admit, though, witches sounded much more laid back than wizards. They seemed to have fewer rules and depended on their own wits to survive, rather than on dusty tomes and family reputation. It was all about deals and trades, charisma and politics. Stuff I was comfortable with. I didn't tell Peter as much. I had no idea if ghosts could have apoplexies, but I wouldn't put it past him to try.

By the time I crawled under the covers, ready to pass out, I felt a little more prepared for my "meeting" with Cassius on Saturday. Peter hadn't known much, if anything, about demonology itself—"what decent person would!" he'd spluttered—but he'd given me some insight on demons themselves, from the wizards' side of things. The main thing he'd stressed was that demons had no goals, desires, or loyalties beyond death and destruction, and they excelled at trickery. I wondered what schemes Rathla'un had up his sleeve, or scales, and whether or not this Prince of Decay even existed. I hoped he did, for Meg's sake if not for my own. I, at least, had a sober parent-figure, even if she was stuffy as an old wardrobe full of mothballs. If things didn't work out, I knew I had to find some other way to help Meg and her mom. I fell asleep plotting daring rescues, not realizing until just before darkness took me that the pain in my chest had eased for the first time since my parents had died.

12

_____

"**S**o this is the squirt, huh?"

I tried not to pat myself on the back too hard. After all, being right about Cassius didn't bode well for me in the long run, especially since I was getting tired of demeaning names. It was as if he thought calling me squirt would somehow erase the six inches of height I had on him.

"Nice to meet you too, Cassius. You know, I have a name. I can write it on your hand if it makes it easier to remember. Oh, sorry, I should have asked first, can you read?"

The older boy's eyes narrowed. "You've got a big mouth for such a skinny runt."

I couldn't help it, I chuckled—mostly because of the generous distance he had to look up to give me the threatening glare he was shooting my way. He might have been several years older—eighteen or nineteen, I guessed—and quite a bit bulkier than I was. But it didn't matter how intimidating you tried to be if you had to look up to do it. "It gets the job done, and that's all I worry about," I replied, keeping cool.

"Well, it's gonna get you in some deep shit if you don't watch out."

I gave him an unconcerned shrug. If I'd been by myself, I might have groveled a little, just to get on his good side. But not in front of Meg. If they wanted my help, it was going to be on my terms, not theirs. I was in full-on soccer-star-cocky mode—not that Cassius cared about soccer, but that was still how I pictured myself for some reason. Thinking about my old soccer days sent a twinge of pain through me, but the memories reminded me that nothing was going to get accomplished without teamwork. Cassius wasn't going to have anything to do with me if I showed him up in front of Meg.

I sighed. "Look, let me worry about staying out of trouble, and you worry about Roger. We're all working toward the same goal here, right?"

"I *am* worrying about Roger, you dumbass," Cassius spat. Well, now I knew why Meg loved the epitaph so much. The older boy continued. "He doesn't tolerate disrespect, and if you start mouthing off to him you'll ruin everything, got it?"

I raised my hands in a placating gesture. "Yeah, okay. Sure. Whatever. Respectful, I can do respectful."

Meg snorted, and Cassius gave her a look.

"Just chill for a second, okay?" the older boy shot at me as he drew Meg away, talking to her in a low voice.

I stared after them, wishing I was a wizard and could just twiddle my fingers to enhance my hearing or something. Not that I knew anything about spells, or if hearing enhancement was even possible, but...wait a sec. I was a witch. Okay, so becoming a witch. I didn't need spells.

"Hey, Peter," I whispered.

"Yes?" His cautious reply made it hard not to grin, as if he knew I was about to get him into trouble.

"Can you hear what they're saying?"

"I'm sure I could."

"Well, then *do* so, if you please." I threw in a little politeness, in case that got him to hurry up.

There was a sigh in my ear, then a moment of silence.

"The ugly one is upset at the diseased girl for picking up such a 'snotty little piece of shit'—his words, not mine. The girl is insisting they need someone strong and smart, otherwise they'll never defeat Roger...now the ugly one has decided that perhaps she's right, as long as the new kid isn't *too* smart, or else they're both in for it."

My brow wrinkled, trying to interpret Peter's rather unflattering translation. Granted, when he said he'd stay and help, he'd never promised to have a good attitude about it. I didn't get to puzzle over it for long, though, and smoothed my expression into a bored mask as Cassius and Meg turned around and came back.

"Alright, shrimp, since you think you're up for this I'll talk to Roger. But if you ask me, you look like some wet behind the ears privileged kid who thinks they'll never get in trouble for anything, even if they get caught. We're not playing with trinkets and sitting around singing. This shit is real. We summon demons, and if we get it wrong, they kill us." Cassius stepped closer, his green eyes glowing suddenly red as he leered up at me. "They love our blood and are always waiting for their chance. Waiting for us to slip. You won't last long if you can't keep it together."

I gulped. "Seems like an odd choice of profession if you want to keep living."

Cassius stepped back and laughed. "Now you're getting it. But the rewards are worth it, right? Power. That's what we're all here for. Ain't that right, Meg?" He gave her a playful slap on the butt, and I almost jumped him then and there, except that I was frozen in shock. Meg didn't say anything, but I saw a muscle in her cheek twitch.

"I'll talk to Roger tonight and get everything arranged. We meet next Saturday at ten. You gonna make it, or is that past your bedtime?" he asked, smirking.

"I'll be ready," I forced out through clenched teeth, unable to take my eyes away from where his hand rested on Meg's hip in a very possessive manner.

"Make sure you are. Meg, take this kid home to his auntie. We've got stuff to do tonight."

Meg moved to step away, but he pulled her back, turning her to face him and kissing her full on the mouth. I knew he was doing it to provoke me, and I stood frozen in fury and indecision. Blood boiled in my veins as I saw Meg stiffen, but then she relaxed and let it happen, so I wasn't sure if I should pound Cassius to a bloody pulp or stay out of her business.

When Cassius finally broke the suction hold he had on Meg's lips, he gave me a mocking salute and swaggered off to his car—a dusty, but still impressive Mustang. I didn't move until he'd revved the engine and roared away, pulling out from under the bridge we'd met beneath somewhere in East Point.

I looked at Meg, searching her eyes, trying to see if she was okay. But everything was closed off. Her walls were firmly in place.

"Come on," she said in a deadpan tone, and turned toward her old Chevy Nova.

"What, that's it? You're just going to let him treat you like that?"

She spun on me, going from cold to blazing hot in a split second. Red flared in her eyes as she slapped me with all her strength full across the face, taking me completely by surprise. "My personal life is none of your fucking business! Now shut your mouth and get in the car!"

I lurched back, startled by her aggression, but then regained my balance, fist clenched against my side. My instinct was to defend myself, but there was no way in hell I was going to hit a girl. I didn't know what to do. I could see she was proud, maybe too proud to admit she wasn't in command of the situation. The blazing red in her eyes seemed to confirm how out of control she was, as if something else was driving her. But I doubted pointing that out would calm her, so I tried a different tactic.

"You deserve respect, Meg," I said, speaking quietly. "Every girl does."

Her bitter laugh rang out and she shook her head as if astonished by the absurdity of my words. Yet the reddish light in her eyes vanished. "You are so naive, Seb. It's kinda cute. But it's going to get you killed." Her face sobered and she looked deeply troubled, staring past me like I wasn't even there.

"Uh, Meg?" I tentatively reached out to touch her hand.

She jerked back, startled, then focused on my face. There was a crack in her mask, and it leaked sorrow. And guilt. "I'm —sorry. I didn't mean to…look, forget about Cassius. Forget about Roger. They aren't the point. They're just a means to an end and when…when we get our parents back we won't ever have to worry about them again. Okay? Now, get your butt in the car and let me worry about my own problems."

She turned and headed for her Chevy Nova and, after a moment's hesitation, I followed.

"Allegiance," Peter said sadly in my ear. "Ties that bind. There are chains around her that she cannot see, even though she herself put them there. Remember, Sebastian, all power has a price."

I didn't reply, but I couldn't help wondering: What would my price be?

———

Meg dropped me off without a word. I trudged into the house and started up the hall stairs, heart heavy. Halfway up, I heard a voice behind me.

"How are your study sessions progressing, Sebastian?"

I turned, trying not to look guilty. "Oh, um, great! They're great. We get a lot of, um, studying done."

"That is certainly good news." Aunt Barrington eyed me from the bottom of the stairs, her eyes piercingly bright even in the dim hall. "I do not believe you have mentioned it before, what was the name of your friend?"

"Oh, no one you would know. Just someone from, um, my soccer team."

"I see," she said in that universally recognized tone of voice that told me no, in fact, she did not see. "I was under the impression that you were no longer on the soccer team, is that correct? At least, I have not been informed of the time or date of any of your upcoming games."

"Er, yeah. I mean, no. I'm not on the team anymore. But that doesn't mean I don't still have friends on it, right?" My stomach twisted as I thought of Cory.

"Certainly not. I am glad your friendships have remained strong during this difficult time. I look forward to your finals report. All this hard work should certainly be reflected in excellent marks."

"Uh, yeah. Probably." I shrugged, pasting a false smile on my face. "Well, I have some algebra homework to finish before bed. Can I go?"

My aunt nodded, but even after I turned I could still feel her eyes on my back all the way to the top of the stairs.

"Sebastian."

I turned back slowly, shoulders tense. "Yeah?"

"You do know, if you need anything, anyone to talk to…" she paused, then cleared her throat. She seemed at a loss for words, which was a first. I waited, uncomfortable and trying desperately to look interested instead of guilty.

"Well…I am here, should you require aid. I am not accustomed to caring for children, but I wanted you to know that you should not feel isolated. You still have family who care for you." With that, she nodded briskly and turned, heading down the hall toward her library.

I stood for a moment, dazed, then continued to my room, trying nervously to figure out what she'd meant. Was she saying she cared? Her? My aunt was pretty much the polar opposite of touchy-feely, so that seemed unlikely. Was it a subtle hint that she knew what I was up to and wanted to help? No, that couldn't be it. She'd wring my neck if she knew my plans. So what was it? I didn't sag in relief until I'd turned the corner, entered my room, and shut the door behind me.

"I really hope Aunt Barrington can't read minds," I commented to the room in general as I collapsed on the bed.

"If she could, she would most certainly lock you in your room. Or in a mental ward," Peter's resigned voice came from the direction of my desk. I looked and found him sitting on top of it, legs crossed, smoking his imaginary pipe.

"You haven't said anything to her, have you?" I asked, giving him a narrow-eyed look.

Peter took the "pipe" from his mouth and blew "smoke" into the air before replying, "Despite my better judgment, I have not."

I lay back down. "Good. She was acting really funny just now, like she knew I was up to something."

"Unlike what most youths assume, adults are not as clueless as you might imagine. Your estimable aunt knows most things there are to know, I shouldn't wonder."

I made a noncommittal noise, eyes staring blankly ahead.

Then I had a thought. "I wonder if Aunt Barrington knows anything about demonology."

There was a beat of silence. "While Madam Barrington is one of the most powerful and skilled wizards in my acquaintance, I would highly recommend against asking her such a question."

I snorted. "Well, of course I won't ask it straight up. I can be subtle."

"As an elephant on Main Street," Peter muttered.

I lifted my head and glared at him, deciding to keep any further plans to myself. Rolling onto my side, I contemplated how to word my question in a way that wouldn't raise my aunt's suspicions. She *had* said to ask her if I needed anything, though a primer course in demonology probably wasn't what she'd meant. Maybe if I came at it from the angle of asking about my parents...I squeezed my eyes shut, not sure I had the strength for such a conversation.

In the end, it didn't matter if I had the strength or not. I was doing this for them, and so whatever had to be done, I would do it. Maybe I'd even find some answers along the way.

13

I t was four days later before I finally got up enough courage to talk to my aunt.

Meg had been unusually subdued at school and refused to talk about anything but the most inane, non-witch-related topics. Peter's coping tactic, on the other hand, was pretending nothing was wrong. His constant bugging was the only reason I did any schoolwork. I was inclined to ignore him until he pointed out that if, by some miracle, I did manage to resurrect my parents, they would be sorely displeased to see me flunking out of school. That got me to at least stop complaining, though it felt strange planning for any future beyond the impossible task that lay before me.

At least schoolwork helped pass the time. It was Wednesday night after hours of work on my modern American literature essay—literally the most boring subject on the planet—when I finally threw down my pencil and decided to brave facing Aunt Barrington as the lesser of two evils. Peter, sitting on my bed and reading a book I'd laid out for him, wished me luck. I turned the page for him before heading downstairs, shoulders squared and a fake smile of confidence pasted on my face.

It was after dinner, but not late enough for bed, so I had a good idea of where she would be. Even though I had no reason to sneak, I still tread as quietly as possible as I approached the library. By the time I stood in front of the door my fake smile had wilted, and I had to force myself to knock.

"Enter," came my aunt's muffled response.

Using my tee shirt to cover my hand—just in case—I gingerly turned the knob, only relaxing once it was clear my appendages were not shriveling into dry husks. Poking my head in, I found a room much larger that I'd expected from the outside. Everything was a deep brown, with blacks and greens scattered throughout. Here and there among the sea of books, gold lettering glinted off leather-bound spines in the light of—whoa…

I stepped into the room, head craning upward as I stared in opened-mouthed wonder at the globes of light floating over my head. For a moment, I doubted myself and checked, sure there were suspension wires somewhere. But no, there was nothing that I could see, just glass orbs hovering in midair, floating at various heights throughout the room. They gave off a warm, yellow glow akin to candlelight, but brighter and without the flicker of flame. Tearing my eyes away from that glorious sight, I turned in place, taking in the walls of orderly bookshelves, the gigantic blackboard covered in strange symbols, and the clear space in the middle of the room where a circle had been carved into the wood-paneled floor, complete with archaic runes.

For the first time in my life, instead of fear, I felt a twinge of respect—or maybe awe—for my aunt. It wasn't that I'd thought she, or my father, were liars, but I guess I'd never really *believed*. It was different when you saw it with your own eyes. Peter, and Meg's demon were different. They were so abnormal, so supernatural, that your only option was to accept them or else assume you were going insane. But with wizardry, I'd been expected to swallow it all without proof. I'd believed Aunt Barrington's threats of curses over the years more because she was downright scary than because I actually believed in magic.

"Did you have a question, Sebastian, or do you intend to gape at my office for the rest of the evening?"

My aunt's dry voice came from behind me, and I spun, swallowing, as I saw her seated behind a large desk of polished wood. Odd-looking instruments that ticked and whirred were ordered neatly to one side of several stacks of books and papers. My aunt was looking at me intently over a pair of old-fashioned spectacles. Several tomes lay open before her and she had a peculiar-looking pen poised over one of them, a glass bottle of ink beside her elbow.

"Er—yes. I…um…" I rocked back on my heels, hands clasped behind me like some nervous schoolboy as I tried to remember the innocent yet subtle questions I'd prepared. Realizing how idiotic I probably looked, I stood taller and put my hands in my pockets where I could wipe the sweat off them without seeming suspicious.

"Yes, I had a question."

"Very well." My aunt laid down her pen and set a stopper on the bottle of ink, then turned her full attention on me. "If you would sit and cease your nervous fidgeting, you might find it easier to ask it."

I gulped. Spotting a chair in front of the desk, I pulled it toward me and sat, its hard wood surface giving no relief to my twitching muscles. "I've been wondering about… about…" I took a deep breath and forced the words out. "I've been wondering about Dad, and about magic. Why didn't he use it? I mean *really*, why not? You're a wizard and you seem to be doing perfectly fine. What was he afraid of?"

Aunt Barrington leaned back slowly in her chair—and by leaned back I mean sat a touch less rigidly, since her chair was about the most severe, straight-backed monstrosity I'd ever seen. Hands folded neatly in her lap, she examined me, as if deciding what to say.

"Your father came from a line of wizards who had, shall we say, forsaken the craft for reasons of conscience. Have you ever heard of pacifists, Sebastian?"

"You mean hippies?" I asked, brow wrinkling.

"Not exactly." I could have sworn her lip twitched upward, but maybe I'd imagined it. "Pacifism is the belief that all warfare, militarism, and violence in general is unnecessary, that conflict can and should be resolved peaceably. Pacifists drafted during the Vietnam War, for example, would refuse to fight. Some pacifists—though not all, certainly—held this belief because they had witnessed the destruction violence could bring and wished to become a part of the solution rather than perpetuate what they saw as the problem. Though not a perfect comparison, your father, and his father, and his father's father before him, viewed magic in a similar way. They believed it did more harm than good, and that such power brought out only the worst in of each of us, tempting us to extremes in behavior that we would not normally resort to. Where there is great power there is great responsibility. Unfortunately, your father did not trust in wizards' capability to live up to that responsibility. It is a view that few wizards share, though ironically, it is becoming more and more popular for completely different reasons."

"What do you mean?" I asked, carefully controlling my voice as I fought to banish the mental image of my father, his skin a waxy grey as he lay, lifeless, in that horrible casket.

"Wizardkind is failing. Why, exactly, is complicated, but

for several centuries now wizards have been having fewer children, and fewer of those children possess magic in turn. In addition, general use of magic is declining with the rise of mundane technology. Contrary to how magic is portrayed in certain children's novels, it is neither easy nor safe. For the careless and undisciplined, it can easily be their death. Against such odds, fewer and fewer wizards are willing to dedicate a lifetime of careful study to master it."

"Oh." I sat, stonefaced, at a loss for words.

Growing up I'd never thought about magic in terms of a wider wizard society. To me, magic had always been a dangerous boogeyman, something to be avoided not only because I was a mundane, but because it was my family's dark secret they seemed desperate to forget about.

"Some of us, however," my aunt continued, "believe that the world is too full of dangerous and evil things to let such important knowledge die. Wizards are born with an incredible gift, a birthright that is both a privilege and a duty. Until there is no more evil in this world, we cannot prevail with words alone."

I stared blankly at the front of her desk, trying to push back the resentment that raised its ugly head. Wizard this and wizard that. What about mundanes? What about me? It wasn't fair that Golden Boy Freddie had magic when he didn't even want it. I'd always been disappointed I hadn't been born a wizard, but not until today had I been angry about it. I was responsible...mostly. At least I knew I would use magic for good. If there was evil out there hurting people, I wanted to fight it. That was more than could be said about anyone else in my family, so why was I the one born without magic?

I wondered if Aunt Barrington had ever been angry at Dad and Freddie for their "dereliction of duty." Well, I wasn't a wizard, but maybe I could still learn something, since my aunt was so adamant about keeping the knowledge of magic alive.

"Aunt B, I know I wasn't born with magic, but maybe I could learn—"

"No!" Her response cut me off mid-sentence. I was left, mouth hanging open, astonished at her sudden outburst.

"But I want to learn! I'm from a wizard family, I already know about magic, I'll do a good job. I'll keep it secret. I'll be responsible, I promise." Even as I spoke, I conveniently forgot about all the completely irresponsible and dangerous things I was planning on doing in less than three days.

"Absolutely not. It does not matter what family you were born into or how responsible a person you are. If you are not a wizard, you *cannot* use magic. It is forbidden."

"But that's not fair! Just because someone wasn't "born" a certain way shouldn't mean they can't do what they want."

"In the case of wizards, it means exactly that. Mundanes are not built to use magic. They do not have the capacity, or the will, to shape and command it."

"You're wrong. Witches can do—"

"What did you say?" Her question sliced out, cutting through my thoughts like a red-hot blade. My body broke out in a cold sweat as I realized what I'd done. I swallowed, determined to play dumb. I could fix this.

"I said that witches can do magic, too, right? I hear about them all the time. They fly on brooms and mix potions in their cauldrons." I tried to say it with a straight face, eyes wide with sincerity.

Aunt Barrington slowly relaxed, resetting her hands in her lap from where they'd gripped the arms of her chair. "That is all nonsense, which you should know full well. And witches can *not* do magic, not in the way you are imagining. What we call magic is simply energy, the Source, present in all things. Wizards are the only humans born with a connection to it. There are other beings with their own link to the Source, but only wizards can command it in its raw form. Witches are simply mundanes who, in their lust for power, have lowered themselves to the point of beggary, trading and feeding off of others to gain abilities which were never meant for them. Mundanes have no business meddling with magic, for their own good as much as for that of others. There are plenty of other ways they can contribute to society without resorting to such vulgarities."

Well, so much for my aunt teaching me about magic. Her words stung, cutting more deeply than I liked to admit. She acted like wizardry was an elite club, and if you weren't born with the right mix of genetic soup, well, too bad, you just weren't good enough. I realized I would have to change my tactics. Words weren't going to get me anywhere. I wondered why my aunt had even bothered to offer me help when she was going to jump down my throat for the simplest of questions.

"Well, thanks for the culture lesson," I said, rising abruptly. "I guess I'll go finish my homework now."

I got up and was halfway to the door when she spoke again.

"Wait, Sebastian. I—I did not mean to sound quite so…harsh."

I stopped, but didn't turn around.

She continued quietly, speaking to my back. "I simply wanted to impress upon you the dangers in your line of thinking. It is not a question of merit: I have known many great men and women, honorable and courageous mundanes, who changed the path of history. I have also known despicable wizards who were a disgrace to our kind. You must understand that magic is a gift and a duty, not a trick to be learned by any clever enough to master it. Those who were not given it, yet try to grasp it all the same, will find themselves paying a greater price than they bargained for."

Her words came too late, annoying pebbles thrown at the adamant wall of hurt I had raised around my heart. But I nodded slowly, back still turned, so she would think I believed them.

She sighed. "Very well. Goodnight, Sebastian."

I took another step toward the door, but hesitated, the memory of Peter's sorrow-filled eyes prompting me to look over my shoulder and ask one last question. "What did Dad and his dad and his dad's dad witness that made them wizard pacifists?"

Aunt Barrington's face tightened and she looked down, shuffling through some papers on her desk. "Nothing that need concern you. Now, go finish your schoolwork."

"But—"

"Go," she said, voice hard.

I left, shutting the door more firmly behind me than was necessary. And this time, I didn't use my shirt.

"Don't say I didn't warn you," Peter's soft voice joined me as I stomped up the stairs.

"Shut up," I growled back. Typical of him to eavesdrop. I wondered what he thought of my last question. I was itching with curiosity about it, but knew I wouldn't get anywhere with him.

"I don't suppose your aunt's words of warning were any more convincing than my own?"

"Go jump off a cliff."

"Well, I can, if it means that much to you. But I'm not sure it will have quite the effect you were hoping for."

"Just shut up, will you? I need to think."

"What, busy planning how to better ruin your life?"

I went through my bedroom doorway and turned to hiss at him. "If you can't think of something helpful to say then keep your mouth shut." With that, I shut the door in his face.

Not missing a beat, he floated right through it, continuing the conversation. "I thought that *was* helpful. After all, if I don't draw attention to the idiocy of your choices, then who will?"

Rolling my eyes in disgust, I crawled under the covers, put a pillow over my head, and sought out the black forgetfulness of sleep.

Apparently, even sleep had decided to be aggravating, because it was a very long time in coming.

14

Getting to my initiation Saturday night turned out to be trickier than I'd anticipated. Meg warned me that I wouldn't be home until past midnight, and I knew my aunt would never allow me out that late. If I said I was staying over at someone's house, she would demand the name and phone number of the hosting parent and probably grill me on our planned schedule of events. So instead, I resorted to that tried and true tactic of teenagers throughout history: sneaking out.

I'd already checked the back-door hinges, surreptitiously listening to see if they creaked as I strolled into the backyard for some fresh air. I'd also made sure I could easily scale the fence, since the backyard gate made more noise than a coop of angry chickens and no amount of grease was going to change that. Lastly, I'd checked out a book on lockpicking from the local library and had focused my attention on becoming a master lockpick. I'd always been clever with my hands, doing better in school with anything that involved hands-on instruction, rather than listening to some teacher drone on. By the time Saturday rolled around, I'd made my own set of picks out of some handy paperclips swiped from a teacher's desk at school, and had practiced enough on the back-door to be confident I could lock it behind me and get back in when I returned. Aunt Barrington's speech when I'd first moved in about house keys and enchanted doors had initially worried me. But I'd thoroughly examined the back-door lock and it worked perfectly fine. Perhaps the enchantments were only on the front door of the house.

Despite Peter's predictions of doom, we made it out of the house without any mishap. I'd already told my aunt I was turning in early so I could get together with friends the next day for an all-day study session. Finals were fast approaching, after all. She'd simply nodded and bade me goodnight. I wasn't sure if she ever checked on me after I'd gone to sleep, so I left some bundled-up clothes under my covers just in case.

Once over the fence, I ran in a crouch until my aunt's house was out of sight, then straightened and jogged the rest of the way to the street corner where Meg was waiting.

Our trip to Roger's clinic was silent and tense. I'd asked Meg what to expect, but she'd just shaken her head. "Either you do it, or you don't," she'd said. "If you can't do it, you're no good to either of us."

Once there, we parked several streets away and walked, since Meg said Roger didn't want people to know clandestine meetings were taking place in his clinic. At the metal back-door, Meg knocked twice, waited, then knocked three more times in quick succession. It opened to reveal a skinny teenage boy, probably my own age, his face illuminated in the red glow of the exit sign overhead.

"Fresh meat, huh?" he asked, his grin more amused than welcoming, and beckoned us inside. I couldn't tell if his eyes were anything but their normal color, not with the red exit sign as our only illumination. No lights had been turned on in the clinic, so we moved carefully down the hall. Once Meg opened the utility closet, though, a glow from the open trap door lit the way before of us.

"Watch your head," Meg warned, stepping down first and tilting her own head so as not to hit it on the lip of the trap door as she descended.

I eyed the steep stairs dubiously, predicting I would have to bend almost double to avoid beaning myself. Taking a deep breath, I grasped the edges of the hole and slowly stepped down. Even with the warning, I barely avoided giving myself a massive concussion. When I finally reached the bottom I looked around, trying to get a feel for what I had just descended into.

My first thought was: not hell.

Okay, so call me biased, or prejudice, or whatever you wanted to, but I had definitely been expecting some cross between a hippie love den and a satanic sacrificial altar. The room before me wasn't even close to either. There were no tribal-looking rugs, drapes, or pillows scattered around. No incense burned—in fact, there were no candles at all—and no spooky music played. There weren't even any pentacles, brooms, or any of the other occult must-haves I had assumed would be included in this ridiculous parade. The space was disappointingly plain, and looked more like a community center multi-purpose room than a den of demonic worship-pers. There was a long, plastic folding table with seven or eight chairs scattered around it, a metal cabinet in the corner, a white board on one wall, and a large, empty section of concrete floor on one side of the room that looked like it had been drawn with chalk and washed clean many times. That was it. No blood, no sacrificial altar, no glowing red lights. It almost felt like I was the butt of some joke. Was Meg pulling my leg?

I examined the table where she'd sat down and was

currently chatting with three other teenagers in a low voice. To my even greater surprise, the table was spread with what looked like a potluck meal. There was a crockpot of chili, a bowl of salad, and a bag of dinner rolls. The three other teenagers were already chowing down as if they hadn't eaten in a week. All three of them were skinny. Meg was just tucking into her food when I walked up and stood silently behind her, waiting for introductions.

"Oh, hey. This is my friend Seb. Seb, that's Frank, Billy, and Sasha." She pointed to each one in turn. Frank might have been in his early twenties, but both Billy and Sasha looked to be barely my age. I gave them a silent nod and sat down beside Meg, accepting a bowl of chili, because why not? Who ever turned down free food? I did, however, sniff it experimentally before I took my first bite. Just in case.

I ate silently while the conversation rolled around me. The other three eyed me curiously, but didn't ask any questions. Maybe it was considered polite not to grill the newcomer. Whatever the reason, I was grateful. Taking my time with the food, I gave my surroundings a more thorough examination. The room itself wasn't very large and the ceiling was fairly low—only about a foot above my head when I was standing straight. So even with a mere five people in the room, it felt crowded.

About halfway through my bowl, there was a lull in the conversation and I felt confident enough to ask Meg a hushed question.

"What's with the food and the whiteboard and the skinny kids?" I muttered. "I thought this was supposed to be a coven of powerful witches or something."

Meg snorted into her chili, drawing looks from the others. They lost interest as she studiously wiped the sauce off her face and the table. When she had control of herself again, she whispered back. "First of all, don't call this a coven. You'll piss Roger off. He says that's a sissy word neopagan religious nuts use. Also, don't use the term witch either, or warlock or sorcerer or magician or anything like that. Those are all 'superstitious titles used by those who have no true under-standing of the powers that control the seen and unseen.'"

"Roger's words, not yours, I assume," I said, resisting the urge to grin at such pompous words coming out of goth girl's mouth.

Meg rolled her eyes in a look of deepest mocking, the whites around her pupils contrasting sharply with her cloud of black eye-makeup. She was in finer form than usual tonight, with skin so pale it looked white and lipstick a dark shade of purple. I was surprised to see a stud in her nose—I couldn't tell if she'd just had it done or if she simply didn't wear it at school. Her earrings were metal monstrosities that I had no idea how she got in, and she had a leather choker around her neck festooned with silver spikes.

"Okay, so what about the other stuff? I didn't expect to get fed chili at a, um, demonic initiation?" I was now unsure what to call it since all the normal words were forbidden.

"Roger has...different sides to him. At the clinic he's all Mr. Philanthropist, counseling troubled teens and helping people get off drugs. At home, though..." She shook her head, as if to rid herself of an image she didn't want to think about. I knew exactly how she felt. "Most of these kids are from the street, or close to it. They're lucky if they get a solid meal a day. He gives them community, food, and even clothes sometimes, and promises them power to take control of their lives. In return, they're loyal to him."

"And you?" I looked sideways at her.

"I'm smart enough to keep my mouth shut and play along."

I thought about that, wondering if she'd voluntarily joined this little group or if she'd been "encouraged." Was this Roger's way of keeping an eye on her? "And Cassius?" I finally asked.

"I'm...not sure. Cassius could leave if he wanted to, I think. But because of whatever is between him and Roger, he won't. Maybe Roger threatened him, maybe he's never known anything else. I don't know. But we're working on a plan—"

A door near the base of the stairs opened and I nudged Meg's leg under the table, silencing her. I hadn't noticed, but there were actually two doors back in that corner. One was partially open and I could see that it led to a tiny, cramped bathroom with toilet and sink. I couldn't see inside the other door because I was at the wrong angle. I eyed Cassius as he emerged from the latter, followed by a much older, much taller man—Roger himself, I assumed. The man was solidly built, as if he worked out, but not obsessively so. He was also blond like Cassius, which would make sense if he was Cassius's father. But then I realized Roger's blond hair was natural, while Cassius had the bleached look of a dye job. So maybe biological father, maybe not.

Overall, I thought Roger looked like a normal enough guy. That was, until a muttered word and jerk of the thumb from Cassius turned his attention onto me.

For the first five seconds, I couldn't breathe. I didn't have words, or even brain cells to come up with the words, to describe what it felt like being caught in that gaze. I felt pinned, stripped, and examined down to the minutest detail. Struggling, I tried to tear my eyes away, until I realized I wasn't actually struggling, I only thought I was. My body was frozen, and I could not look away. Not from those eyes. One was hazel green. The other was a shocking electric blue.

When he finally blinked, I sagged in my chair, clutching my chest. My heart was racing like I'd just sprinted a mile. I lowered my eyes, avoiding his gaze and focusing instead on his square jaw and full, almost pouting lips.

"So this is our newest member?"

Meg nodded silently beside me.

"Meg has spoken highly of you, Sebastian. She says you have the perfect skills and temperament to become a valuable part of our group. It's an honor to have you among us."

Roger spoke slowly, deliberately. Some might have called his manner down-to-earth and assumed he was a no-nonsense, honest man. I thought it made him seem cold and calculating, as if each word was carefully calibrated to achieve a specific result. And the way he said my name made me shudder. Like he owned it. I didn't know how to respond, so I just nodded, still avoiding his eyes.

"Please, relax. Finish your meal. You're among friends." With that, he turned away and started talking to the other teenagers.

I hunched over my bowl of now lukewarm chili, all hunger gone. But pretending to eat gave me an excuse to not talk to anyone. I watched as the other three kids fawned over Roger. And, to give him credit, Roger seemed to really care. He asked how they were, sympathized with their troubles, and offered words of wisdom and an encouraging squeeze to their shoulder before moving on to the next person.

Hearing footsteps descending the stairs, I glanced behind me to see the boy who'd been watching the alley door. I felt a twinge of unease as he turned, reached above his head, and pulled the trap door shut after him. This was it. For better or worse, I was stuck.

After another five minutes of "fellowshipping" together, Roger called us to order. We all grabbed chairs, arranging them in a circle. The way things were situated I sat across from Roger with Meg on my left and Cassius on hers, and one of the other kids between him and Roger. The older

man's back was to the stairway, as well as to the door to his
office, or whatever it was. I wondered at this, since I would
never willingly sit with my back to a door—I might have had
some status in high school, but middle school had been a
living hell. Then I noticed that Roger's chair was the only one
with a padded seat, and I remembered Meg pulling it up and
offering it to him. Sneaky little thing. I assumed the Book of
Names was in Roger's office, and hoped Cassius was good at
distractions, because it would be hard to miss even one
person in a group so small.

The next thirty minutes were probably the weirdest half
hour of my entire life. Roger seemed to think himself some
sort of guru or wise man, but shouldered the mantle of a
school counselor so as to better connect with his "followers."
The first ten minutes felt suspiciously like a group therapy
session, and I swear I made up every single word that came
out of my mouth. No way was I going to open up to that
creep and let him psychoanalyze me. The further we got into
it, the more it turned into a sermon as he talked about what
he called "the precepts of self-empowerment." Everyone else
knew what they were, Roger explained, but a refresher
wouldn't hurt as he went over them for my benefit.

He explained that we were all our own masters, our own
gods, and that it was up to us to take control of our lives,
instead of letting circumstance and other people manipulate
us. Empowerment began inside yourself through believing
that you deserved better, that you deserved to be in control.
But you had to overcome self-doubt before you could attain
"true power."

As much as I'd raged at fate, or chance, or whatever it was
out there that had decided to take my parents away from me,
I wasn't stupid enough to think I could ever truly control my
life. Life was chaos, uncontrollable circumstance. Or was it? I
kept listening, half weirded out, half curious.

True power, as it turned out, only came to the strongest. The most deserving. These weren't physical attributes, but the strength of will within to control one's destiny. And, conveniently, only he could show us the path to true power.

I thought the whole thing made about as much sense as a book written by a monkey rolling around on a keyboard. No one else seemed bothered by the fact that he spoke of finding self-empowerment and independence, while simultaneously assuring us that the only way to such things was through loyalty to him and his "path." Apparently, he wanted his followers to be independent of everyone but him. I stole a glance around, expecting everyone's eyes to be glazed over in disinterest. But what I saw made my skin crawl. Everyone, even Meg and Cassius, was laser focused on Roger. Their eyes were bright and intent, and they leaned forward as if hanging on his every word.

Feeling creeped out, I sincerely hoped Meg and Cassius were pretending just to fit in. They had to be, with the drivel coming out of this guy's mouth. I mean, finding the power within yourself to take control of your life was all well and good. But I knew where this was going, and was pretty sure the last thing demons cared about was you finding "inner strength" and fixing your life. I wasn't really sure what demons wanted, but happy, healthy people probably wasn't high on their list.

Caught up in my thoughts, I missed Roger's last few sentences, but my ears perked when he said, "And when you're ready, you can summon your own spirit of power."

Spirit of power? I assumed that was a PG code word for demon. I started listening more carefully.

"There are many different kinds," Roger was saying. "Each one is unique and will strengthen a different part of you. At first, I will help you discover and call these spirits to yourself. Once you become familiar with them and have molded them to your will, you can progress to more and more powerful spirits, each one simply waiting to be found. They might seem hostile at first, but only because they wait to see you prove yourself, prove your strength and become worthy of theirs.

"And this is my work, which I dedicate to you. Many in this life struggle, oppressed under the strength of others, or under circumstance: drugs, poverty, bullying, abuse…loss of loved ones. But once you have mastered your own inner strength and start collecting spirits of power, no one will be able to hurt you again. You will be the master of your own destiny, able to control death itself."

Silence rang throughout the small room, and it took me a moment to realize Roger had stopped talking and was staring at me. I looked away, embarrassed that even I had become enthralled by his words, or maybe just the slow but melodic rhythm of his speech. It was all ridiculous, of course. And yet, the promise of that kind of power…I couldn't deny it was tempting.

I squirmed in my seat, self-conscious that he was still staring at me, though no one else was. Their eyes were fixed on him.

Yeah, whatever. No matter what kind of power he promised, this whole thing was one huge, stinking pile of creepy. I didn't know what nonsense he'd been feeding the four others, but Meg and Cassius clearly knew they were meddling in the affairs of demons. These "spirits of power" were no benevolent wisps of potential, waiting for you to prove yourself "worthy" before granting you immeasurable power. They were nasty, grimy, lying, sneaky, devious little demons who would probably eat your eyes out the first chance they got. And yet, here I was, about to let myself be initiated into this group of demon-loving wackos.

What the heck was I thinking?

"Are you ready, Sebastian, to join our fellowship?" Roger's voice echoed, ominous, in the little room.

My eyes darted around, glancing first at Meg, then the stairs, then back at Meg. Couldn't I just stand up and walk out? They wouldn't stop me, would they? I mean, they wanted willing participants, right?

I'd warned Peter earlier to stay quiet, to watch only and not interfere, not unless our lives were in danger. But as my heart thumped in my chest, adrenaline pumping, I wished he would start yelling then and there, protesting at the top of his lungs. In the confusion, I would slip quietly up the stairs and run as fast as I could all the way home.

Then Meg turned to looked at me, and I swear her eyes crushed what was left of my heart, my very soul. They were desperate. Haunted. Begging me to stay, to not leave her alone.

With him.

"Yes," I said with as much confidence as I could muster, looking Roger straight in the eye.

A smile spread slowly across his face, those full lips curving, mismatched eyes alight with triumphant pleasure. "Very well. Let us begin."

15

With a gesture, Roger had everyone stand, surrounding me in a tight circle as they laid their hands on my arms and shoulders. My skin crawled at their touch and I had to resist the urge to push them away. Because I was looking for it, I noticed Meg shift so that Cassius's thick body was blocking her from Roger's sight. Her fingers were wrapped around my bicep, and they gave it a reassuring squeeze.

Roger drew something out of his pocket and I almost flipped when I saw that it was a small knife. I was about to start kicking and biting people when Roger caught my eye and my limbs felt suddenly leaden.

"Calm yourself, Sebastian. No one here will harm you. I am not here to burden you, nor to ask for more than you can give. *I* give to *you*, pouring out my blessing so that you can find your true power. All you must do is repeat after me."

He didn't break his gaze, and I was rivited in place, unable to look away as he took the knife and nicked his wrist in one quick motion. Dipping a finger in the tiny rivulet of blood that flowed from the cut, he touched my forehead, then my eyelids, then my lips. I shuddered, revolted, but couldn't move. I couldn't even blink, and my eyes started to sting.

With slow, unhurried movements he lifted my left hand and positioned it palm toward him, as if I were about to swear an oath. Using more blood from his wrist, he drew a symbol on my palm, still not breaking eye contact with me. I couldn't see the symbol, but his motions felt convoluted. Twisted. Finally, he drew something on his own palm and lifted it to press against my raised hand. The blood between us felt hot and sticky.

"Repeat after me, Sebastian. I, Sebastian Logan Blackwell."

Panicked thoughts raced through my head—how did he know my middle name?—but I felt my mouth open, repeating the words even as I told myself to stop. "I, Sebastian Logan Blackwell."

"Do solemnly swear loyalty to this fellowship."

"Do solemnly swear loyalty to this fellowship."

"To keep its secrets and protect its members."

"To keep its secrets and protect its members."

"And obey its leader unto death and beyond."

Whoa, what? To death and beyond? My brain was yelling bloody murder by this point, but my lips kept moving. "And obey its leader unto death and beyond."

Still holding my eyes, Roger began speaking in the same guttural language I'd heard Meg use. I had pretty much worked out it was demonese, or whatever you called the language demons spoke. At least, it was the language these people used to control them. He didn't speak long, which was good, because my knees were about to buckle. Something shot between our eyes, like a spark, and I felt a tug in my chest. Or was it in my soul? I didn't have time to wonder, because I suddenly felt nauseous and dizzy, as if the earth beneath me was shifting. I knew with immediate, shocking clarity that the words I'd just spoken in English were only a paltry lip service, a performance. This was the true initiation.

Ties that bind.

And then it was all over. Roger blinked, and the spell, or whatever it was he'd done to me, released. I sagged, only the hands of the people around me keeping me on my feet. I heard Meg's voice in my ear as she helped lower me into a chair.

"Relax, Seb, it's all over. You've done it. *We've* done it."

And with that, I fainted.

———

"SEBASTIAN? Sebastian, lad, are you all right? Oh goodness gracious, I don't know what to do. Please wake up!"

The teensiest, tiniest of urgent whispers tickled my ear and I sat up, looking around frantically. "Wha—"

"Calm down! You're fine." Meg put a hand on my arm. "Sheesh, you are such a drama queen."

"Oh, thank the heavens above. You gave me quite the scare, young man." Peter's relieved voice did more to relax me than Meg's hand, and I quickly realized I was on the white plastic table, still in that basement room. As far as I was concerned, though, I was not fine, and wouldn't be until I was very far away from that creepy place.

"Ah, Sebastian. Feeling better?" Roger's disarmingly smooth voice slithered down my spine. "Don't be concerned, the initiation can take its toll on the body, especially for those not used to physical strain."

Swinging my legs over the side of the table, I glared at him. Okay, so not exactly *at* him, more like in the general direction of his left ear. I wasn't sure if he honestly thought I was a weakling, or if he just enjoyed implying it under the guise of fatherly concern. I didn't care, I was just ready to get out of there.

"Don't worry yourself. You'll feel fine in no time." He smiled at me, the expression not even beginning to reach his eyes.

I suppressed a shiver, looking away to scan the room, expecting to see teenagers giggling behind their hands at my fainting stunt. But the room was empty.

"I sent everyone home for the night. A short meeting, I will admit, but the induction of a new member is a momentous occasion. We will work on our strengthening exercises and summoning symbols next time."

There wouldn't *be* a next time, if I had anything to say about it. But no need to tell him that. I hopped off the table, clutching it for a moment as a last wave of light-headedness passed through me. Meg stood nervously at my elbow, her hand still on my arm.

Roger waved a hand at the stairs. "Now, why don't you go outside and get some fresh air. I need to speak with Meg for a moment."

I glanced down at Meg and she just barely flicked her eyes at me. I didn't need to see the terror in them to know she didn't want me to go. Her grip on my arm had gone from gentle to viselike.

So I very carefully stared Roger down without meeting his eyes. Being an inch or so taller than him helped bolster my courage. "You guys can talk later, right? Because I need her to take me home, ASAP. We wouldn't want my aunt asking questions about why I was out so late, would we?"

His brows drew together at the implied threat. "It's rather important, actually. I'm sure another minute or two wouldn't hurt."

Well, so much for subtlety. Steeling myself, I looked him in the eye. For some reason, whether because I was ready for it, or because he wasn't really trying, I could stare straight into that mismatched, creepy gaze, and not feel like he was about to mind control me.

"No," I said flatly. "I feel really sick, and I need her to take me home, *now*."

I turned my back on him, even though every instinct in me screamed not to. "Come on, Meg. We're leaving." Keeping my body between her and that slime ball, I herded Meg toward the stairs.

"Safe travels, Sebastian," Roger called after us. "I look forward to our first lesson."

I didn't turn to look, but I could imagine the mocking smile he had on his face. As soon as I reached the utility room, I "accidentally" bumped the propped-open trap door with my foot, making it slam down on the hole with a bang. "In your dreams," I muttered at it, suppressing another shiver. "Come on," I said to Meg, and half led, half dragged her out of the building. Once we were out in the open I released her arm and let my stride widen, eating up the ground between us and where we'd left her car. I had long legs and was soon several paces ahead of Meg.

"Seb, wait!" she called, trotting to keep up.

I didn't slow down. I. Was. Furious. Not to mention fuming, seething, and incensed. Oh, and scared, don't forget scared. The problem was, I didn't know who I was furious at. Or perhaps the better question was, who *wasn't* I furious at? At the moment, I wanted to punch someone and didn't really care who it was. Roger, Meg, myself—all seemed like good candidates.

Peter must have gotten over his shyness of Meg, because his pearly white form suddenly appeared beside me, his dressing gown eerily *not* fluttering in the wind. He seemed even more upset than I was. "Sebastian, what is the matter? Is your mind your own? Can you tell me how many fingers I'm holding up?"

Meg let out a surprised yelp behind me, but the sound was quickly cut off as if she'd clapped her hands over her mouth.

I swiped furiously at the misty image, ignoring Peter's raised digits. "Of course my mind is my own, you idiot, no thanks to you! Why didn't you stop me?" I didn't know why I was shouting at him. I knew it wasn't his fault. I had let this happen.

"Because your life was not in danger!" Peter spluttered back at me. "Your instructions were quite strict, if you recall. I thought you said friends did as instructed, or whatever that saying is."

"Friend also don't let friends do stupid, idiotic things no matter how much they think they want to." I gritted my teeth, perfectly aware of how hypocritical I sounded.

"Then *why*, in the name of heaven and earth, didn't you tell me that before? We could have avoided a mountain, no, a whole continent, of trouble if—"

"Never mind. Just drop it, will you? It's over and done, and I have a headache. Go away. Go on, get out of here!" I yelled at his wispy shape floating in front of me, and, as I'd asked, he vanished, a hurt look clearly visible on his face.

We were almost to the car and Meg must have finally gotten over Peter's abrupt entrance and exit, because she caught up with me and grabbed my arm.

"Calm down, Seb. What's the big deal?"

I whirled on her, wrenching my arm out of her grasp. "Calm down? Calm down?! You didn't tell me your precious leader would be putting some sort of demonic spell on me! You didn't tell me he'd hypnotize me and splatter blood all over my face!"

Suddenly remembering that warm, sticky feeling I

reached up to scrub my face, expecting to find flakes of dried blood. But there was nothing there. I looked at my hand, faintly visible in the light of a distant streetlamp. Clean.

"Did you wash the blood off after I fainted?" I demanded.

Meg shook her head.

"What do you mean? Of course you did. Where did the blood go?"

"It was taken," she said quietly.

"Taken where?"

"The blood was an offering, and it was accepted. Who knows where it goes. I don't, and don't want to, either."

Something dark stirred inside me, and I absolutely lost it. "What the fuck, you crazy bitch!" I screamed, getting right up in her face. "What the fuck did you do to me? This is all your fault!" My arm lifted of its own accord, and I didn't realize what I was doing until Meg screamed.

I froze.

Staring down into her dark, frightened eyes, I saw tiny glints of red reflected there. The sight sent a jolt through me and I blinked. The red vanished.

I deflated with a whoosh of air as if someone had punched me in the stomach. Shaking, I sank to the ground and sat with my back against the Chevy Nova. I had no idea what had come over me. There'd been so much tension inside and I'd felt the irresistible urge to let it out. Something inside me had told me I *should* let it out, that I should punish Meg. Where had my self-control gone?

"What's happening to me?" I asked, head in my hands.

I felt her sit down beside me, but she didn't touch me.

"Something given, something gained. That's the witch's way." Her voice was quiet, but hard. I thought there might have been a bit of sadness in it, too, but I could have been imagining it. I didn't look up to see what story her eyes told.

"You can't say I didn't warn you. Did you expect it to be easy? Did you expect us to just swoop in, save our parents, and fly off into the sunset to live happily ever after? Nothing is ever free. Power has a price and…sacrifices have to be made. You have to give something in return."

Breathing deep, I got my emotions under control and finally looked at her. Her face was a hard mask of determination. She didn't give an inch, and the defiant fire that had seemed smothered in Roger's presence resurfaced in full force.

"But…are you sure it's worth it?"

She didn't hesitate. "My father's life, my mother's health, they're worth *everything*."

"But what about your life?" I asked quietly, reaching out to touch her cheek. She flinched, but then let me stroke it with a featherlight caress. At the touch, her mask seemed to crack. Her eyebrows shifted, angling down in uncertainty and…was that guilt? But then her eyes hardened again and she looked away.

"My life is already hell—I thought yours was too. Or are you having second thoughts?"

I was, but not for the reasons she imagined. I would do anything to get my parents back, including destroy myself. But Meg? Could I live with destroying her as well? What would there be left of us if we succeeded? I didn't know what Roger had done to me, and I doubted Meg knew either. But whatever it was, it wasn't something we could just pretend had never happened.

"We're going to do this," I promised, reaching out to take her hand. It twitched at my touch, but she didn't pull away. "And we're going to do it *together*. That means I need to know the whole plan. No more keeping me in the dark. I can't help if you don't tell me what's going on."

There was a long silence. Finally she gave a curt nod.

Pulling her hand out of mine she stood up, then offered it to me again. "Have it your way, squirt. You've gotten this far, so I guess you're not going to flake on me, huh?" She gave me a sardonic look, to which I made a rude gesture. But I still took her hand and hauled myself to my feet.

On the way home Meg explained how she'd managed to slip away from the group and into Roger's office, just as planned. The book had been lying there on his desk in plain sight, and Meg had wasted no time finding the right page and taking a picture of it. Once she slipped back, she'd dropped the camera into Cassius's pocket, just in case Roger got suspicious and searched her.

When I asked her what our next move was, she told me I wasn't going to like it one bit.

"How bad can it be?" I asked.

"Studying. A *lot* of studying."

I groaned.

Since I'd already told my aunt we were going to have an all-day study session the next day, Meg said we might as well use that as an opportunity to start teaching me about demonology. The sooner we memorized the necessary information, the sooner we could get the show on the road and be rid of Roger. And Cassius, I added silently to myself.

When we finally reached the street two blocks from my aunt's house, I got out, then went around to her side of the car and waited. After giving me an arched brow, she finally rolled the window down. "What? You expect a goodnight kiss or something?" she asked, voice full of sarcasm.

Well, if she was offering…I mentally shook myself. Focus, Sebastian, focus. "No, I just wanted to make sure you were gonna be okay. Later, I mean. At home. Roger didn't seem too happy when I insisted you take me back."

"Oh, that." Meg sighed and looked away. "I'll…be fine. I've dealt with worse."

"Do you need somewhere to stay? I'm sure my aunt wouldn't mind. We have an extra bedroom," I said, words tumbling out of my mouth in a rush.

Meg's lips quirked, but her eyes were full of sadness. "That's…nice. But no. Things would be even worse if I didn't come home. And besides, my mom needs me."

"Well, okay. But call me if you need anything, alright? Even if it's in the middle of the night. You have my number."

"Sure, Mr. Knight in Shining Armor. Don't jump on that horse too fast, you might miss the saddle and fall off." She gave me a truly impressive eye roll as she closed her window, but softened it with a wave before driving away.

I stared after her, watching her taillights disappear into the night. I'd wanted to kiss her. Not the kind of kiss you daydreamed about giving a hot girl at school you watched from afar but never talked to. No, I'd wanted to kiss her softly and tell her everything was going to be fine, that I would protect her. "If I were a knight, I'd never miss the saddle," I said to no one in particular.

"I don't doubt it."

"Seriously, Peter? You little creep, you were eavesdropping, weren't you!" I gave him a disgusted look.

Peter threw up his hands. "Do this! Don't do that! Let me be an idiot, but wait, now I'm going to yell at you for letting me be an idiot. At this point, I don't know *what* to do, you insufferable little—little—" He puffed up bigger and bigger, apparently at a loss for words.

"Teenager?" I offered.

"Yes!" His explosive reply deflated him and he sank, pulling out an invisible handkerchief from his pocket and wiping his forehead with it. "Young people these days. Absolutely insufferable, I tell you."

"I'm pretty sure we've always been insufferable," I said,

starting off down the street toward home. Hm, since when had I thought of Aunt Barrington's house as home?

"Now wait just a minute, young man." Peter's voice interrupted my thoughts as he hurried to catch up with me. "We are not finished."

"We never started. Now hush, or you'll wake everyone in the neighborhood with your hollering."

"I most certainly will not—Sebastian!"

I ignored him and kept walking, but this time he zipped in front of me and stood his ground, wrinkled hands on hips, mustache fairly quivering in outrage. I hesitated a moment, then kept going straight through him. It was like being dunked in an ice-covered lake. I gasped and bent over, hands on my knees as I caught my breath. Peter took the opportunity to give me a piece of his mind.

"We need to have a serious discussion, young man. I don't know how all this friend business works, but I know that I will not allow you to continue down this path. You'll end up a demon-possessed shell, damned to eternal torment!"

"Nah—you'll probably nag me to death long before that." My body gave one last convulsive shiver, then I straightened and started off again.

"Listen to yourself, Sebastian. Just listen! Not thirty minutes ago you were furious that I did not stop you from participating in an unholy ritual. You were shaken, nauseous. You even fainted! Yet now you are brushing me off like it was all a game. Listen to yourself!"

I halted, finally, and sighed. "Look, I know it's not a game. I haven't forgotten what happened thirty minutes ago. But nothing fundamental has changed." I knew that was a lie, but Peter didn't need to know about the spark that had jumped between me and Roger, or that tug I'd felt afterward. "No matter what, I can't give up, especially not now. Meg is depending on me. This isn't just about the dead anymore, it's about the living."

"And I am trying to *keep* you alive. You and that sickly girl—"

"She's not sickly, she's a goth."

"What? She's descended from the barbarian tribes of eastern Germany? How very odd, I would have expected her hair to be a shade lighter—"

"No! She's a *goth*. You know, the subculture where they wear black and have strong opinions about rock music?"

"I shall have to take your word for it, lad. The point is, this is suicide. You haven't a clue what you're getting into, and you have only a fool's hope that this girl has half an idea herself."

"I'm sure Meg knows what she's doing."

"Is that so?"

I crossed my arms, jutting out my chin. "Yes."

"Then you're lying to yourself."

"It doesn't matter. I'm not turning back. I won't let her down."

"And what if turning back *is* not letting her down? What if helping her pursue this foolish course is sealing her fate? Are you not her friend? Then why are you allowing her, even encouraging her, on this suicidal quest?"

My heart clenched at Peter's words, at his implication. I had already lost both my parents, I couldn't lose Meg, too, the only friend I had. Wait, were we friends? I thought about it. It felt like we were. Or was she just using me? Maybe, but if so, I was using her just as much.

Yet, I couldn't let her down—or myself, for that matter. What Peter didn't understand was that I wasn't just driven by longing for my parents. I was consumed by guilt. I'd killed them. Me. And if I couldn't fix my mistake, then I couldn't live.

"We're doing it, whether you like it or not, Peter. Now, are you going to help us? Because if not, I don't need you hanging around messing things up."

The ghost hesitated, and I wondered if he would finally give up on me this time. Or perhaps he would go blabbing to Aunt Barrington and I would have to run away. Either way, I braced myself for the betrayal.

But he didn't leave. Instead, he grew closer, the glow of his spectral form fading as he did so. I expected to feel cold, but to my astonishment there was a touch of warmth on my skin, like the sun on a cool spring morning. His old and wizened face peered into mine, brows drawn in concern and translucent eyes full of so many things I couldn't describe.

"Now, now, my boy," he said softly. "Don't be quite so hasty. 'I will never leave you, nor forsake you,' as the old saying goes. Well, that's my lot, or privilege, as you might say. And I plan to stick to it. You manage to get into enough trouble all on your own without my help, so I don't suppose my presence can make it any worse. But see here, you can't go tottering blindly into something as dangerous as this. Let's put our heads together and see what we can come up with. Some sort of failsafe or back-door. What do you say?"

I swallowed hard, blinking back tears that I felt ashamed of, but couldn't stop. Ignoring them, I spoke, keeping my voice as chipper as possible. "Well, now that you mention it, I do have an idea. But you won't like it."

He didn't, but listened anyway as I turned to walk slowly beside him toward home. Yes, home. Of a sort, anyway. I wasn't sure if I'd ever truly feel at home again anywhere on earth. But for now, it would do.

16

My idea involved breaking into Aunt Barrington's library to see if she had any books on how to defend against demons. Or defeat demons. Or generally not get your butt kicked by demons. The tricky part was, they couldn't be books of wizard spells, since obviously I couldn't use those. They had to be books on demonology. Now, I thought it unlikely my aunt would have such "unclean" knowledge in her library after she'd made it clear she considered witches the dregs of the earth, but Peter disagreed. He said that while Aunt Barrington *was* a wizard, she was also, well, a wizard. And wizards hoarded knowledge like dragons hoarded gold, whether they approved of the subject matter or not.

Although we had the beginnings of a workable plan, we wouldn't get a chance to test Peter's theory for a while. I needed plenty of time to plan my foray and practice my lock-picking skills, plus the next day was Demonology 101 with Meg. Our highly dangerous plan to break into a cranky wizard's private sanctum and "borrow" forbidden lore would have to wait.

Meg came to pick me up around eleven. Not quite the crack of dawn I'd implied to my aunt, but then, we were teenagers. Peter was annoyingly perky in the mornings, and I often wondered if ghosts ever got tired. That particular morning, though, I was in too much of a hurry to worry about it. I only popped into the kitchen to grab an apple and a non "off-limits" blueberry scone before heading out the door.

Spring was fast becoming summer and we drove with our windows down, enjoying the breeze under the bright Atlanta sun. Despite the heat, Meg wore a black leather jacket, perhaps to protect her "delicate" skin from the rays of the "cursed day-star," as I'd heard her call it. Personally, I was impressed. She had to be cold-blooded or else have a will of iron to wear that much leather on such a sunny spring day.

I'd been hoping Meg would take us to her house so I could meet her mom and get a feel for her in her home environment. But when she finally slowed the car, pulling on to a back street, I recognized the brick building she'd brought me to the first time we'd hung out. Even though bare weeks had passed, that day felt like a lifetime ago. I'd been hopeless then, with nothing and no one to live for. Now? Well, I wasn't fixed, or healed, or even marginally less screwed up. But at least I had a plan and a little bit of desperate, stupid hope.

I shook my head and got out of the car, remembering how Meg had almost left me stranded. Back then, I'd suspected she'd done it just to mess with me. Now that I knew her better, I was absolutely sure of it. Meg came across as the kind of person who got to know you by pushing all your buttons at once, then stepping back to see what happened. Not the most subtle or diplomatic strategy, but who was I to judge?

I was pleased to note the absence of a certain Mustang as

I followed Meg into the taller-than-ever weeds. I didn't think I'd get much studying done if our partner in crime, Mr. Scumball, joined us. I'd be too busy resisting the urge to make his ugly face uglier. On the other hand, why *wasn't* he here?

"I'm sorry your boyfriend couldn't join us," I quipped, fishing for answers as I followed Meg into the dim coolness of the building. "I don't know how we'll ever manage without his charming wit and gentlemanly behavior."

Meg didn't turn around. "He's not my boyfriend."

My traitorous heart picked up at her words, completely undaunted by her suppressive tone. "Then what is he?"

There was a long enough silence as we navigated the first-floor debris that I began to think she wasn't going to answer. Then her terse reply echoed in the dark space. "Useful."

"Well," Peter muttered, "that is certainly reassuring."

"Tell me about it," I murmured back.

So, if Cassius was useful, then what was I? Expendable? I called out to Meg, "You might want to let Cassius know. I don't think he's gotten the memo yet."

She didn't respond, simply mounted the stairs and headed for the second floor. I shrugged and followed. Peter had decided to stay out of sight, he claimed because Meg was obviously nervous around him and he didn't like scaring people, though he could have fooled me. I'd told him he was a miserable excuse for a ghost, but he'd been adamant. I wondered if he just liked sneaking around. Or, more likely, he still held a grudge against Meg. That would explain why he only spoke to me, and only in a whisper, so Meg couldn't hear.

Instead of going all the way up to the roof like we'd done before, Meg led me to a room on the second floor that had several east-facing windows. Plenty of light streamed in, and the floor was more or less free of debris.

In the middle was a clean spot with several pillows scattered around.

Meg plopped down on one and took off her backpack, pulling out a large folder. I sank into a crosslegged position beside her and watched with interest as she also pulled out a mini dry erase board and some markers, all of which she pushed in my direction. Then she set the folder on the floor in front of me, opening it to the first page. I peered down in interest, but the paper was just covered in a bunch of squiggly drawings, as if a two-year-old with a crayon had gotten ahold of it.

"What's that?"

"Those are the symbols you need to learn. They're the basics used in any kind of demon summoning ritual. Once you've memorized all these, we can move on to more complicated ones."

I stared at her, waiting for the joke.

"Why are you looking at me like that? It's not rocket science. Just start copying the symbols again and again until you've memorized them."

"What symbols?" I protested, pointing at the page. "These are a bunch of squiggles. And besides, there's no translation here. I can't just memorize stuff without knowing what it means."

"Yes, you can. You sing along with 80's songs don't you? And the symbols are supposed to look like that. I'll worry about what they mean, you get memorizing."

"She is right about the symbols," Peter said softly in my ear. "I never learned any of them myself, of course, but I've seen them a time or two. I suppose demons, being rather twisted themselves, would have a similarly untidy script."

"Will you stop looking over my shoulder?" I muttered out of the side of my mouth. "Make yourself useful. Go keep an eye on what Meg is doing," It wasn't that I didn't trust

Meg—well mostly—but only an idiot passed up a chance for more information, and I happened to have an invisible friend at my disposal.

Peter fell silent and I glared at the page before me, trying to separate one symbol from another. Delaying the inevitable, I looked up and watched Meg pull out a notebook and a large photograph from her backpack. She stared at the picture intently, holding it close to her nose, then started scribbling in the notebook. I assumed the photograph was from the Book of Names. Hopefully it contained what we needed, especially after the trouble we'd gone through to get it. Well, that I'd gone through. Resigning myself, I finally bent my head and concentrated on memorizing demons' excuse for a legible script.

We worked in silence for several hours. The task Meg had set me to was mind numbing, but I was determined. Nobody said bringing your parents back from the dead would be easy, and I wasn't going to fail just because of some stupid little symbols. The more I worked with them, the more I realized they weren't random, or really even that squiggly. They looked like they could have been different at one time, graceful curves and sweeping lines instead of squiggles. But at some point they'd become distorted.

Ten pages of symbols in, I looked ahead, saw I still had a good thirty pages to go, and threw down my marker in disgust. I needed a break.

Meg looked up at me, eyebrow raised.

"What?" I said. "You're telling me you don't find this mind-numbingly boring?"

She shrugged, focusing again on her papers. "Doesn't matter if it's boring or not. If we mess up any of these symbols, draw one even slightly off, we could all die. That's motivation enough for me."

Glaring at her, I opened the folder again. But I couldn't

force myself to pick up the marker. I really did need a break. "Look, why don't you tell me about this summoning spell we're going to do. There's tons of stuff I need to know. I can come back to the symbols later. I thought you were going to give me a lesson on demonology. A 'beginner's guide to summoning demons' or something."

"There's not much to it," she said just a bit too casually. "You draw some symbols, say some words, and as long as you know the name of the demon you're summoning, they have to do what you want."

My eyes narrowed. "Uh-huh. So their name is like a magic word? 'Open sesame' or something?"

"More or less."

"I thought you said you had to have a stronger will than theirs. How do you keep them from ignoring you and, I dunno, possessing you and dragging you back to hell with them?"

"Oh, Cassius and I will worry about that."

"So I'm just a third wheel, is that it? Just a lightning rod? A power conduit? Why even teach me these symbols, then?"

She still wouldn't look at me. "The summoning circle will take long enough to draw as it is—I figured you could make yourself useful and help out with the symbols."

Now that didn't sound right. I stood up. "Stop pulling my chain, Meg. I thought we'd agreed no more keeping me in the dark. Are you going to explain this stuff or not? What if something goes wrong? How am I supposed to help? Maybe I should go ask Roger to teach me. He'd probably love an attentive apprentice, for once, since you've obviously never been one."

That got her attention. She slammed her pencil down and got up, eyes narrowed at me as she pointed a threatening finger. But there was something behind the glare. Was it worry?

"If Roger got wind of this, he'd have us locked up. Convince people we were insane and get us committed. Or maybe he'd just send a demon to murder us in the night. I don't know. But he doesn't like competition, or disobedience."

"It sounds like you need a loyal, *informed* ally at your side. I can't help if you don't tell me what's going on, Meg. I'm tired of you dancing around the point." I crossed my arms, planting my feet and steeling myself for a fight. I didn't want to do this, but I knew whatever we hoped to accomplish would fail miserably if things kept on like this.

Meg sighed and looked away, crossing her own arms. I waited, giving her a chance to decide if she was going to trust me or not. Finally, she looked back, face unreadable. "Cassius doesn't want you knowing too much. He thinks if we teach you demonology, you'll backstab us or tattle to Roger."

"And what do you think?"

She gestured toward me. "Well, you just threatened to go to Roger. What am I supposed to think?"

"She has a point," Peter chimed in from beside my ear. He seemed to be enjoying the show.

Ignoring Peter, I dropped my arms and stepped closer, lowering my voice. "I said that to get a reaction out of you, Meg. You know you're kind of an ass, right? Like, if you and a mule went head to head, the mule would lose."

Meg snorted, but I saw her lips twitch. "Yeah? Well, you're a nosy snoop."

"Don't forget intelligent and wildly handsome," I added, grinning.

She rolled her eyes.

"Look," I said, getting serious again. "Cassius is paranoid because he knows I'm smarter than he is. All he's worried about are power and position, so of course he sees me as a threat. But you know very well I couldn't care less about him, or Roger, or their stupid power play. All I want is my parents back, that's it. Then I'll gladly kiss this witchy stuff goodbye. Maybe we both can, and go back to being normal teenagers. So, do you want to put your trust in a,"—I used a few choice words that even Meg raised her eyebrows at—"who treats you like his property? Or in a friend who's just trying to help?"

Her lips tightened, but she didn't yell or deny my assessment. I stepped closer, almost close enough to reach out and touch her.

"When was the last time someone stood up for you?" I asked quietly.

Meg's eyes went somewhere far away. "Not since Dad died…at least, not until last night…" She looked at me, and for the first time something in them softened, though she quickly covered it up with pursed lips and a mock scowl. "You are annoyingly persistent, like toe fungus."

I stepped back and gave a theatrical bow. "Then this humble toe fungus is at your service, m'lady."

"Yeah, yeah. Whatever. Now grab your folder and come here."

Nothing had been said out loud, but the atmosphere in the room had changed. We were making progress.

"Impressive, young man. I see you are skilled at charming the damsels," Peter observed. Though I couldn't see him, I could hear the grin in his voice.

"That's me," I whispered back, "The lady charmer." I tried not to smile too widely.

My crash course in demonology was quite the eye-opener. There were times when Meg openly admitted she didn't know something, but overall she seemed to have the basics well covered. Hers was a purely practical knowledge. She didn't know much about demons themselves. She didn't care where they came from or what they were here to do. All that mattered to her was that she could call on certain ones and they would do as she bid them.

"You've got to know the right words and symbols," she told me. "But beyond that it just comes down to willpower. I can't really describe it, but do you remember any time when your parents told you to do something and you really, really didn't want to, but eventually did it because you knew you had to? Or because you knew you couldn't get away with refusing? You have to exert that kind of willpower over the demons."

"I have to act like their parent?"

"No, dummy. You have to absolutely know that you are in charge and they *will* do what you tell them. They can smell fear a mile off. You can't be afraid or you'll lose control."

"Well, that's comforting to know," I muttered. "What about this demon prince we're trying to summon? He's not some little imp. How are we going to control him?"

Meg hesitated. "Alone, I don't think we can do it, but with all three of us we should be fine. Plus, we'll make a deal, right? The ones you can't force to obey, you make a bargain with. Roger always uses blood as an incentive,"—I gave her a startled look—"no, not anybody else's blood. Sometimes he uses his own, but mostly he just buys pig's blood or some- thing when we need a lot."

"So, he sacrifices things?"

"Ew, no!"

My skeptical expression made her pause.

"Okay, so maybe at his house. But not at the clinic. I know fresh blood always works the best, but I've never seen him work with anything bigger than an imp. I'll have to research what we need to summon a greater demon."

"You realize this demon prince could ask for literally

anything. How are we going to know what to bring ahead of time?"

"We might have to do it in two stages," Meg admitted. "Summon him once to figure out his bargain, then do it again when we have what we need."

"Delightful," I said, too chicken to voice what I was really worried about: What happened when the demon asked for our souls? Yeah, I'd been flippant about it in the past, but that had been before Roger had done…whatever he'd done. That time I'd almost hit Meg, it had shaken me. What would it mean to give up your soul? Could you live without it? Would whatever controlled your soul also control you? I didn't know the answer, and almost didn't want to, lest the knowledge weaken my resolve.

"Don't worry about it," Meg was saying, unaware of my inner turmoil. "Right now, focus on memorizing these." She pointed to the folder open between us. She'd been telling me the meaning of each, explaining that they were pictograms, like Chinese, not an alphabet like English. With each new meaning, she warned me that demons were tricky and experts at finding loopholes, so it was important to use the combinations and incantations she taught me, not attempt to make up my own.

Of all the things I was learning, though, there seemed to be one particular area lacking: protective symbols. Everything was about gaining power and demanding obedience, closing loopholes and laying down the letter of the law. There seemed to be no straight-up shields, or protective wards, or whatever you'd call them.

When I pointed this out, Meg shrugged. "Either you're strong enough to control the situation or you're not. I mean, to summon them in the first place you have to open yourself up enough to exert control, and that makes you vulnerable to them. There aren't any one-size-fits-all protections. If you made a ward that just said, 'don't hurt me,' that's super vague. A demon could think of all kinds of ways to mess things up without technically 'hurting' you. You gotta be smarter than them."

That did not sound encouraging at all, and after a long afternoon of stuffing squiggly lines and dire warnings into my head, I was even more determined to find something, anything, to give me an advantage.

17

Meg sent me away with homework, and once I'd returned home and was in the privacy of my own room I had to wrack my brain for a safe place to hide it. If my aunt ever caught sight of it she'd skin me alive. I seriously considered my sock drawer—a perfectly respectable hiding place—until I remembered Aunt Barrington did my laundry. Finally, I decided I would just have to keep it on me at all times, hidden among my school papers.

I spent the next week plotting how to get into my aunt's library, half-heartedly dabbling at homework, and enduring mind-numbing hours of memorizing symbols. On Sunday, my aunt allowed me another all day "study session with friends" without asking too many inconvenient questions. Ironically, I really was studying, just not anything she'd have wanted me to know.

Safely in our abandoned building, Meg grilled me on the symbols, pouncing on any little mistake and demanding perfection. I buckled down and met the challenge, weary, but grimly determined. After hours of hard work, she begrudgingly admitted my progress was impressive, and rewarded me with an evening on the roof, watching the sunset as we reminisced about happier days. I was glad Peter had decided to stay home that day. I didn't want his disapproving comments ruining my mood.

Things were tentative at first, but it had been a good day and we were both feeling optimistic. It made our reminiscing more cathartic than painful. I regaled her with tales of my mischief-making middle school years when I barely went a single day without a note sent home from my teacher. She fondly recalled the one time her father had taken them to visit relatives in Mexico City and how she'd tricked her little brother into eating a jalapeño pepper by promising it tasted like candy. We laughed and groaned together, and though our mirth was brief, it felt good to remember a time when our lives had been better.

Inevitably, though, things turned somber again. Meg surprised me by admitting she wished her father had shared more of his cultural heritage with them. He'd wanted to raise them as "normal" as possible, and she regretted that. It was ironic how similar I felt about my own father, except that while she could take pride in her heritage, all I could do was feel a conflicted mix of longing and shame. Even if my father hadn't hated his own culture, it wasn't something I could ever be a part of, mundane as I was. So, not only was I an orphan, I was an outsider to my own identity. A child apart. A homeless misfit. I wondered if Meg felt the same. A child of two cultures, yet at home in neither.

It *had* been a good day, and I treasured the bond forming between me and Meg, fragile though it was. But by the time I got home I felt more empty and depressed than I had in weeks.

The memory of my parents was fading. Life seemed to think it could go on without them, as if they'd never existed.

But I couldn't allow that. I was lost without them, and not even a friend who could understand my pain was enough to fill the hole they'd left behind. I went to bed even more determined, resolving to work harder than ever to bring them back.

———

THE NEXT WEEK I got serious about preparing for Operation Library Infiltration. Peter helped, but I could tell his heart wasn't in it. No doubt he felt guilty about aiding and abetting the theft of wizard lore. At first, I'd hoped he'd be able to detect and neutralize any spells we encountered, but he rather touchily informed me that dead people couldn't use magic, wizard or no. Once I got him on the topic, though, Peter waxed eloquent about special wards that could prevent wizards magically breaking and entering, and alarm spells that would sound should anyone but the owner attempt a spell close by. Finally, I got tired and asked if there was anything stopping me from just picking the lock and walking in. After all, I wasn't a wizard. He looked surprised, then coughed.

"Well, wards against mundanes *do* exist, but mundanes would hardly know the value of your aunt's library, now would they? A simple lock would keep out such unwanted visitors. Therefore, in theory, it would be logical to assume she had not bothered with wards against mundanes. Wizards would be her main concern."

I looked at him with suspicion, but it did make a kind of sense. The books about lockpicking that I'd read said people put more trust in locks than they should, making the false assumption that locks kept things safe. In reality, most locks were absurdly easy to pick, and acted more as a passive deterrent to the casual snooper. In some stores and businesses the locks weren't even there to keep people out. They were just necessary to cover legal liability. If someone broke in, the security system would alert the police and cameras would record the incident, providing all the needed evidence for a nice insurance payout later on. In light of Aunt Barrington's opinion of technology—best avoided if at all possible—I doubted she had her own security system. There was no TV in the house and she'd refused to buy me a computer, even though I'd had one at my old house.

So, with Peter promising to act as a lookout, I decided simplicity was best and laid my plans for a daring break-in. Ideally, I'd wanted to sneak home during school while my aunt was at work. But if I went missing at school, or even left pretending to be sick, the teachers would call her. So instead, I decided to do it in the dead of night when she was fast asleep.

I'd told Peter to wake me up at 3 AM, hoping he'd manage to do it more quietly than my alarm clock. I woke to a freezing cold touch on my neck and almost yelled as I sat straight up, rubbing the spot.

"Sheesh, did you have to be so physical?" I hissed.

Peter's form glowed faintly in the darkness, arms crossed. "You were as dead as a particularly old and rotting log. I tried whispering your name, but you just muttered something about cheese scones and rolled over."

Glaring daggers at him, I slipped out of bed and donned my tools of the trade: black sweatpants, socks, and turtleneck, black gloves, and a black ski mask to cover everything but my eyes. Paranoid? Possibly. I slipped my home-made lockpicks into my pocket along with a small penlight. Then I took a deep breath.

"Okay, Peter. Let's do this."

"Heaven forgive us," he muttered, but followed me as I carefully opened my bedroom door—I'd surreptitiously oiled the hinges earlier that week—and crept down the hall. Fortunately, I didn't have to pass my aunt's door to get to the stairs, as her bedroom was at the opposite end of the house.

I'd carefully mapped out my route, making note of all the squeaky boards between me and the library. The stairs were the hardest part, since most of the steps squeaked like a choir of mice—this being a house older than even my aunt. Using the railing, I managed to avoid the worst, skipping several steps at once near the bottom and ending up crouched on the hall rug. Peter went on ahead, giving me a faint glow to see by as I crisscrossed the floor, navigating the house's built in alarm system.

Near the library door I miscalculated a step, and as I shifted my weight a loud creak of antique wood rent the silence, muffled only slightly by the rug. I froze and waited, hoping my aunt didn't have magically enhanced hearing. When nothing happened, I carefully lifted my foot, wincing at another creak that seemed to mock me with its complete unconcern for my secrecy.

Finally at the library door, I had Peter take a peek inside and look for any unpleasant surprises. I wished I had a way to detect spells, but I was only a simple mundane, no matter how brazenly I toyed with demons. One of these days, I needed to find someone who would make me useful artifacts that anyone could use, wizard or no.

Peter returned, reporting nothing suspicious in the library, simply darkness and the quiet ticking and shuffling of the devices on my aunt's desk.

Moving carefully, I pulled out my picks and got to work. It wasn't as easy as I'd thought. Whether because of the nervous tremble in my hands, or the true superiority of the lock, it remained completely unfazed by my basic techniques. After several minutes of tense fiddling and no budge from the lock, I took a break. Taking out my penlight and shielding the beam, I peered inside the keyhole, trying to figure out what I was doing wrong. Almost at once the answer slapped me in the face and I felt like an idiot. The past few weeks I'd been practicing on modern mechanisms, but this was a ward lock, not a tumbler lock. I'd sort of skipped over the history of locks in my library books. If I hadn't, I probably would have realized sooner that such an old house would be equipped with antique locks on the inside, even if the front and back doors had been updated.

Putting away the picks I'd been using, I pulled out a jury-rigged skeleton key. I might have skipped the history part, but I'd read and re-read the section on different types of locks and prepared every sort of pick I could create, hoping my aunt wouldn't notice the randomly missing implements around the house.

With slow, probing motions, I slipped my skeleton key into the lock and began turning and jiggling, silently begging the lock to have mercy and let me in. To my utter astonishment, it did. I felt the resistance give and there was a soft click.

I breathed out a sigh of relief.

Just as a precaution, I called softly to Peter. "Are we good? Did I set off any alarms?"

There was a moment of silence, during which I hoped Peter was checking out the library and possibly flitting up to my aunt's room to make sure she was still deep in oblivious slumber.

Finally, I heard: "To the best of my knowledge, you have not been discovered."

I slipped my tools back into my pocket and ever so carefully opened the door. With no windows to let in light from the street lamps outside, the interior of the library was pitch black. Closing the door, I switched on my penlight and looked around, getting my bearings. Everything was as I remembered from my previous visit. Curious, I swung my penlight toward the ceiling and marveled once again at the glass orbs floating above me like frozen soap bubbles, now devoid of light.

Turning my attention to the bookshelves, I headed for the one closest to the desk. I figured my aunt would keep the most important and dangerous books near at hand. Earlier in the week, I'd asked Peter to pop into the library when my aunt wasn't there and check the titles of the books to see if he could spot anything useful. Unfortunately, the books on magic either didn't have titles on their spines, or else their titles were cryptic and unclear. Some were even in different languages. He hadn't been able to find anything of particular interest beyond a history of the occult during the Enlightenment era.

And so, with the penlight in my mouth, I began the process of carefully examining each book on the shelf by the desk. I handled them all with the utmost care—I knew better than to mistreat my aunt's prized books. One by one, I took each volume down, reading what I could from the first few pages. At least half of them were complete gibberish. Some were in languages I faintly recognized like French or Spanish. Others, though written in English, spoke esoterically of visual conveyance, transmutation, thaumaturgy, essence fascimilification, and other big, magical-sounding words that were unlikely to help protect me against demons. A smaller subset involved history of magic and magical theory topics that seemed quite interesting, but I forced myself to return them to the shelf. If I indulged my curiosity, I'd be there all night and get caught red-handed in the morning. The sight of me engrossed in a book—a rarity indeed—probably wouldn't keep Aunt Barrington from flaying me within an inch of my life. Or turning me into something dreadful, like a slug. Or a chihuahua.

Dragging my mind away from such horrifying thoughts, I refocused on my search. A few of the books were extremely old, their worn leather covers cracked around the edges and their yellow pages as delicate as gossamer to the touch. These were in a variety of languages including English, but the English ones sounded worse than Shakespeare with all their thees and thous and even weirder words I didn't recognize. One book I pulled down had a magnificent, red leather cover inlaid with gold filigree, and I opened it excitedly, wondering what powerful knowledge lay within. But the book was completely blank. Not a single mark on any of its pages. Mystified, but knowing I would find no answers on my own, I replaced it and moved to the very bottom shelf, my last chance at finding something useful.

The first book I chose was a stuffy exposition on the art of crafting, and I put it back hurriedly. The second and third books were more of the same, as if the shelf had been relegated to hold the most useless and boring tomes that Aunt Barrington possessed. But on the fourth book I struck gold. As I let the slender, brown volume fall open in my hands, the title stared up at me from the first page: *A Wizard's Guide to Nonhuman Magic Users*. Underneath, there was a smaller subtitle: *The Customs and Habits of Fae, Demon, and Celestial Hosts*.

A shiver ran through me and for a moment I just stared at the book, trying to wrap my mind around the idea that all these creatures existed. It seemed preposterous. This was real life, not some fairy tale or angst-filled paranormal romance. And yet, I'd seen a demon with my own eyes. If such things existed, then who was I to say that fae and celestial hosts didn't? I assumed the latter referred to angels, and I wasn't sure I'd ever want to run into one myself—I doubted they would approve of my life choices. But the fae sounded fascinating and I couldn't wait to learn about them. The idea of little fairies flitting about among emerald leaves and bright flowers made me think of my mother and her garden.

Carefully slipping the book into a bag I'd brought, I continued looking. I was nervous about taking any of Aunt Barrington's books with me, worried she might notice them missing. But it was a risk I had to take. Unlike Meg, I couldn't snap a picture of just one page. I needed to read the whole thing, and I couldn't do that crouching in a dark library. I would just have to read quickly and return it surreptitiously, rearranging the books on the shelf to cover the empty space. Fortunately, since the book was so thin, it would be easy to cover its absence.

There were almost a dozen more books on the shelf, and I carefully went through each one, just in case. On the very end was a plain, black volume that seemed ordinary enough. But when I thumbed through the index, I found a chapter titled, "Alternative Warding Methods." I wasn't sure what "alternative" meant, but if it was anything besides spell-casting, it would be worth a look. The only hitch was that the black book was quite a bit thicker than the brown one I'd already taken. Looking around the room for a solution, I noticed that the lower shelf of a bookcase beside the fireplace was completely hidden behind an arm chair. Treading carefully around the large circle of magic symbols carved into the floor, I moved the arm chair and bent down to examine the books. To my relief, there was a black book almost identical to the one I was "borrowing." Repositioning the armchair to hide the gap, I went over and slid the replacement book into the empty space I'd made, then stepped back to examine my handiwork. Everything looked normal.

Now with two forbidden spell books secreted into my bag—somehow, they felt as heavy as bricks, or maybe that was just my guilty conscience—I crept back to the door and slipped through, closing it quietly behind me and using the skeleton key to re-lock it.

———

UNSURE how long I'd be able to keep the books, I started reading that very night. The little brown one was quick, but fascinating, even if I didn't understand some of the terms it used. Then again, there were a lot of "it has been said" and "according to ancient record," so I wondered how much wizards actually knew about fae, demons, and angels, and how much was simply oral tradition and myth.

I was reading lying on my stomach under the bedcovers, penlight out and ears pricked for any movement in the hall. As I finished the last page of the little brown book I switched off my light and poked my head out, looking for Peter's glow. He was by the window, staring out at the dark night that would very soon turn to dawn.

"Psst, Peter."

"Hmm?"

"Could you explain the difference between demons, fae, and angels? This book used a lot of mumbo jumbo that didn't really make sense."

His pale form floated over, passing through and then seating itself in my desk chair. He adopted a scholarly expression. "As I understand it, there are three species of beings able to manipulate magical energy: humans, fae, and angels."

"Wait, what about demons?"

"Good heavens, boy, be patient. As my father used to say, you have two ears and one mouth. Use them accordingly."

I closed my mouth and crossed my arms, resisting the urge to roll my eyes.

"Ahem, as I was saying. There are three *species* of magic users. Demons are not a separate species, simply corrupted angels. Fallen, as you might say. According to the old tales, angels were granted the most power, but it was to protect and serve only. The fae, while not as powerful, could do many things, and they were given as stewards to the earth and its living things. Man, a creative being in the image of *the* Creator, did not have specific powers either great or small bestowed upon them, but was given direct access to the Source—that is where magic comes from, lad—so that they could truly delve the depths of their creative calling. But man's form was more frail than that of angel or fae, and so how much raw power they could command at once depended on their skill, strength, and whatever magical devices they invented to aid themselves.

"Now, in the beginning, certain angels were jealous of mankind's power and sought to steal it. For their betrayal, they were cast down from heaven, corrupted and cursed, bound to the very magic which they had scorned. That is why demons are so dangerous to wizards. They have always been jealous of our access to the Source and will use any means necessary to gain control of us, whether through subtle corruption or direct possession."

I was silent, trying to digest this glut of information. It made a lot more sense now that Peter had explained it in plain English. Well, mostly plain.

"So, have you ever seen a fae or angel?" I finally asked.

"Not personally, no," Peter admitted. "There exist ancient records recounting their forms and deeds. But it has been many long millennia since they walked the earth alongside man. Some more modern accounts exist, claiming to have had dealings with them. But I cannot personally say what is to be believed and what is simple fancy."

"Huh." I thought about that for a long time, wondering where those accounts were and how I could get ahold of them. My mind drifted, and then I remembered something that had been bothering me. "So why can't all humans use magic? Why are there wizards and mundanes?"

Peter hesitated. "No one really knows. Legends say it was a gift to one of the first men that ever lived, and his descendants were the fathers of wizards. Some accounts point toward Gilgamesh as being that man, though historical records are too sparse to tell for certain. Others say it is random genetic evolution." The ghost shrugged. "Who can know for certain?"

"But if mundanes can't use magic, then how can they be witches?"

"Ah, well, that comes down to the inaccurate nature of the English language. You see, witches don't 'use' magic, not in the way wizards do. When a wizard casts a spell, they are directly channeling and controlling energy flowing from the Source: magic. Witches, on the other hand, especially those who specialize in controlling demons, do not channel magic. They simply take advantage of the demon's own magical properties. Demonology is the study of demon magic, the very essence which binds and controls them. It is how they rule each other, and if spoken and written correctly, can be used by humans to control them—in theory, at least.

"Yet, demonology affects nothing but demons themselves, no matter who uses it. Demons can use their own magic to many devious purposes. In theory, they could gift their power to other beings, yet has anyone ever heard of a generous demon? Even were some wizard or witch to acquire such power, demonic magic can only corrupt and reshape what has been made. It cannot create or give life, only harm and destroy. Knowing this, it is no surprise the type of people who gravitate toward demonology," Peter finished delicately.

I frowned, wondering if what I was trying to do was harmful. All I wanted was to have my parents alive again. Was that so bad? But if demons could only harm and destroy, would they be able to bring back my parents? Make their bodies new again? I rather hoped Peter didn't know what he was talking about.

"There are other witches, of course," Peter went on, "who are simply mundanes in possession of magical artifacts crafted by wizards. Some such artifacts can work independent of their creators and may be controlled by physical, rather than magical, means."

My ears perked up at that, but I was impatient to move on to the most interesting topic. "What about the fae?"

"Long, long ago, there were tales of druids—those befriended by the fae. But I know little about them. Keep in mind, lad, that 'witch' is a general term we wizards use to mean anyone not a wizard themself who is impertinent enough to meddle in magic."

"Because, of course, anyone *not* a wizard is incapable of being moral, responsible, or intelligent?" I said, giving him a sarcastic smile that I knew he could see, despite the darkness.

"Well, I wouldn't exactly put it that way, but…yes, that is the view of most wizards. Many of the older family lines have become rather, shall we say, elitist?"

"Just what the world needs, more people who think they're better than everyone else," I muttered, shaking my head. Looking out the window I could see that the sky was beginning to lighten. "I'd better get some sleep," I told Peter, lying down and trying to get comfortable.

Despite a long night with no rest, I felt wide awake, images of demons, fae, and angels dancing around in my head. I only indulged in fanciful imaginings for a few minutes, though, before refocusing on my mission.

Today, well, yesterday, had been Friday, the second to last Friday of the school year. I'd been studying hard all week—not my finals notes, of course, but the rest of the symbols Meg had given me. If I could keep my door locked and Peter on the lookout for my aunt, I'd have all that day to perfect the last few. I might even have time to crack open that black book and find out what "alternative warding" was before night fell and I had to go to Roger's stupid meeting. On Sunday, however, assuming all my symbols were perfect, Meg had promised to let me practice summoning on her little demon, just so I'd know what it felt like and what to expect. That was what I was most excited about. Well, excited was not quite the right word. Terrified was more accurate. But knowing we were getting closer to our goal made my heart somehow lighter.

One thing at a time, I told myself, and tried to get some sleep.

18

The last place in the world I wanted to be on a Saturday night was in the cramped secret basement of a shabby therapy clinic, surrounded by wackos. But, following the general pattern of unfortunate events in my life, that's right where I found myself. Meg had warned me that if I didn't go, Roger would get suspicious and might start questioning her and Cassius, since they had vouched for me. Who knew what he could worm out of them with his piercing, hypnotic gaze. It was better not to chance it.

So, Saturday night, I dutifully snuck out again, Peter following along, silent and invisible. I was beginning to have a sixth sense about when he was around. It wasn't the chill in the air he sometimes caused, rather that, when he was around, I didn't feel so alone. And when he wasn't around, I could tell something was missing.

Of course, by something, I mean a busy-body nag. He was a regular little conscience, that one. Whenever I was being "disreputable"—from checking out girls, to making faces at my aunt behind her back—he made sure I knew what he thought. Not that he *did* anything about it. But perhaps he could be excused, being incorporeal and all.

The funny thing was, I didn't mind. I'd always been pretty immune to scolding, and most of the time his stuffy ramblings were more amusing than anything else. Quite possibly it was because he reminded me of my parents. Even if it hurt to remember them, I didn't want to forget. So, his nervous mutterings in my ear as I followed Meg down the alleyway toward Roger's clinic were more of a comfort than anything else. I kept trying to get him to talk to Meg, but he insisted it was better he keep to himself, especially when we were around Roger.

As we exited the alley to cross the road beside the strip mall, I saw Cassius's Mustang parked on the street. And leaning against it was none other than Mr. Scumball himself. Resisting the urge to give him the finger, I instead quickened my pace to walk beside Meg instead of behind her. As soon as he spotted us, Mr. Scumball pushed himself off his car and caught up—to my great annoyance. Even though I'd strategically positioned myself between Meg and him, he deftly swerved around us and came up on Meg's other side, putting a possessive arm around her and grinning at me over her head. Well, not really over her head. He just had to look up and there I was.

"Ready for your first lesson, runt?"

"As long as it doesn't involve you opening your mouth, yes."

"I'd watch it if I were you. Roger trains the newbies. He'd love a reason to put you in your place just like he did Meg."

By his leering grin I could tell *he* would love a reason to put me in my place as well. My temper flared and I wanted to grab Meg's hand and pull her away from the piece of filth. But one look at her tight jaw and flashing eyes told me such an action would get me a tongue lashing. And probably a black eye. She didn't want to be rescued, not from Cassius. That didn't mean she liked what was going on, but I had to remind myself that he was "useful." I hoped how she acted at school was the "real" Meg and not this part she was playing with Cassius. She was so vibrant, so fiery with me, but whenever she was around Cassius, or Roger's stupid "fellowship," she seemed…diminished.

True to Cassius's word, as soon as the various members had gathered in the little room and eaten some food—hotdogs and baked beans this time—Roger set them about their various tasks and turned to me.

"You'll be practicing with me, Sebastian, so I can start teaching you the basics of self-empowerment. You must master yourself before you can hope to gain power over your environment."

"Sure, whatever," I muttered, glancing around the room at the other kids. They were paired off, heads together, talking in low voices. No blood or sacrificial chickens in evidence.

Roger offered me a chair and then sat across from me. I scooted as far away from him as I could without looking like I was doing it on purpose.

"Now, Sebastian. Look into my eyes."

I thought about saying no. But a glance to the side told me that Meg and Cassius were deep in conversation and so there was no escape there. I could either follow Roger's directions or leave. So I looked.

Man, those eyes were creepy. Even as I watched, the whites turned blood red. I wanted to jerk back, to yell, to run. But I was stuck.

I felt a presence. Not Peter, whose nervousness beside me was almost palpable, but something behind Roger's eyes. It was looking at me. Without knowing how, I was absolutely, positively certain that a very powerful, very scary demon was present. And it liked what it saw.

"Good, good. Relax, Sebastian, there is nothing to fear." Roger's voice was soft and soothing. My body relaxed, reacting to whatever calming power was in his voice, even as my mind buzzed in panic. I knew I shouldn't be relaxing. I was a rabbit caught under the claw of a tiger that, sooner or later, would get hungry. But there was nothing I could do, so I took a deep breath, commanding my brain to stop bouncing around in circles and focus.

"There. That is better. I can see we are going to be very good friends, are we not?" The sibilant voice was no longer Roger's. It was far older, and far more powerful.

Its question pressed on my neck, urging me to nod my head in agreement. I fought it, gritting my teeth.

"Gooood. You are strong, and I will make you stronger. If you wish to control others, you must first control yourself. Stand."

My muscles obeyed before the thought of resistance could even cross my mind. They contracted, pushing me forward and upward. But then my brain caught up and I fought back, straining to sit down. I must have looked like an idiot, leaning forward, halfway out of the chair, frozen in a silent battle.

Slowly, inch by inch, I sank down into the seat. But it took every ounce of willpower and strength I possessed. By the time I finally felt the command relax, I was gasping for breath.

"Was that not amusing? Surely you are not tired. Not yet. We have much, still, to do."

Again and again he, it, whatever it was, told me to stand and I had to resist. Each time I did better, reacted faster, but it was exhausting work, both physically and mentally. I had no idea how much time had passed, but finally, I stopped fighting, tired of the stupid game he was playing.

"Tut tut. You are not trying, Sebastian. Do you no longer wish to gain power? Would you rather be controlled, perhaps, than learn to control? What if I told you to gouge out your eye? Since you are so content to obey, surely it would be no hardship."

To my horror, my hand lifted and turned, my pointer finger extended and headed straight for my eye. Panic exploded in my brain and I pushed back with all my might. My hand slowed, but didn't stop, inching closer and closer to my wide-open, terror-stricken eye. I told myself he wouldn't go through with it. He was only playing with me, right?

"Yeees. A delightful game, no? Think of how amusing it will be when you have only one eye? Or perhaps none? I hear blind men have marvelously sharp hearing. Would that not be a splendid thing to experience?"

The evil, sadistic pleasure in that voice told me he was not going to stop. By this point I could almost feel my fingernail, it was so close to my eye. I pushed and pushed, terror turning to anger as I cursed the twisted bastard for toying with me like I was his plaything. Looking into those mismatched, red-ringed eyes, I could see my own eyes reflected there, narrowed in rage. I couldn't tell what color they were, but I could guess, and I knew I hated this creature for it. I hated it and I hated Roger and I'd be damned if I let them play with me.

I yelled and pushed, lashing out with every bit of pain, anger, and frustration inside me. The thing's hold was broken and I felt suddenly light as a feather. I panted for breath, my hand dropping to my lap where it lay, trembling, while I glared at Roger. He grinned back, showing white, perfectly straight teeth.

Sensory information flooded in to my brain, as if I'd been

in a cocoon of laser sharp focus, ignoring the rest of the world. My muscles were exhausted, demanding I slump in the chair and give them relief. Soft voices spoke in rhythmic tones around me and I realized the struggle must have all been in my mind. Nobody looked startled as if I'd just yelled at the top of my lungs and tried to punch Roger, even though that's what I'd done in my head.

"See? It feels good, does it not, to know you have the power to resist?"

Roger's voice was still smoother than normal, and his eyes still red. I could tell the thing was watching me, just beneath the surface. And it was pleased.

So was I, but for a completely different reason. I had not, in fact, been thinking about how good it felt to resist. I'd been worrying about Meg and what this sicko might have made her do, or done to her, with such a powerful force at his disposal. But neither he, nor it, seemed to know that. Which meant they couldn't read minds, as I had at first feared. They were just good at guessing. Except now, they were wrong.

Well, far be it from me to burst their bubble.

"Yeah, it feels—it feels great," I panted, still trying to catch my breath.

"Excellent." Roger let out a long breath and closed his eyes. When he opened them, they were back to normal. He smiled disarmingly and stood, raising his voice. "I think that's enough for tonight, boys and girls. I wouldn't want to keep you out too late. We'll meet again in two weeks for more practice."

I stumbled as I got up, catching myself on the chair. My legs felt like jelly. Looking up, I could see Meg stealing glances in my direction, her brow furrowed. But she didn't come over to help, perhaps not wanting to draw Roger's attention.

As we were leaving, Roger called Cassius back to talk to him. I did an internal victory dance—I didn't have the energy for an external one—happy to not have to look at either of their worthless faces any more that day.

"Come on, Meg," I muttered, heading for the stairs. We made our escape and walked back to the car in silence. I could feel Peter hovering anxiously, but he didn't speak, either. It wasn't until we arrived at the Chevy and I moved to circle around to the passenger side that Meg stopped me, grabbing my arm and pulling me back.

"Are you okay?" Her voice was low, worried. I couldn't see much of her in the dark, but her pale, upturned face seemed to have lines where before there'd been none, and her grip was tight on my arm.

"I feel like I just ran a marathon and I have a splitting headache. Other than that—yeah, I'm fine."

Her grip relaxed, though her hand stayed where it was. "Okay. It's just…I know how it feels." She didn't say what *it* was, but she didn't need to.

I held those deep brown eyes with mine, wishing I could get inside her walls. I'd had glimpses of a funny, interesting girl who was fiercely loyal to her family. But the tiny windows that occasionally appeared always shut quickly, and then she would push me away. Who was Meg Garcia, really, under all that makeup, black clothes, and spiked boots? Who was hiding behind those walls, so tall and strong?

I wanted to know—to know *her*.

I was afraid I would never get the chance.

Something prompted me to move. I wasn't sure if it was my head or my heart, or the hot blood pounding through my veins. Whatever it was, I took a chance, raising one hand to cup her cheek as my other hand sought hers, twining our fingers together. She didn't pull away.

"I'm more worried about you," I said, hoping the

genuineness in my voice told her I wasn't trying to be patronizing.

Meg sighed, looking more tired than I'd ever seen her. She seemed far older than seventeen, the pain adding weary years to her face. "I'll be fine. I'm used to it, I guess."

"You shouldn't have to be," I said, squeezing her hand.

She snorted. "We don't all have well-adjusted, responsible family members to shield us from reality, Sebastian. Some of us live in the real world."

I pulled away, stung, like she'd slapped me in the face. I had to squash the urge to strike back, hating my petty anger and hating more where I suspected it came from.

But she wouldn't let go of my hand and gently tugged, drawing me back. "No—I'm sorry, Seb. I wasn't thinking. Of course you live in the real world. I just meant…I guess I meant that some of us are luckier than others. And we unlucky ones have to deal with what life hands us."

I let her pull me in, wanting more than anything to be close to her, but unsure if it was the right thing. We were both so broken—what if all we did was break each other further? So I waited, anxiously trying to read her body language.

Meg looked up at me, studying my face. After a moment, she smiled. It was very small, and her eyes were still sad, but it was a smile. "I don't know, maybe I'm not so unlucky after all."

She tipped her face back farther, and it was all the invitation I needed. I let go of her hand and raised both of mine, one cupping her face and the other tangling in her thick, silky hair. Bending down, I stopped when my lips were just above hers, pausing to breathe in her scent as I waited, wanting to be sure. Wanting *not* to be Mr. Scumball.

I needn't have worried. She let out a sigh of impatience and stood on tiptoe, mashing her mouth against mine.

Her lips were warm and soft, and oh so full. They were the hottest lips I'd ever kissed, and let me tell you, I'd kissed plenty. The cheerleading team's pants might have belonged to the football team, but their lips were all too eager to make the rounds.

Meg's lips were smooth, and as they pressed against mine I slid my tongue along them, just barely caressing their silken surface. At my touch, they opened in a soft gasp and I felt Meg press against my body.

The slow fire that had been growing inside me exploded. I was caught off guard by this new feeling, so intense and all-encompassing. My fingers tightened, gripping her hair as I resisted the urge to reach down, pick her up, and pin her against the car. I had no idea what I would do next, just that part of me ached with the need to grind against something, anything. But I held back, my already exhausted will struggling to retain control.

With an effort, I broke our kiss, letting my hands drop to her shoulders. "Not that—I'm not having—the time of my life," I panted, "but if Cassius happens to—to see us, I suspect our little conspiracy won't—stay secret for much longer."

Meg pouted, and man if I didn't almost lose it again right there. Those lips made my brain go all fuzzy and made my body, well, throb. It was almost embarrassing.

"Cassius can go fuck himself. But...I suppose you're right." She gave me an apologetic look and stepped back, allowing me the space I needed to get certain, ahem, parts of myself under control.

Suddenly self-conscious, I turned away, rubbing the back of my neck. "So, uh. I guess we should go home?"

"Yeah," Meg agreed. "Let's."

19

Peter, to his credit, did not say a single word after Meg dropped me off. Of course, he didn't need to. I could sense his stuffy disapproval a mile away. On the other hand, he didn't come right out and scold me, so maybe he was recalling his own youth and similar nights spent with lovely young ladies. I bet if I'd asked him, he could've told me dozens of stories of wooing women with his fine speech and dapper mustache.

I had more important things to worry about, though, so I didn't dwell on Peter's past love life. For the short walk home, I let myself remember Meg's soft lips and curvaceous body pressed against mine. But as soon as I'd snuck back into my room, I was all business. I still had that second book to go through, so after undressing and checking that the house was quiet, I crawled under the covers, got out my penlight, and started to read.

Most of it went over my head, I had to admit. But based on the little I could pick out from the academic mumbo jumbo, I knew my guess had been right. The chapter I'd noticed about alternative warding discussed warding without spells. It mentioned, among other things, the properties of iron and its effect on magic, as well as several species of plants. The last bit, though, was where I focused my attention. It was barely a page, but opposite it was a black and white illustration with numbered figures demonstrating what it called "celestial emblems."

"Psst, Peter," I whispered. "If something is celestial it has to do with angels, right?"

"Indeed. What have you found, young man?"

"Take a look at this."

I felt a chill pass through me and I squirmed. "Hey, turn off the air conditioning, will you?"

"Ah, pardon me."

The chill vanished, and I barely needed my penlight as Peter's glowing form joined me under the covers. His dressing gown-clad figure floated, or sat, or lay, I had no idea which, so that part of him was in the bed and part of him was in *me*—that was creepy—and a few bits of him no doubt stuck up above the covers. What mattered, though, was that his face ended up next to mine, examining the page.

"Fascinating…"

"What?"

"…oh, yes, this *is* quite the find…"

"Will you stop muttering to yourself and tell me what it is?" I hissed, seriously considering shutting the book and not opening it again until he deigned to explain himself.

"What? Oh, pardon me. I have heard of such things, but there are very few texts, I think, which still address the existence of celestial emblems. It is truly a magnificent find. I wonder if Madam Barrington has any more volumes on—"

"But what *are* they?" I interrupted him.

"Why, they are the symbols of power which angels use, their magical runes. Though the rules of their magic differ, of course, they are the same as the demonology symbols you've been learning, only in their uncorrupted form. Demons, after all, are simply fallen angels, cast down and cursed for their attempt to usurp man's power."

"Huh." I stared at the page, fascinated.

"My boy, if this is indeed what I think it is, you might have just found the ward you were looking for!"

I spent an hour reading and re-reading that page, asking Peter dozens of questions as I unraveled each academic, overly complicated sentence, until I was satisfied I understood what it said. Then I spent several more hours copying down the emblems over and over, making sure they were exactly the same as the illustrations on the page. According to the book's brief explanation, they couldn't be cast or controlled like a wizard would normally manipulate a spell, but rather could be combined in certain ways to take advantage of the emblems' innate magical properties. That was fine with me since I wasn't a wizard anyway. I just needed to make sure I had all the emblems memorized exactly: not only their form, but also their proper placement.

Around dawn I finally dropped, exhausted, into a deep sleep and snored the morning away until my alarm clock went off at ten thirty. My body screamed at me when I tried to get up, every muscle sore from the previous night's exertions. I considered briefly a certain, pleasurable exertion I wish I'd had, but quickly shook the thought away.

I was meeting Meg at eleven for another Sunday of "study" and needed to get ready. The thought of my neglected finals preparation gave me a twinge of guilt, but I pushed it away. School wasn't important right now. Yes, maybe it was important in the larger scheme of things, but I would have plenty of time to catch up later...after I got my parents back. Everything would be fine then, and I could actually enjoy it. Maybe even get back on the soccer team. The thought of my former teammates gave me another stab of guilt. Yesterday had been their final soccer game of the year. Cory had begged me to come, but I'd brushed him off. At this point, I didn't even know if they'd won or lost. That life felt so far away, now. Part of me wished I could get it back, but mostly I just thought about it with sad resignation. Things would never be the same. Hopefully they would get better, one day. But I'd endured too much pain to ever be the same careless, happy-go-lucky teenager I'd been before.

With another shake of my head I crawled out of bed and into the shower, then rushed downstairs for a bite of toast before heading out the door.

"Do try and slow down, Sebastian. You will give yourself a stomachache."

My aunt's stern tone made me jump. I turned, mouth stuffed to the brim with jam and toast, and flashed her a sticky smile and two thumbs up. She gave me a pointed look from her position in the kitchen doorway, but then turned back to the dining room and whatever she'd been doing before her "suspicious teenager" radar had gone off. I sagged in relief against the counter. Her very presence made me feel guilty. Of course I had reason to be, but that couldn't be helped.

With Peter trailing glumly behind, I got to our meeting spot just in time and jumped into Meg's car as she pulled up. We drove in a silence that was only slightly awkward. I was happy simply being around her, but I wasn't sure what to say. Should I mention last night? Or pretend it hadn't happened? I decided to keep my mouth shut and take my cues from her. Since she didn't say anything herself, we were quiet for the whole ride to the abandoned brick building where we'd set up our "witchy" headquarters.

We wasted no time in getting up to the second floor, clearing everything away, and practicing drawing the circle we would use to summon the Prince of Decay. It had taken

Meg and Cassius weeks to work it out using their information stolen from the Book of Names. While I didn't like the
idea of Meg and Cassius alone together—or together at all
for that matter—at least I'd been spared having to put up
with him myself.

After practicing the circle, we went over the incantations
we would use, Meg making me repeat them dozens of times
from beginning to end to check my pronunciation. The
words felt dirty as I spoke them, dropping heavy from my
tongue and leaving a bitter taste in my mouth. We were
careful to practice each of the symbols, each of the words, in
isolation. I didn't know exactly what kind of power they held,
but I knew I didn't want to get anyone—or anything's—
attention before we were good and ready.

Once Meg was satisfied with my performance, she helped
me clean everything up and then sat us down across from
each other, cross-legged on the floor, our knees almost touching. Up to this point she'd been all business, not giving me
even the tiniest of coy looks or flutter of eyelashes. So I was
good. I did not pounce her and suck her face off like a part
of me was begging to do. Instead, I focused all my mind on
the task at hand. If I messed any of this up, it would put my
life, but more importantly her life, in danger. There was no
way I was going to let that happen.

Now, though, as we sat across from each other and I
caught her eye, I saw she had to purse her lips to keep from
smiling. "What are you looking at, dumbass?"

I couldn't help the silly grin that spread across my face.
"Oh, just the prettiest girl in town."

We both froze, like deer in the headlights.

"Well, now you've put your foot in it," Peter's whispered
voice tickled my ear, and it sounded more than a little
amused.

Drat. I knew my "don't make a complete fool of yourself" filter should have caught that thought before it ever got to my lips. But the filter seemed to have switched off when I wasn't paying attention.

Despite my embarrassment, I held her gaze. It was true, after all, even if I hadn't meant to say it out loud. She *was* pretty, and all the more so for her scars and walls and prickly exterior.

At first, she glared at me. But as the moments passed her face softened, and finally she lifted an eyebrow as if to say, "can we get back to business, please?"

"When did you stop smoking?" I asked, suddenly realizing I hadn't seen her with a cigarette in weeks.

Meg actually blushed. Ducking her head, she cleared her throat and answered in a level voice. "After I first met you. You seemed like a nice guy. I didn't want to make your clothes smell like cigarettes and tip off your aunt that you were hanging out with one of 'those' kids."

I stared at her, amazed.

"I mean, it's not like I've completely quit. I wish I could. But it's a start. Seems like the polite thing to do."

That prompted a snort. "Since when do *you* do polite things?" I asked, almost-but-not-quite laughing.

She leaned forward and punched me in the shoulder, at which point I gave up pretending not to laugh.

"Oh, shut up. Quit your cackling and pay attention. We have work to do."

Remembering our mission sobered me up quicker than a drunk man dunked in ice water. Expression serious once more, I got comfortable and paid attention. Meg drew in the dust on the floor, showing me several new symbols and teaching me their names. These were what I would use to practice summoning Rathla'un—Meg made sure I pronounced his name correctly, otherwise he'd just sit there and laugh at me when I told him to do something.

Once she was sure I had everything right she dug in her jacket pocket—she was still wearing that insane leather jacket—and took out a small pocket knife.

"Whoa there, Sweeney Todd! Put the knife down. I like my neck just the way it is, thanks."

"Oh, stop being a baby. You'll barely feel a thing." She reached for my hand, but I pulled it protectively out of reach.

"There is no way in hell I want a demon getting ahold of my blood. Why do we need it? You summon the little wretch just fine without it."

"That's because the bond has already been formed, the bargain already set. You can try to summon him with just his name, and if you're really, really strong-willed you could probably force him to do what you wanted. But he'd fight you the whole way. Why wouldn't he? There's nothing in it for him. Remember, something given, something gained. Even with demons. Nothing is free in life, genius."

I glared at her, not liking what I was hearing. It felt like every time I turned around, I learned of some new way I was being shackled to this dark road, bound in ways I could never undo. Maybe it was naive of me to imagine things could ever go back to normal, but once this was all over I would gladly leave it behind. I didn't *want* to be a witch. Okay, so parts of it were cool, but in general, witchcraft seemed like a string of foolish decisions to get something you could really live without. I didn't understand how anyone who wasn't as desperate as Meg and I would ever go through this stuff.

"While I am not fully fluent in the methods of demonic rituals, her reasoning is sound and I would not be surprised if this is indeed how it must be done." Peter's scholarly assessment of the situation, even if it was for my ears alone, did not make me feel any better about it.

"This is the only way?"

Meg nodded.

"Fine," I snorted, giving her my hand. Her warm touch sent tingles up my arm and I shifted, trying to focus on very platonic, non-sexy things. The sight of her flipping open the knife did the trick. I half looked away, not wanting to watch, but unable to take my eyes off the blade.

"Ouch!" I jerked, but she held my hand still as she made the quick, tiny cut on my finger.

"Alright, Mr. Squeamish, hurry up. Draw the symbol I showed you."

Using my throbbing finger, I drew a set of squiggles on the floor between us, leaving streaks of blood on the dusty wood. I hoped Meg had a disinfectant wipe around somewhere, or there was a good chance my finger would end up infected.

"Good, now call his name while it's still fresh."

"Ohhh, dear," Peter muttered. "I have a bad feeling about this."

Ignoring him, I obeyed Meg and closed my eyes, concentrated, then spoke the incantation she had taught me. Translated roughly, it went something like, "Come, Rathla'un. I offer my blood in return for service. Attend to me and obey my words."

I'd already said the words individually more than a dozen times in practice, but this was the first time I'd spoken them all together, finger throbbing and leaking a few last drops onto the floor as my blood started to clot. And this time, I could feel it. The power in the words. They rang as they left my mouth, and I could actually taste their filth, like I'd just bitten into a rotten egg. I struggled not to gag, forcing the last few words out with all the will I could muster.

I knew the moment he appeared. The aura of his presence broke over me in a wave that made my skin crawl, and even though my eyes were still closed, I could see him. He seemed to be both a physical and spiritual being, invading my brain and boring behind my eyes until there was nowhere left to escape.

"You called us, massster."

"Oh my goodness gracious! That *thing* is here again."

My eyes popped open at the sound of the demon's hiss and Peter's disgusted exclamation.

There it was. Though slightly less impressive in the light of day, I recognized its decaying wings and scaled flesh. It was crouched on the floor between myself and Meg, looking up at me expectantly. The blood was gone. Every smudge, every drop, vanished as if it had never existed, leaving no stain.

I shuddered. I could feel it there, waiting, its wings fluttering occasionally in that creepy way that reminded me of a wasp.

Gulping, I tried to wet my dry throat. "Go stand in that beam of sunshine," I said, pointing about five feet to the side where light streamed through one of the windows and painted golden squares on the dusty floor.

Rathla'un shrank back, hissing. "Noo! Demonss do not like the sun. It burnsss us. We will not do this."

I hesitated, glancing at Meg for support. To my surprise, she was staring intently at Rathla'un with red eyes and an uncharacteristically nasty smile on her face.

I looked away, suppressing a shudder, and focused on my task while trying not to wonder if my own eyes were red. Gathering my thoughts, I bore down on the creature's will, noticing now how the connection we had went both ways. He seemed almost in my head, but I could push back, reaching out to touch his reluctance and squash it flat.

"Heavens, boy, is this really necessary?" Peter whispered. "Surely you could set him a less, um, painful task?"

"Go!" I commanded, unsure if I was talking to Rathla'un or Peter. Or both.

Peter quieted and the small creature before me quailed, limbs trembling as it crawled slowly, inch by inch toward the light. I tried not to feel pity for it. Meg had assured me that sunlight didn't actually kill them, just hurt. A lot. Surely this miserable creature deserved the pain, didn't it? It had probably hurt people and done terrible things. Plus, this was the only way I could prove I had control, by making it do something it didn't want to.

The closer it got to the sunbeam, the harder it became for me to push it farther. It began to moan pitifully, begging me to stop. Sweat broke out on my forehead and I leaned forward, putting my fingers in my ears to block out its cries. Closer and closer I forced it, ignoring everything but the goal, the one thing I had commanded it to do.

A sudden scream of pain broke my concentration and I started, sitting up and looking around. Rathla'un crawled away from the patch of sunlight, dragging the left side of his body as he wept piteously.

"Master hurtsss us. We obeyed, we did nothing wrong, yet he hurtss us and burnss us. Burnssss us!"

Peter made a noise beside me. "Oh dear, I think I'm going to be sick." His presence vanished.

I felt ashamed. Dirty. What kind of monster was I? It was just a miserable little demon, and I shouldn't have felt sorry. But I did.

"Oh shut up, you little prick," Meg said to the demon, then looked at me. "Ignore him. He's just moaning to get attention. He's not really hurt, not much anyway. But look, as soon as you got him where you wanted, you let go. Why did you do that? You have to be able to maintain control. Make him do it again, and this time hold him there."

"No!" I scrambled to my feet, needing to get out of that

room. If I hurt that poor creature again, I would throw up. "I was perfectly capable of keeping him in the sun, I just saw no reason to make him scream any more than necessary. It hurt my ears. Anyway, I need some fresh air. Let's go up on the roof for a bit."

She gave me a long look, but finally shrugged and got up. I turned to leave, but her voice stopped me.

"Wait a minute. Aren't you going to release him?"

I realized Rathla'un was still curled up on the floor, sniffling and cradling his left arm.

"He's your slave. He came at your command, took your blood, accepted your bargain. He can't leave until you release him."

"Er, go home, Rathla'un." When it didn't move, just glared up at me with hate-filled eyes, I glared right back, feeling a bit less sorry. Giving the wretch a firm mental nudge I tried again. "Go on, beat it!"

It vanished, leaving behind nothing but a wisp of smoke and the smell of rotten eggs.

"Congrats. You've summoned your first demon. You're now officially a witch."

"Yippee," I mumbled, feeling wretched.

"Is it gone? Thank heavens. I must say those little creatures are absolutely repulsive."

Peter was back in my ear, but I barely noticed, caught up as I was in my own tortured thoughts. If a little pipsqueak like Rath made me feel this bad, what would it be like summoning the Prince of Decay?

I shuddered, feeling the sudden need for sun on my skin. "I'm going up on the roof." I eyed Meg. "Do you need an umbrella to join me?" In that leather jacket of hers I couldn't fathom how she hadn't overheated yet.

Meg rolled her eyes. "There's some shade around by the chimneys, remember? Besides, it's not like I melt in the sun.

That's the Wicked Witch of the West, and she only melts in water."

Chastised, I shrugged, and led the way up the second-floor stairs to the roof. Meg sat in the shade while I settled down next to her, half in shade and half in sun. It was warm out, but not so hot that I couldn't take the direct light. The beams felt good on my arm and face, which I tipped back, eyes closed to soak up more of the sun's rays.

We talked for a long time, hours probably. I wasn't supposed to be back until the evening, so we had time to kill. Our conversation was about everything, and nothing. It wasn't so deep, or so close to our loss, as it had been the last time we'd reminisced on the rooftop. There seemed to be an unspoken agreement between us not to stray too close to raw memories. Instead we talked about school, our friends —and enemies—our strengths and weaknesses, even our favorite music. Meg wasn't a chatterbox, but by sharing first I goaded her into telling me perhaps more than she had intended. It was nice. Up there on the roof, we were above our troubles. Even our plans for the future and the pains of our past seemed to fall away. The day felt timeless, never-ending.

As the sun finally dipped toward the horizon and the shadows began to lengthen, our talk turned back to demonology. I learned more details about greater and lesser demons—the former you avoided unless absolutely necessary, the latter you could usually work with, for a price. I discovered that once a demon had accepted your bargain, you could usually control it with only your willpower. But sometimes, for the more stubborn ones, you needed to know how to command them in their own language. So it was important to always continue studying demonology, learning more words and phrases in case you needed them to control an unruly demon. Meg shared all the tips and tricks she'd learned for persuading lesser demons, which was usually easier than outright forcing them by will alone.

By the time the sun had sunk behind the trees, we'd run out of things to say and I knew it was time to head home. I stood, shaking out the kinks in my muscles, then turned to give her a hand up. After she pulled herself up, though, she didn't let go, just stood there, looking up at me. She was close enough that I could feel her body heat in the quickly cooling air.

"What is it?" I asked, voice soft in the silence. Occasional cars passed on the street below, but by and large it was a very quiet neighborhood.

"I...just don't want this day to end, I guess." She shrugged. "I haven't been happy this many hours in one day for, I dunno, years probably."

"Well," I said, inching closer. "I'm delighted to have helped you break a personal record. Maybe we should get together sometime and try to beat it again."

"Goodness, boy, you are incorrigible. Have you no shame? If things are about to get...delicate, I believe I shall wait by the car." And with that, Peter was gone.

I grinned and Meg—not privy to Peter's hushed grousing—smiled back.

My heart skipped a beat.

"Yeah. Maybe we should...sometime," she said in a teasing tone and turned to go, still holding onto my hand.

I pulled her back, slowly drawing her close and leaning in for a kiss, giving her plenty of time to push me away. She didn't.

The kiss, when our lips met, was soft and chaste, without the desperate passion of the night before, yet holding promises of better things to come.

I was still thinking about that kiss when Meg dropped me off two blocks from my house. I was still thinking about it as I climbed the porch steps and pulled open the front door. I didn't stop thinking about it until I went to step over the threshold and ran smack dab into my aunt. Stumbling back, I looked up to see her terrible face, pale with a fury so great her eyes seemed to radiate energy, as if lightning bolts would leap from them and incinerate me where I stood. In her hand, she held two antique-looking books, one brown, one black.

My body washed cold, then hot, then cold again.

I'd forgotten to take the spellbooks with me.

20

"Oh dear."

I barely heard Peter's stunned comment. My ears were ringing and my mind fluttered helplessly, trying to come up with a plan, an excuse, an explanation.

"Uh...Aunt Barrington, I can explain."

"Is that so? I cannot imagine what set of circumstances could possibly explain the presence of books from my *private* library appearing in your possession. Without. My. Permission." Her words were lethally sharp, each one cutting into me like the lashes of a whip.

I swallowed, then opened my mouth, hoping that by the time words came out I would know what to say.

But she didn't give me the chance. "Did you think I would not know if someone violated the privacy of my personal sanctum? That I would not be aware of the comings and goings in my own house? Did you think I would not miss even a single one of my precious bo—"

She halted abruptly. Her brows furrowed and her nostrils

flared as she breathed in deep, like she'd caught a scent. Then her eyes widened.

I had assumed my aunt was as mad as she'd ever been in her life.

I was wrong.

Her expression went from angry, to deadly cold. And when I say cold, I mean the kind of cold you see on the face of your murderer right before they stab you in the heart. A muscle twitched in her cheek, and she looked at me like I was the lowest scum of the earth.

"You foolish, arrogant, reckless wretch! You have been consorting with demons. I can smell their foul stench on you." Her voice had become dangerously quiet.

Like a rabbit that smells a fox, I remained frozen. Waiting. I thought of the demonology notes tucked away in my backpack among my school things. Each slender piece of paper felt like a glowing, red coal—a flashing beacon of guilt.

"Come," she snapped, following that with a string of words in a language I didn't recognize. I felt a sharp pain in my left ear as it was yanked upward, like I was a little boy and some adult had grabbed my ear and was pulling me along by it.

"Ow, ow, ow, ow! What are you doing? Stop it!" I stood on my toes to alleviate the pressure, flailing against whatever was holding me. But there was nothing there to fight, just empty air.

Aunt Barrington whirled about and marched down the hall, and the pain pulled me after her. I protested loudly, and colorfully. How else was I supposed to fight against wizard magic? I was a good head taller than her and yet she had me by the ear, literally.

"Better go along quietly, my boy. You can't win. Believe me, I tried a time or two—in my younger, more foolish years, of course—and she always won the argument. Fiercer than a she-tiger when she's angry, that one." Peter's gloomy voice didn't make me feel any better, and I stumbled along down the hallway, following the invisible, and painful, pull on my ear.

My aunt marched me into her library and stood me in front of her desk while she took her seat behind it, a metaphorical cloud of thunder and ice about her head. The objects on her desk were clicking and whirring furiously and my two stolen books lay side by side on the polished wood before her.

She made me stand there, on my tiptoes, wincing in discomfort while she examined me, perhaps deciding what to do. I wanted to tell her to lay off and leave me alone, but I sensed that such unrepentant rudeness from me at this point wouldn't make the situation any better. So I took the pain, until she finally barked a single word and the invisible force released me. Back on the flat of my feet again, I massaged my ear, eyeing her and waiting for the axe to fall.

"I am speechless, Sebastian. I cannot believe that the son of Thomas and Alison would be so selfish, so foolish, so utterly disdainful of everything they sacrificed. Do you have any idea what you have done?"

I crossed my arms, feeling an outburst building inside. I tried to keep it in. I knew it wouldn't help. But I also wasn't going to stand there and be scolded like I was twelve years old again. I was an adult—mostly—and could make my own decisions.

"I thought not," Aunt Barrington's lip curled in disgust. "You are young, immature, and ignorant."

"Hey, now, wait a minute—"

"SILENCE!" Her voice, magically magnified, boomed through the library and my mouth slammed shut.

"You. Are. Ignorant. You have no inkling of the forces you are toying with, Sebastian. In your youthful arrogance you presume to know what is best for yourself and, even worse, for others."

My insides burned, but I kept my mouth shut, glaring at my aunt as she glared right back at me.

"You parents sacrificed their *lives* to protect you from the dangers of magic. From the hate and greed and jealousy it can engender in the undisciplined and foolish heart. They sacrificed *everything* for you, and yet you repay them by tainting yourself with the most deadly, despicable magic one could possibly imagine. How could you, Sebastian? How could you dishonor them so?"

"You don't know what you're talking about!" I burst out, pushed to my breaking point. "All they ever did was hide things from me and make me live a normal life—"

"Exactly!" she cut me off again, hand slamming down on her desk. "You have no idea how hard they worked to protect you, to give you a semblance of normalcy, of safety—"

"What do you mean safety? Safety from what?" I spread my arms wide, mocking her. "From an annoying sibling and a grouchy old aunt? Well, too bad they failed miserably at that."

Both my aunt's hands were on the table now, fingers splayed, fingertips white as they pressed against the wood. Her voice grew quiet again, controlled by a will of iron. "You know not of what you speak. You have *no idea* of the forces which have sought, and still seek, to harm you, because your parents did their job so well."

I hesitated, doubt growing as I remembered their sudden and mysterious trips. They'd never told us where they went, and had always came back looking tired and worn. What had they been doing? What was out there?

"Well it—it doesn't matter anymore. They're gone, and now I have to find my own way. And I have. Just because you don't agree with it doesn't mean it's bad, or stupid."

"The very fact that you think that, boy, tells me you have already been blinded. Blinded by greed and the lust for power." Her quiet words and piercing eyes cut through me, hitting their mark. I thought of mismatched eyes, green and blue ringed by circles of glowing red.

"The power isn't for me," I protested. "It's to help someone else." There, that was true enough.

"It matters not who the power is for!" My aunt stood abruptly and pointed at me, her eyes wide and almost fearful. "Your intentions mean nothing, Sebastian. Nothing! You are giving yourself into the control of something evil beyond compare, and you can do nothing good with its power, no matter how hard you try. Do not believe the lies that such a thing can save you or bring you your heart's desire. It will bring you only death."

I gritted my teeth, stomach churning and chest burning. "Well, I've had plenty of that lately, so I guess it'll be nothing new."

"Listen to yourself, Sebastian! What lies has some filthy witch been whispering in your ear?"

"Back off, old woman!" I uncrossed my arms and took a step forward, fists clenched by my side as an image of Meg flashed through my head. "You don't know what *you're* talking about. Not all witches are bad. Some are good, some are bad, just like people. And they've been the only ones helping me in all this mess. All *you* do is give orders. Do this, do that. You don't care what I feel or what I want. You just tell me to shut up and obey. But I won't. You're not my mom or my dad, and I don't have to listen to you. I know what I'm doing and my *friends*, these witches you're too ignorant and stuck-up to admit might be decent people, are helping me fix my life. So shut up and leave me alone!" By the time I was done, my voice had risen to a yell and I'd taken another step forward. Everything before me was tinted red, and I wanted to attack, to strike her down and prove I was right. Trembling, I clenched my fists harder, nails digging into my flesh as I tried to control myself.

Not at all intimidated by my display, Aunt Barrington slowly leaned forward, fists on her desk, eyes dark and face contorted in pain. "I know exactly what I am talking about. Witches are liars. They are murderers. They care only for their own selfish purposes and destroy everything you love if you get in their way. Do not tell me I do not understand. They—" she cut herself off, lips pressed together as if holding back something that wanted to come out. When she spoke again her voice was hard as iron. "They are evil beyond compare and I will *not* have my nephew consorting with them or being pulled into their web of lies and deceit."

She came around her desk, eyes flashing, and got right in my face, not the least bit bothered by my height. "Since you are acting like a willful child, I shall treat you as one. You are grounded—"

"What?" I yelped.

"—you will be confined to your room indefinitely. I will decide what punishment is fitting after your school finals. Until then, you will spend every minute of the day studying. I will be informing the teachers of this so that they can ensure you have sufficient material to keep you occupied—"

"Now wait a minute. You can't do that—"

"—and whoever this witch or witches are that you have been "studying" with, be warned, I shall be asking your teachers whom you spend time with at school. You can be sure I will raise this matter with their parents. We will put a stop to this devilry. Now go to your room!"

"You're crazy! I am not going to—" I began, but my aunt said a sharp word and the pain was back, pulling me up to my tiptoes as she reached into my pocket and confiscated my cell phone. I grabbed for it, but the force pulling my ear hauled me out of the room and toward the stairs. I fought back, trying to turn around and head for the front door. But it felt like my ear was in danger of ripping from my head, the force was so strong. I couldn't escape.

Cursing, yelling, and kicking I fought it all the way up the stairs and into my room. As soon as the pressure vanished I spun back around, but the door slammed in my face and no matter how much I tugged, it wouldn't budge. The red tint was back in my vision and I attacked the door, kicking and punching and calling my aunt every obscene name I could think of. I cursed her, I cursed my parents, I cursed the world, and fate, and even Meg.

At the thought of her, though, I started to calm. The red in my mind raged, wanting blood, but I pushed it away, wrenching back control, trying to clear my head.

Meg. I needed to warn her. My phone was gone, but maybe Peter—

Spinning, I pointed an accusing finger at Peter, who hovered anxiously behind me. "You! You *knew* she'd find out, didn't you? This is all your fault!"

"Well, I—that is—I might have suspected, but—"

"Why didn't you warn me?"

"And what good would that have done, young sir? Would it have stopped you?"

I glared daggers at him, arms crossed. No, of course it wouldn't have, but at least I could have been prepared. My eyes burned, the betrayal leaving me off-balance and vulnerable. I lashed out in thoughtless anger. "A fat lot of good you are. I don't know why I even bothered being friends with you in the first place."

As soon as the words left my mouth, I regretted them. But it was too late.

Peter drew himself up to his full height, his whiskered face angrier than I'd ever seen it. "Well! I do *apologize* that you got in trouble for *stealing*. I tried to warn you that it was unadvisable, but did you listen? No! I tried to tell you that consorting with witches would only lead to trouble, but did you listen to that, either? No! It does, indeed, seem that I am useless. Good for nothing but blathering on, giving advice that is ignored and unappreciated. Why am I even here? Madam Barrington was right. I have obviously failed to protect you. It was from yourself that you needed protection, and I was not good enough, not wise enough, not persuasive enough to fulfill my duty. Perhaps I should just leave. My task is already doomed, and I will spend forever wandering this desolate plane, never having peace."

"Woah, hey, don't talk like that," I said, alarmed. "What do you mean task? Why won't you have peace?"

"It matters not. Not anymore," he intoned, anger spent and face now a mask of gloom. "All is vanity. Mist in the wind. This family is doomed to make the same mistakes, and I am to blame for them all."

"Now wait a minute. You're not—Peter—"

But he was gone.

"Peter? Come on, you old grouch, come back!" I waited, listening, but there was no pompous muttering or chill in the air. I couldn't feel him anymore, and that sense of total isolation was creeping back over me, a cold counterpoint to a fresh wave of hot guilt.

"Come on, Peter. Don't be like that. I *do* need you. I need you to warn Meg. I need you to remind me when I'm being stupid. Okay, so maybe I don't always take your advice, but that doesn't mean it isn't useful." I paused, listening.

Nothing.

"Peter? PETER!" I didn't care that my aunt would hear me. I was suddenly desperately afraid of being alone. Why had I lashed out? I was such an idiot!

But there was no reply, and with the silence came a

weariness and despair greater than I could bear. I dropped to the floor, back to my bed, head in my hands. Everything had gone wrong.

I spoke into my hands, tired voice faint even to my own ears. "I do need you, Peter. I need someone to care. I need...someone..."

And there I was again. Alone.

It was my own fault. Everything was. But I couldn't think about that or I'd lose my grip and spiral back into that darkness that I knew all too well. I needed to focus, to make a plan. Now that I had calmed down, maybe I could talk to my aunt, explain things, show her that Meg wasn't so bad. No, who was I fooling? She was too angry. She wouldn't listen to me, wouldn't understand. But why was she so upset? What did she have against witches? Was it simple prejudice, like Peter? Or had something happened to her?

Guilt constricted my chest, making it hard to breathe. I wondered why my aunt had always been alone. No husband, no children, no family at all—at least that I knew of. But why did she have to be so cross all the time? Why couldn't she be gentle and understanding like my mother had been? Yeah, my parents would have been furious at what I'd gotten up to, but Mom, at least, would have heard me out. She would have asked for the whole story, beginning to end. She would have tried to understand.

But she wasn't here. If I'd been a better person, less petty and argumentative, we wouldn't have had that crash, my parents would still be alive, and I wouldn't be in any of this stupid mess. It was all my fault.

I was a total screw-up.

The tears finally came, leaking past my fists as I pressed them angrily against my eyes.

I had to fix this. Our plan was my only hope. I'd see Meg tomorrow at school, and we'd figure out what to do.

21

———

The silence between us was glacial as my aunt drove me to school the next morning. After my first week back, I'd started riding the bus, but apparently my aunt wanted to make sure I was actually *going* to school. She'd decided to drive me herself until the end of the year. The night before, I had promised myself I would apologize to her, in memory of my mother. But I'd woken that morning in a foul mood, hungry from skipping dinner and stiff from falling asleep leaning against my bed. Any virtuous feelings I'd had were buried under a mountain of sullen anger. And, of course, Peter, who probably could have talked some sense into me, was gone.

Aunt Barrington didn't say a word when she dropped me off, but the silent threat was there: come straight to pickup as soon as the bell rings. Or else.

At least she hadn't thought to inspect my backpack. I had no idea if she would recognize any of the demonology symbols, but with the meanings Meg had written down for me, she could have guessed what we were planning to do. If she got even an inkling she would probably chain me to my bed.

I made a beeline for the back of the school where Meg and I usually met every morning before the bell, trading snarky comments to psych ourselves up for a day of misery. Rounding the corner, I trotted along the sidewalk, passing the back doors and heading for that grassy spot where the school building bent in an L-shape, creating an alcove with a few trees and a lunch table. I spotted Meg ahead, already sitting at the table, chin in her hands. Today was buckle pants day, topped with a complicated-looking lace-up-vest-thingie over a long-sleeve shirt with more holes than Swiss cheese. The expression on her face promised terrible things to anyone who so much as breathed in her direction. I hoped she wasn't too cranky, because I certainly didn't come bearing joyous tidings.

As I strode toward her, though, I saw a group of people round the end of the building in front of me, heading for our alcove. They were big guys, and I recognized several of them from the football team.

Uh-oh.

I called out a warning to Meg, and she looked up at me, then past me. Her eyes widened, and I had a sinking feeling there were more coming up from behind.

My spin got me around just in time to meet Bryan's haymaker as he hauled off and punched me right in the face. I heard—and felt—something in my nose pop. I rolled with the blow, letting its momentum continue my spin, sending me stumbling away from the group and toward Meg.

"Get out of here!" I yelled, hoping she could slip away before the two groups met and had us cornered.

"Hell no," Meg said, a predatory grin spreading across her face. "It's Monday, and I was just wishing I had some punching bags around to take the edge off. Hello, girls. Miss me?"

Reaching her, I turned, putting us shoulder to shoulder as I took stock. My nose hurt like heck, but it didn't seem to be bleeding too badly. I could taste blood on my lips, but thankfully it wasn't streaming down my face.

The two groups met and spread out. There were ten of them in all, Bryan and his gang of thugs. The idiot had finally taken off the nose bandage he'd been wearing for weeks, as if it would somehow elicit sympathy for his poor, abused self.

"I guess we're even now, lardbutt," I said to Bryan, touching my nose gingerly. "But I'm pretty sure I'll pull off the rakishly handsome, crooked-nose-look way better than you."

Bryan growled. "Shut up, punk. We're not even. I'm going to pound you to an inch of your life. You and that slut have it coming, and I'm gonna give it to you."

"Don't you mean pound him to *within* an inch of his life?" Meg asked, clearly unimpressed. "And the next person who calls me a slut, I'll shove my foot so far up their ass that their tongue will have athlete's foot."

"Shut up, bitch."

Meg grinned evilly. "Now *that* you can call me, because it's true."

Bryan glared at her and motioned to his cronies. "Get her."

No one moved.

I spread my arms wide. "Come on, you bunch of pansies, she's just a girl. You're not scared of a girl, are you?" I laughed, but inside I was trying not to panic. There was no way we'd win, not with ten of them. We'd give as good as we got, certainly, but we'd probably end up with broken bones, maybe worse. And there was no one here to stop them. All the teachers and students were inside getting ready for class. I didn't know if Bryan and his friends would get away scot-free, but whether or not they got caught wouldn't un-break our bodies. For Meg's sake, I had to try diplomacy.

"Look, guys, surely this is overkill. We're sorry for embarrassing you in front of the whole school, okay? There's no need to get yourselves incarcerated for assault and battery."

Some of the guys looked nervously at each other, and I had a spark of hope.

"You and your little slut are a bunch of losers. You don't even deserve to go to this school. And we're going to make sure you don't."

"That doesn't even make sense—" I tried to say, but Bryan pushed one of his thugs toward me, yelling angrily.

"Get 'em, guys. The girl too. She's the one that broke my nose."

Like a pack of dogs, they descended. Meg and I backed up, trying to stay together as we blocked their first few swings. What they lacked in skill, however, they made up for in sheer numbers.

It wasn't a fight, it was a massacre. I think we both blackened a few eyes and bruised a few groins along the way, but they simply crowded in and grabbed us, hands reaching out to pin our limbs. Before I knew it, I was back to where it had all began that day in the cafeteria, held between two thugs as Bryan punched me first in the stomach, then the face. He didn't seem to have enough creativity to branch out from there, but his punches were heavy enough that it didn't matter.

This time, though, things were different. This time, they had Meg, too, and as Bryan hauled back once again, I saw her over his shoulder. Three guys held her, one on each arm and one with a fistful of her hair. She was struggling, kicking and spitting like a wildcat, and the guys who were supposed to be beating her up were having trouble getting close enough to land a blow. But then the one holding her hair punched her savagely in the kidney, and she doubled over with a scream of agony.

I went berserk.

Kicking out viciously, I caught Bryan in the shin and he backed up, limping and cursing. Now with some room in front of me I surged forward, then dropped suddenly to the ground, throwing the two guys holding me off balance. Coming back up with a twist I wrenched from their grip and lunged at Bryan, attacking in a murderous rage. Everything in front of me turned red as I slugged him across the face, splitting his lip and sending blood flying.

"You want blood, Rathla'un? I'll give you blood!" I screamed, calling the demon to me with every fiber of my being, feeling for that familiar presence and commanding it to obey.

Bryan stumbled back, shocked, and reached up to touch his lip.

I felt a tug, a response in the bond I'd made with the miserable creature of sulfur and hate. "Make. Them. Bleed," I commanded.

There was a whir of wings and a flash of red and Bryan fell, clutching his face. Yells rang out behind me and I turned to see the other football players screaming, holding their faces and arms, blood leaking out from between their fingers.

I threw back my head and laughed.

Meg's scream brought me back to myself and I spun, ready to take down anyone who was still hurting her. But she wasn't screaming in pain. She was screaming in horror, looking down at the bodies of her attackers, moaning, rolling in their own blood.

"Stop it, Sebastian! Stop it! Call him off!"

Cold realization washed over me and I frantically reached

out with my mind, grabbing for the destructive, vindictive, gleeful whirlwind of evil I'd let loose. It strained against me, wanting more blood, wanting death.

"Stop, Rathla'un. Leave! GO!"

He laughed, high and wicked, then vanished.

Silence spread out around us, broken only by the pitiful moans of Bryan and his teammates, every one of them oozing blood onto the grass. I stared at Meg, her wide eyes full of fear as she gaped at me.

Then yells and running feet sounded inside the school. Doors banged, and I came back to myself. Lunging forward, I grabbed Meg's hand and pulled, dragging her after me as I sprinted toward the end of the parking lot where she always left her car.

"Stop, Seb, what are you doing?"

"We can't stay here, we have to go!" I yelled behind me. "No one saw Bryan initiate the fight, they won't know we acted in self-defense. They'll expel us for sure and probably put us in juvie or something. We can't let that happen!"

Reaching her car, I hauled open the driver's side door and pushed her in, then raced for the passenger seat. By the time I jumped in she had the car started and we roared out of the parking lot with a squeal of tires and cloud of exhaust. Looking back, I could see a dozen or more people rushing out of the school, some going to help the injured football players, some standing there and screaming. A few pointed at our quickly disappearing car, but we were too far away for them to do anything about it.

Well, at least the bullies who attacked us would get immediate medical care. They'd be okay. I hoped.

"What the fuck just happened?" Meg yelled at me, swerving around cars and completely ignoring several stop signs as she barreled away from the school.

"I don't know! I just—I just saw them punching you and

I—I lost it. I couldn't let them hurt you. I didn't mean to—I didn't mean to—"

"You didn't mean to summon a demon and command it to 'make them bleed'? Seb, you freaking moron! It could have killed them all. In fact, I have no idea why it didn't. Maybe it was just getting warmed up, having some fun before it really got serious about the bloodletting. You can't give such stupidly broad commands like that! If you give a demon an inch, they'll take a mile, and more."

"Sorry…I just…I was so mad."

"Obviously," she scoffed.

"Well, what else was I supposed to do, let them beat you to a bloody pulp?" I asked, clenching my fists at the very thought. My right one still throbbed from when I'd punched Bryan.

"No, obviously, but they wouldn't have gone that far. They just wanted to rough us up a little. You know, scare us. You shouldn't have gone all apeshit on them. Talk about overkill."

I shook my head. "No. They were going to break bones. I know Bryan and his thugs. There was this time when they lost a game, one of the kids on the other team was found with a broken collar bone, a cracked rib, and two black eyes. They never caught whoever did it, but I know it was Bryan. I've seen him and his friends beat up other kids before. We humiliated them in front of the whole school, Meg. Didn't you hear him? 'I'm gonna make sure you don't.' I mean, his grasp of the English language is pathetic, but his point was pretty clear."

Meg snorted, then fell silent, seemingly out of things to say. I was glad, because I didn't want to think about what had almost happened.

I had almost murdered ten people.

Witches are murderers.

The memory of my aunt's pain-filled face made me wince, and I sank lower in the seat, feeling filthy. Things were getting out of hand. We needed to summon that prince, make our bargain, and end this so things could go back to normal. I was digging a deeper and deeper hole, and with each passing day I was growing less sure I could climb out of it.

Meg finally slowed to barely legal speeds, now that we were on main roads and a good distance from the school. I took advantage of the silence to probe at my nose and face, wincing at the sore spots. I didn't think my nose was broken, but it was hard to tell with it so swollen. Everything else seemed pretty much in order except for a split lip and some aches and pains around my torso. I looked over at Meg. Her face looked fine, if seriously pissed off. I didn't think she'd appreciate me asking if she were okay, so instead I said, "So uh…where are we going?"

"I dunno, genius, where *are* we going?" she echoed. "We're pretty much outlaws. We can't show our face again at school, your aunt will throw you in jail herself if she ever catches you, and the school will probably report us to the police, so being seen anywhere right now might get us picked up."

My heart sank, realizing the bleakness of our situation, and I had a sudden longing for Peter. For his advice, however annoying it was. He would know how to get out of this mess.

"Tonight."

"What?" Meg asked.

"We have to do it tonight. It's now or never. Especially if we have to come back and summon the thing a second time. We need to get this ball rolling."

Meg was silent, eyes focused on the road.

"Uh, hello? Meg?"

"Wha? Oh, um, right. Tonight…" She trailed off.

"What do we need? Can we get everything together in time?"

"Cassius is, um, in charge of getting the supplies. He has easy access because…well, Roger."

I nodded. "I'm sorry, my aunt took away my cell phone. How are we going to contact him?"

Meg let out a long, disgusted sigh. "We'll have to lay low at my place. There's a phone there."

"But won't the school know where to look for you?"

She shook her head. "We never updated my school records. They still have our old house on file, the one we lived in before…" She fell silent.

I knew how she felt, so I didn't say any more.

22

We drove the rest of the way in silence, each a prisoner of our own dark thoughts. I kept an eye on Meg. She seemed unusually fidgety, drumming her nails on the steering wheel and shifting uncomfortably every few minutes. It looked like she was nervous, but about what? It could have been any manner of things, so I tried to distract myself by watching the scenery.

By now, I was used to our normal route to the abandoned brick building Meg used as hideout-slash-home away from home. This time, though, as we entered the south part of Atlanta, she veered more east. I'd never spent any amount of time in that part of the city, so I had no idea where we were. We passed through some nicer-looking neighborhoods, but then I started seeing more corner liquor stores and apartment complexes with less individual houses and charming little yards. Most of the people out and about were black, brown, or somewhere in between, and while I certainly wasn't a stranger to diversity, I wasn't used to quite so much of it at once. Atlanta as a whole had a very ethnically diverse population, but it seemed things were pretty segregated within individual neighborhoods. Where I grew up in North Atlanta we had a black neighbor here and there, but most of the people around me had been white.

I looked at Meg and wondered where her old house was, what kind of neighborhood she'd grown up in, and if her white makeup and goth persona were just a rebellious facade or part of something much deeper. I also wondered why I had to resist the urge to sink lower in my seat, as if the people on the street were staring at my skin. It was a ridiculous, stupid feeling. People were just people, right? But no matter how much I told myself I was being an idiot, the feeling was still there, a sort of vague discomfort, the thought that I didn't belong.

Meg finally pulled into a rundown apartment complex that consisted of several long, two-story buildings painted a dull, muddy brown. The grass around them was worn away in many places, creating a patchwork of dust that was liberally covered with trash and the occasional plastic toy.

After she parked her car next to a rickety metal stairway, Meg got out and jerked her chin at me to follow. She waved at an old man sitting on the second-floor overhang wearing nothing but boxers and a ball cap, with a beer can in one hand and a cigarette in the other. The old man waved back, grinning with all four teeth in his mouth. We passed the stairway and headed farther down, passing an open door from which a woman's shouts and a man's curses emanated. Meg didn't bat an eyelid. A couple of kids on bikes circled in the lot between Meg's building and the next, and Meg waved at them too. They waved back, shouting questions about the "new guy." She yelled at them to mind their own business, and they laughed and rode off.

Finally, she stopped at a door on the first floor and pulled out some keys from one of her many studded pockets. "Mom, I'm home!" she called as we entered the apartment.

Everything was dark and I had to suppress a cough. The smell of cigarette smoke was overwhelming. Meg flipped on a few lights, illuminating a dingy living room that opened up into a kitchenette. A hallway was in front of us, with what looked like three doors leading off it.

"Ma?" Meg called, dumping her backpack on the floor and heading for the hall. She disappeared into one of the doors as I stood awkwardly in the living room, looking around at the yellowing furniture and small TV. The walls were mostly bare except for some cheap landscape prints. The picture hanging over the couch caught my eye, though. It was no print. It looked like a large, beautifully painted picture of a mother holding a baby. Both were swathed in flowing clothes, hers blue and the baby's white. I had stepped forward for a closer look when I heard Meg exclaim from the other room.

I rushed for the door she'd disappeared through and found her, kneeling on the carpet, fighting with a withered-looking woman who didn't seem to want to get up.

"Come on, Ma, stop it! Will you—just—"

The woman started shouting, words slurred, obviously drunk. It looked like she'd thrown up on the floor and herself, but was resisting Meg's attempts to get her up on the bed.

Not saying a word, I entered the room and helped Meg lift her struggling mother onto the bedcovers. The woman couldn't have been more than fifty, but she looked decades older. Her pasty white limbs were emaciated and some of her teeth were missing. Her stringy hair hung from a sallow face with far too many wrinkles for a woman with such a lovely, vibrant daughter still in high school.

I gently held the woman while Meg got a wet cloth and cleaned her off, crooning, comforting, and scolding her all at the same time. We worked together to clean the floor, mopping up both vomit and spilled alcohol. Then I helped Meg make some soup and hold her mother down while she forced the woman to eat. It wasn't long before the fight had left the woman's withered limbs and she stopped struggling, but instead of eating more she just passed out, mouth open and snoring. I took the soup back to the kitchen while Meg tucked her in.

"Sorry you had to see that."

I turned from the sink to see Meg leaning against the doorframe, arms wrapped around herself, eyes on the floor. Going over, I put a hand on her shoulder, half expecting her to shrug it off. When she didn't, I used my other hand to tilt her face up so I could look her in the eye.

"You have nothing to apologize for."

Tears welled in her eyes and she swiped at them angrily, looking away. "It's—it's not fair," she said, voice hitching. "Adults are supposed to be strong and have it all figured out. It's not fair that Mom gets to fall apart and I have to hold everything together."

"Maybe adults don't actually have it all together. Maybe they're just better at pretending than we are," I said quietly, sliding both my hands down to rest on her arms. We were standing very close.

She sniffed, still looking away. "Well, they should have it all together. They're adults. It's their job."

I chuckled. "And it's our job to go to school, get good grades, and obey authority. I think not doing what we're supposed to do is a pretty universal problem."

"Yeah, whatever," Meg grumbled, then pulled away. "There's not much around, but you'll find soda in the fridge and some crackers or something in the cabinet if you're hungry." She paused then, examining my face. "You won't be winning any beauty pageants any time soon."

I struck a soulful pose. "I need not fear. My inner beauty is undimmed."

"Alright, Shakespeare, settle down. Let's get something to bring down that swelling." Rummaging through the freezer she found some ice which she crushed and put in a bag. She handed it to me, then disappeared down the hall for a minute, coming back with a bottle of pills. "Take two of these and help yourself to anything in the fridge. I need to call Cassius."

I retrieved a coke, took my pills, and retired to the couch to watch TV while Meg used the wall-mounted phone by the hallway. It'd been weeks since I'd watched TV, but I barely noticed the screen, too busy trying to eavesdrop on Meg's conversation. I caught a few words, but besides Meg being annoyed and Cassius not being happy, I couldn't pick out much. I missed Peter.

Hanging up the phone with a more force than was probably necessary, Meg stomped over to join me on the couch.

"So?"

"He's not happy, but we can make it work."

"Okay, how long until we get started?"

She tossed her hair back, seeming agitated. "We'll head over after dark and meet him there."

"Right…" I shifted uncomfortably. "Do we, uh, have to worry about Roger showing up here?"

Meg shook her head, expression grim. "He doesn't usually come over on school nights."

"Ah." There was an awkward silence. "So…what, we just sit around here all day?"

"Pretty much."

I could think of some very…engaging things to occupy our time, but Meg was obviously in a foul mood, so it was unlikely I'd get far with any of them. She didn't say anything else, so I turned my attention back to the TV and tried to let it distract me as I held the bag of ice on my nose. No luck. Meg's presence was much more distracting than any TV show, and my eyes kept drifting away from the TV and back to her.

"I'm gonna change," she said abruptly and stood up.

I gave her a blank look.

"What, you think I wear all this stuff because it's comfortable?" she asked, gesturing to her unwieldy boots, buckle-and-stud-festooned clothing, and heavy makeup.

Shrugging, I kept my mouth shut, knowing better than to comment on anything involving girls fashion choices.

She rolled her eyes and left, disappearing down the hall. I stayed where I was, watching the TV, but not paying attention to it as I listened to the snoring coming from her mother's bedroom. My mind was completely distracted by the thought of Meg changing clothes, and I couldn't help imagining what would happen were I in the room while said wardrobe change took place.

Things in my head got pretty steamy, pretty fast. Embarrassed, I shook myself and focused again on the TV, glad Meg couldn't see inside my head.

It took her a good twenty minutes to do whatever she'd decided to do, long enough that my ice melted and the painkiller kicked in. I heard water running a few times, but it sounded like a sink, not a shower. Finally, I heard a door open and soft footfalls coming down the hall. TV forgotten, I watched the hallway and, when she emerged, couldn't help but stare.

She wore a simple tank top and jeans, nothing special there. But the way they fit her form, hugging all her curves without unnecessary hardware getting in the way, was just plain hot. Her bare feet—which were adorable, by the way—paused in the entrance to the living room and I raised my eyes to examine her face. She'd taken out the spiked earrings she usually wore and had done away with her plethora of studded necklaces and bracelets. Her hair was smoothed down from its normal hairdo of spiked messiness and now it wreathed her face in soft waves. And her face, oh man her face. She'd washed off all her makeup so that now, for the first time, I could really see *her*. And she was beautiful. Her skin was creamy and smooth, and her lips looked much better pink than black. Her large, uncertain eyes looked out at me, elegantly framed by simple lashes instead of a cloud of black makeup.

My mind turned to instant mush and I think my jaw hit the floor. "Holy cow…"

Meg looked self-conscious. "Don't be an idiot."

"No, really, Meg. You look amazing. Cross my heart, hope to die." A silly grin spread across my face, despite my best efforts.

She shook her head. "You're just saying that to be nice."

"No, I'm not." I got up from the couch and went to her. Lifting a hand to run it over the fishnet-free skin of her arm, I marveled at its softness. That's when I spotted the bruise. Multiple bruises, actually, in the shape of a handprint.

Every part of me stilled, even my breathing. Gently, ever so gently, I took her wrist and lifted her arm, turning it so I could see the whole bruise. Well, that explained why she'd been wearing a leather jacket in almost 80-degree weather.

"Who did this?" Calm, I told myself. Stay very, very calm.

She looked away, pulling her arm out of my grasp and covering the bruise with her other hand. "It doesn't matter."

"It matters to me."

"Well, it shouldn't."

"Why not? I—I care about you." I gulped at the admission, only just now realizing the truth of my words. "I want you to be happy and safe. If someone hurt you, that matters to me."

She was silent, and I could feel the tension radiating off her. I wondered if she was deciding between yelling at me or just throwing me out of her house. Finally, she looked up, her eyes hard, but not unkind. "I can take care of myself, Sebastian. I've been doing it for years, long before you ever came around. I"—she swallowed—"I appreciate your concern, I really do. But forget about it. I fight my own battles."

I looked into her eyes, knowing sadness filled my own, and wished things were different. Wished she would let me in. I had a pretty good idea who had left the bruise, but I couldn't help someone who refused to admit they needed it.

Taking a deep breath, I forced myself to relax. Baby steps. She was right, she'd been on her own for a long time. I just had to stick by her. Win her trust.

Raising a tentative hand, I gently ran my fingers up and down her smooth arm, endeavoring to take her mind off the bruise. "So...I think we were talking about how hot you are..."

Meg's lips pressed together as if to suppress a smile, but she needn't have bothered. Her eyes betrayed her as they danced with hidden laughter.

"Is that so?" she asked.

"Yup." I nodded, feeling emboldened. "You know, you're much more beautiful without the makeup and goth clothes. Sure, you look great in all that getup, but it's just a costume. It's the you inside that makes it look good in the first place, and I can see you better once you take it all off."

Looking up at me, her eyes went a bit misty. "No one's ever said I was beautiful before," she breathed.

Something squeezed my heart, and I stepped closer. "Well, then, 'no one' is obviously a blind nincompoop, because anybody can see how beautiful you are." Feeling the time was right, I bent my head and kissed her softly, reverently. I wanted her to know that she was special. Valuable. Worth fighting for.

Whether or not she got my message, I didn't know, but she must have liked something I was doing, because she grabbed my shirt and pulled me down toward her, deepening the kiss. All my attention zeroed in on her lips, drowning out even the painkiller-dulled ache in my face. My hands came up of their own accord, one settling at the small of her back and the other sliding into her hair at the base of her neck.

She moaned against my lips, pressing close, and my brain officially stopped working. Every bit of me was on fire and a particularly urgent ache was forming below my waist. I liked the sensation, but it drove me with a need for more, and I didn't really know what to do. At the moment, I had no specific plans, just an overwhelming need to touch her, smell her, taste her.

Meg, however, did have a plan. She pushed me and I, surprised, gave way. It wasn't enough of a push to separate us, but it backed me up, and she kept going until my heels hit the couch. Her mouth still on mine, she suddenly gave me a firm shove, breaking my hold and sending me down onto the couch.

I stared up at her, amazed at how beautiful she was with that sly half-smile on her face. Slowly, she climbed onto my lap, straddling me, and took my face in her hands for another kiss. I had no idea what to do next, but I knew better than to just sit there, so I ran my hands up her legs, over her butt and hips, and up her back, feeling every curve and swell. She moaned against my lips, so I did it again, pausing when I got to her butt to give it an experimental squeeze. Yep, she definitely liked that, judging by how she pressed harder against me, grinding down on my crotch, which—inconveniently—

drove every single coherent thought out of my brain. Or perhaps conveniently, I wasn't sure which it should be.

Letting go of my face, Meg reached down to grab the edge of my shirt and pulled up, tugging when it met my arms and could go no farther.

I hesitated. Things were moving a lot further and a lot faster than I was used to. I knew the general theory of it all—what teenage boy didn't?—but that knowledge seemed little help here and now with a beautiful girl on my lap trying to take my shirt off. Especially since my brain had long ago stopped functioning and I couldn't remember any details of what was supposed to happen, just vague, slippery impressions that made me blush.

But Meg obviously knew what to do, part of my brain argued. Why not just follow along? That thought, surprisingly, was what pulled me out of the overwhelming wave of desire clouding my brain. Because that thought led to another, much less pleasant thought.

Bruises.

I slid my hands from Meg's back to her wrists, trying to get her to let go of my shirt as I gently broke our kiss.

"What?" she asked, looking disappointed.

"I—I don't know if—if this is best," I hedged, not sure what to say and afraid of hurting her feelings.

"What do you mean?"

"I mean…well…I…" I stopped, screwing up my face as I tried to find a way to explain that didn't sound terrible.

Meg dropped her hands, looking at me in confusion and not a little impatience. "What, is this your first time? Afraid you won't do it right and I'll be underwhelmed?"

Well, yes, that was obviously a valid concern that had crossed my mind. But it wasn't why I'd stopped her. And it certainly wasn't anything I'd willingly admit to a girl. "No, of course it's not that. I've had plenty of practice."

She raised an eyebrow and I knew she didn't believe me, so I hurried on.

"Look, it's not that I don't want you, or that you're not *amazingly* hot. It's that—I don't want to be just another guy taking advantage of you."

Meg scoffed. "You're not taking advantage of me. I brought you to my house. I pushed you on the couch, and I'm going to take your damn shirt off if you'd just let me." She gave me a smoldering look and I felt something between us twitch. I looked down, embarrassed, then realized that the view of her very full, curvaceous breasts straining against her tank top wasn't any better, and looked back up.

"Meg…you're…special to me. I want to help you, to be your friend. And maybe, yes, someday, er, you know. But right now…well…I want *you*. Not your body. You. We have plenty of time for the other stuff, right? I don't want to rush into something that should be more than just a whim."

I felt silly saying it and half expected her to laugh and call me a baby. She might have been only a year older, but sometimes she acted so grown up. And I wanted to be grown up, too, but there was grown up, and then there was *grown up*. My mother hadn't been the best at talking about the birds and the bees, but she'd never left me any doubt to the sanctity of that bond, that intimacy. She'd loved my father with all her heart and showed it in everything she did. Somehow, I knew that getting naked with a girl I'd only known for a few weeks, no matter how beautiful she was or how much I wanted her, wasn't honoring that memory.

I didn't know what was going on behind those dark brown eyes as Meg stared at me, brow creased in thought. But she didn't call me a baby. "You are one strange boy, Sebastian Blackwell," she finally said. "But I think…I think that's all right. I've never had a friend before. Maybe I'll give it a try."

That made me smile, and I expected her to smile back, but her face remained troubled. Worried, I pulled her in for another kiss, wanting to smooth that trouble away. She didn't resist, but the fire wasn't there anymore, so I stopped.

Meg shifted and slid to the side off my lap, curling up on the couch and leaning against me as I extracted my arm and put it around her shoulders. She snuggled up to me and we sat that way for a long time, silent and pensive as the TV played quietly in the background. I thought about love, about my parents, and about what the night would bring.

Whatever happened, I hoped it would be the end of this crazy road full of pain and darkness. All I wanted was to go back to being normal, to having family around me and living life. And maybe even getting a girlfriend.

Maybe.

23

Night found us back at the old brick department store, setting up some flashlights and a battery-powered lamp on the second floor in a room facing the alleyway, so people on the street would be less likely to notice the light. Cassius had yet to arrive.

Meg hadn't spoken a word since earlier that day, and she moved in jerky motions, often starting and looking at me nervously. It confused and worried me. I tried asking her what was wrong, but she'd only shaken her head. Maybe she was just nervous about what we were preparing to do. I was nervous too. In fact, I didn't think my internal organs had ever formed so many knots at once. It was like some competition to see if they could make me throw up. So far, I was winning.

It was stupid, but I missed Peter. His presence, while annoying at times, had assured me I had backup, had *someone*, should I need it. Now, though, I was on my own. I had very little idea what was in store for us, and I only hoped this demon prince wanted something easy, like a pint of blood or a sacrificial goat.

Speaking of goats…I heard a car pull up outside and looked out the window. Cassius was silhouetted against the light of his car door as he got out. He went to open the trunk and pulled out something that wiggled and thrashed, and made muffled, bleating noises. I shuddered and got back to sweeping the floor clean of debris. I really, really didn't want to know what Cassius was bringing up.

It was a goat. I had no idea where he'd gotten it, and I couldn't bear to think about what we were going to do with it. The poor thing was trussed up like a Thanksgiving turkey with a cloth tied tightly around its mouth and over its eyes. My stomach churned at the sight of the large, sharp butcher's knife Cassius took out of a slender box. I kept telling myself, better the goat than me, but it didn't make me feel any less queasy.

Once we had the space cleared, I stepped back and looked away, unable to watch as Cassius slit the goat's throat. After it was done he used a large bowl to collect the blood that poured out. Seeing the life drain slowly from the goat's twitching body made me finally lose the competition with my stomach. I rushed to a corner of the room and threw up all over the floor. When I turned back, Cassius was mixing something into the bowl of blood. It looked like salt. I wondered if that was to keep the blood from coagulating.

Meg still hadn't said a word, but she didn't look happy either. Her face was stony as she and Cassius dipped brushes into the blood and got started painting symbols on the cleared floor. I wiped my mouth on my shirt and moved to join them. Everything felt surreal. Was I really doing this?

I tried to ignore my troubled thoughts and concentrate on completing my circle. I had to get everything exactly right. Cassius kept looking over at me, his leering face worry-ingly smug. I didn't like that he was perfectly comfortable killing a helpless animal—and what was with the happy face?

It seemed odd that he wasn't insulting me every few minutes like he usually did out of whatever pathetic need he had to feel superior. Something felt off.

We worked as quickly as we could, but it still took us over thirty minutes to finish all the symbols. The final product was a large circle in the center of the room about ten feet across. Evenly spaced around it in the shape of a triangle were three smaller circles, each joining the larger circle at a single point, their symbols commingling where they touched. Meg examined our work with a critical eye while Cassius went outside to get something else from his car. She added a few touches here and there where we'd left a gap or forgotten a dot. I shifted nervously as she examined my markings, knowing there was no way to hide the extra symbols I'd added.

"What the heck are these?" came the inevitable question. She sounded angry, obviously afraid I'd messed everything up and ruined our chances that night.

I rushed to explain. "They're something I found in my aunt's library. Just extra protection. See how they're completely inside the circle? They're not blocking anything or interrupting any of the other sequences. They're harmless. Either they work and help, or they don't, and nothing changes. We could even add them to your circle if you want. You never know, they might be useful."

Meg glared at me, and I could see the questions behind her eyes. I had, quite deliberately, neglected to inform her my aunt was anything but a normal mundane, so she was obviously wondering how magical symbols had ended up in the old woman's library. But asking such a question would delay things and draw Cassius's attention, and we didn't exactly have another goat.

I held her gaze, trying to project calm confidence. Meg seemed to be having an internal battle. When Cassius walked back in, found us crouched over my circle and asked what the holdup was, Meg glanced back and forth between us. She hesitated for a long moment before straightening and giving him a casual brushoff.

I didn't know what was going on between her and Cassius, but I wasn't going to complain. Peter's absence meant I had no one to watch my back, but at least my fail-safe plan had survived. I hadn't the slightest clue if the celestial emblems I'd added would do any good or if they'd even be needed. But at least they were there. I wished Meg had taken me up on my offer to add them to her circle. I was worried about her.

The only remaining step was to use the last of the blood to paint the demon prince's name on the back of our hands. Meg said it didn't matter which one, so I put it on my right, since I was left-handed. Putting the name on our hand would give us a stronger connection, a better way to gain control, should the demon actually show up.

Finally, everything was ready. It was time to summon this greater demon, an immensely stronger and more dangerous being than little Rathla'un. I had a really, *really* bad feeling we had no idea what we were getting ourselves into. My insides echoed that, cramping tighter and tighter until it was almost too much to bear. There was a moment after we'd each stepped into our respective circles that we paused, looking at each other. This was the moment to say no. To give up and back off.

None of us said a word.

"The time has come. Let us begin," Cassius finally said in an overly pompous voice. I wondered if he imagined himself to be like his father, the son now stepping up to lead his own little cult. There was no time to wonder about it. Cassius had started chanting and Meg and I caught up, repeating the incantation she'd gotten from the Book of

Names. Cold chills ran down my spine as I spoke, a sharp counterpoint to the heat that started in my right hand and spread up my arm and into my heart. My chest was on fire, and my mouth felt full of soot, dry and bitterly foul as the words left my lips.

We called the name of Afnergu'alak, Prince of Decay, entreating him to accept our offering and come to bargain with us. We intoned and chanted, repeating the name over and over. I shuddered each time I said it, stomach roiling with nausea as my chest continued to burn.

I was beginning to think, almost hope, that this was all a silly waste of time when the lights flickered, then went out. And it wasn't just our lights. I could see nothing at all, not even the outline of the window or the starry sky outside. Everything was pitch black. Had I gone blind? Our voices died and we waited, shivering in the dark.

"Who calls? Who speaks my name?" A slow, melodic voice flickered through the darkness, echoing as if its owner was speaking to us down a long tunnel. I trembled when I heard it, the sound both transcendent and utterly horrifying.

Nobody spoke. My tongue felt glued to the roof of my mouth.

"Come now, mortals, do not be afraid. Fear is useless. It will not save you now, nor aid you. Speak. What is it you desire?"

The darkness lifted, and I gasped in a lungful of air, not even realizing I'd been holding my breath. Our lights came back and they now revealed not three, but four figures in the room.

He, it, the thing, was...not as I had expected. Somehow, I'd imagined the Prince of Decay would be revolting. An oozing mass of rotting flesh, or perhaps a twisted, wart-covered creature with many eyes and horns and...whatever else demons had. But Afnergu'alak was none of these things.

The only word to describe him was beautiful. Or terrible. I couldn't decide which.

He appeared in the form of a man, but with skin as black as night and long hair as white as the moon. His skin reflected the light, but was dull in places around his chest, torso, and legs showing where he wore a vest and pants the same color as his skin. His physical form flickered and wavered, as if it wasn't physical at all, but merely a mirage or reflection of something that existed elsewhere. There was an aura of darkness all around him that swirled and broke, forming and reforming into phantoms of horror that played tricks on my eyes. The blackness moved about us in threatening tendrils, like fingers, making the lights flicker as they tested our circles, seeking a way inside. Everywhere the darkness touched—the floor, the walls, the ceiling—shifted, bubbling and warping into contorted shapes. Everywhere, that is, except our circles. The symbols painted in blood were unaffected by the shadows' touch.

"A—a—fnergu'alak," Cassius finally stuttered, and the demon glanced at him, one perfect eyebrow lifted in question.

"W—we come to ask f—for power. Power to c—control our destiny."

I glanced at Meg, confused. Was this part of the script? Or was Cassius horning in on our request for our parents' lives? But Meg wasn't looking at me, or at Cassius. She was staring at Afnergu'alak in horrified fascination.

The demon's eyes glinted, twin wells of hell's red glow. "I do not give power to the weak, foolish one. Only to the strong. The weak are not worthy, and serve better as slaves to those who are."

Cassius quailed, but seemed determined to give it one last try. Straightening, he thumped himself on the chest. "I—

I *am* worthy. I tricked my father and stole his knowledge. I will take his place. I am strong!"

The demon's laugh began low and quiet, but grew louder and louder, finally filling the room to the brim with its terrible, echoing sound. "Your father, little human, *let* you look at his book." He chuckled again. "He knows your heart, your lust for his power. He thought this would be a useful lesson…if you survive. If not, well…he has no use for a weakling."

Cassius gaped at him, mouth opening and closing like a dying fish.

Seeming bored, the demon shifted, eyes settling on me. He turned away from the others and moved slowly in my direction, like a lion stalking its prey. I made the mistake of glancing at the floor, and my stomach turned at the sight. Radiating out from the demon's feet was a patchwork of putrid rot, as if the wood beneath him had been transformed to flesh and was afflicted with some vile disease. Pustules and sores appeared, festered, then disappeared, forming anew amid veins bulging with black, diseased blood. It was a kaleidoscope of nauseating decay that seemed to herald his approach.

He halted where his and my circle met, a wicked smile playing on his lips. "Hello, Sebastian." He said it slowly, as if tasting each syllable and savoring their flavor. "So delightful to see you again. I enjoyed our little game the other night. Did you?"

I didn't respond. It took all my willpower to simply meet his gaze and not cower.

"Do you know what your name means, Sebastian?" The demon smiled and answered his own question. "It means venerable. Ironic, is it not? But perhaps you will grow into it…some day."

He didn't give me a chance to reply, but instead turned to

Meg, red eyes intent as he surveyed her from head to toe. "And you, little girl...I have long been watching you. What have you come to ask of me?"

Aside from a tremble in her hands, Meg didn't seem intimidated. She glared at the thing as it approached, crossing her arms. "I want my father back. Your servant, Rathla'un, said you can do it. Bring people back from the dead."

A knowing smirk touched the demon's lips. "Did he now? And did he say what price such a deed would require?"

Meg shook her head, not taking her eyes off the flickering, shadowy form.

"But you already know, do you not? It is written in the book." The demon's grin was now broad, and he stared intently at Meg, who glanced guiltily at me.

Uh-oh. My feeling of unease grew, now almost stronger than the nausea in my stomach and the burn in my chest. She'd already known what the Prince wanted? Why hadn't she told me?

"Your father's being, I can give you, reknit and reformed. But who, I wonder, do you intend to offer me in return? The weakling? Or the boy?"

Horror froze me where I stood and I stared at Meg, eyes wide and heart pounding. She'd known all along. She'd planned this whole thing. Which meant—she'd never wanted a friend, or an ally. She'd wanted a sacrifice.

I staggered, pain shooting through my chest as if Meg had stabbed me there herself. The agony—physical, emotional, mental—was so intense that my concentration broke and my defenses fell. I felt my vision darken as Afnergu'alak's reaching tendrils surrounded my circle, hovering just outside the line of symbols, waiting to pounce.

I found I didn't care. Let them take me, if it would just make the pain stop. I had absolutely nothing left to live for.

There was no way I could pay the price demanded for my parents, and the one person who had given me hope, who had eased my loneliness and pain, had just stabbed me in the back.

It had been a lie all along. A cruel, merciless lie.

"No! Wait!" Meg's voice sounded frantic, yet so far away.

The shadows paused. "Yes?"

"Take him. The weakling. The boy is mine, don't touch him!"

Darkness drew back from me and I could see once again. The demon's red eyes glinted as he looked back and forth between us three, seemingly delighted at the turn of events. "How very interesting."

"W—what? No!" Cassius seemed to have finally found his voice, and he stared at Meg, looking as shocked as I felt. "What's going on? Don't do this! We had a plan. We were in this together."

"You're an idiot, Cassius. A big, stupid, disgusting idiot." Meg's voice was scornful, yet I could hear a tremor in it.

"But I helped you! I protected you. I *saved* you. You can't turn on me like this!"

At that, Meg's eyes flashed, glowing red and full of hate. "You *used* me. Used me like I was a toy that you could have whenever you wanted, expecting me to be grateful that you even noticed me. Well, now I'm using *you*."

"No! Please! Meg—"

"Take him, Afnergu'alak! I offer his life in return for my father's."

"As you wish…"

Cassius screamed, falling to his knees and swiping frantically at the tendrils of darkness surrounding him as if he could bat them away.

Witches are murderers.

Be kind.

"Stop!" A commanding voice rang out over the clamor and the demon paused, then turned, his darkness drawing back in hesitation. As he stared at me with blood-red eyes I realized that *I* had spoken. I had imposed my will, using the bond painted in blood on my hands to force Afnergu'alak to halt.

"Seb, what are you doing?" Meg hissed, eyes normal again and full of fear.

"The right thing," I told her, not taking my eyes from the demon.

I wanted more than anything to give Meg her father, to see my own mom and dad again. But I would not, under any circumstances, kill someone in cold blood. Not for anyone, and especially not for my parents. The knowledge of such an unholy sacrifice made on her behalf would break my mother's heart.

"You will not harm him, Afnergu'alak. You will let him leave. Now."

The demon looked at me appraisingly, one eyebrow raised. He seemed to be considering his options.

I pushed on the bond that connected us, forcing my will down it.

"Very well. If you insist on throwing away your only chance, far be it from me to stop you." The shadows flitting in circles around Cassius faded away, oozing back into the demon prince. The terrified young man rose unsteadily to his feet, eyeing the shadows, then made a break for the door.

"No! Sebastian, this is our only chance! Stop him!" Meg stepped forward, but halted as the tendrils reappeared, now swirling around her own circle, hungry and dark.

"You mean *your* only chance, Meg? What about my parents?" I felt angry—furious, actually—but my head was clear, maybe for the first time in months. "Were we going to trick two other people into 'joining' us and bring them back here to sacrifice on that same bloody altar?"

"Of course not! We were going to make the demon accept one life for all of them. We could do it, together."

"Says who? I can't trust anything that comes out of your mouth, since you've been lying to me this whole time!"

"No! I mean, well, sort of...at first. But you weren't what I expected." She hurried to explain. "You were kind. And brave. I had already decided before tonight to double-cross Cassius. I promise!"

I shook my head, disgusted at the both of us and knowing I had to end this madness. "Listen to yourself, Meg. Is this really what your father would have wanted? Did he fight for law, and truth, and justice, for you to start murdering people in his name?"

Meg stood frozen, pain, desperation, and sorrow all warring on her face. Her lip trembled, and silent tears began sliding down her cheeks.

"No," she choked out, finally admitting the truth. "No. He wouldn't want this." I could see the hope die in her eyes, the same cold, bitter death my own hope had already suffered.

"We can't do it, Meg. Not like this."

She nodded, the tears falling faster as she struggled to hold herself together.

I straightened, pushing back against the terrible despair that seemed determined to crush me. "Let's end this. Let's go home. At least—" I hesitated, the pain of betrayal still raw in my chest. But she hadn't picked me to die. Maybe in the beginning, before she'd known me. But in the end, she'd chosen me to live. "At least we have each other. We'll figure something else out. I promise."

"Boooriiiing."

We turned in surprise, having almost forgotten the

demon we'd summoned. He stood in the center of the circle, elbow propped on his crossed arm and chin in his hand, looking supremely unimpressed.

"All this love, and sacrifice, and disgusting morality is terribly boring. You summoned me with the promise of a bargain, and yet now have changed your minds? That is not how these things work, dear mortals. I came for something tasty, and something tasty I will have. Time for a little game." His eyes glinted maliciously, and my stomach dropped down to my toes.

"Meg, concentrate! We have to banish him. Now!"

Afnergu'alak laughed, moving swiftly toward me as he gathered darkness about himself in a whirling rush. It cascaded over me like a wave. I tried to concentrate, tried to push back, but it swept aside my pitiful shields like they were cobwebs. It came for me, coalescing, then—

Stopped.

I gasped, staring at the floor where the seven celestial emblems glowed faintly in a circle around me, holding back the darkness. I was surrounded on all sides, but not overcome.

"What is this?" the demon hissed, his tendrils jerking back as if burned. "What filthy trick are you playing?"

I ignored him, concentrating on Meg. I was desperate to grab her and pull her into the protection of my circle, but I knew the moment I stepped outside those emblems, I was doomed. I almost shouted at her to run, to make a break for it. But she could barely see me through the swirling shadows, and I doubted Afnergu'alak would simply let her pass, not if she put herself directly in his grasp.

The image of him wavered and he hissed again, backing away from my circle and moving toward Meg's instead. He halted just outside of it and the shadows returned in full force, blocking her from my sight.

"No! Afnergu'alak, stop! I command you!"

He completely ignored me, chuckling as he did so.

"Meg," I called out, shifting from side to side, trying to spot her. "Come on, focus! We can do this if we work together!"

But I could no longer see her through the darkness, and she made no sound. I closed my eyes, concentrating with all my might as I hammered at that bond, the thing that was supposed to give me control. But it was useless. There was no response, not even a twitch of acknowledgement.

Finally, the darkness lifted, and what it revealed sent me stumbling back in shock, barely catching my balance before I tumbled out of my circle. Meg now stood just outside my glowing celestial emblems, her eyes shining blood red and the butcher's knife in her hand, raised, poised to strike.

"And thus love ends. What a pity," chuckled the demon, looking on, clearly pleased.

"Leave her alone! Let her go!" I screamed, ready to jump out and tackle him if I thought it would save Meg. But it wouldn't. The echoing, shimmering thing in the central circle was no more than an image of its master. Somehow, I knew that if the demon had fully coalesced, we would have been utterly crushed under its power. Which meant Meg had known, had planned for that accordingly in the symbols and words she had chosen. Perhaps the circle constrained him so that only a shadow of himself was able to answer our call, even if the symbols could not completely contain his tendrils of darkness.

I eyed Meg's trembling form in fear, my mind scrambling, begging me to come up with a plan. At first, I thought she was trembling with rage, but now I saw she was shaking with exertion. Her face was contorted and strained as she fought back against the demon's control, the symbol on her left hand glowing brightly by her waist as her right held the knife aloft.

"Fight it, Meg, fight it! You can do it! I know you can…"

But she couldn't, not for long. Soon, her strength would fail and she would try to kill me. Or slice into me slowly, bit by bit, until I bled to death. Whatever the demon prince desired.

"Help! Anyone! Please, help!" I yelled, hoping someone might be passing by outside and would hear me and come to investigate. Though maybe Afnergu'alak would just possess them too.

A thought struck like a bolt of lightning, and I grabbed onto it, desperate. "Peter? Peter! PETER!!" I screamed until my throat was raw, reaching out with all my senses and begging him to come.

Slowly, the point of the knife inched closer and I backed up, careful to stay within my little circle.

"All right, all right, stop your yammering. If you insist, I suppose I could—" the misty form of Peter materializing beside me paused, as if sensing all was not right. "Good heavens above, what have you gotten up to this time? I—" Just then he caught sight of the knife. And the demon.

"Jumping Jehoshaphat! Quick, boy, banish it! Rebuke it! Something!"

"I can't!" I told him, almost crying in relief. "I'm not strong enough. Go get Aunt Barrington. Quick!"

"But—"

"GO!"

His white glow winked out, and I was alone again.

"Absolutely fascinating. Was that a ghost? What is one of those doing here, I wonder? You are quite the interesting mortal, I must say. What a pity I am going to kill you. But never fear, once we rid you of that weak body of yours, you will feel much better. Everything is much more vibrant and exquisite as a pure soul, without the mortal form to muddy the waters."

"Leave me alone!" Though helpless and hopeless, I stood defiant, refusing to let him toy with me.

"Hmm, perhaps I will, after a thousand years or so of torture, once I have grown tired of your screams. But that is a long way away. Right now, this little girl is going to slice you into ribbons. Slowly. While I force her to watch. Oh yes, she knows what is happening. That is what makes this all the more fun. And when she is done with you, she will carve herself up. It will be quite the fascinating sight."

I turned away, trying to block that leering smile of pleasure from my mind as I searched Meg's face.

"Meg, can you hear me? Fight him! You can do it."

Her eyes flicked back and forth frantically, searching for a way out.

"It's your hand, Meg. He must be controlling you through the bond you created. You told me it was a two-way street, remember? Push back. Push him out of you! I know you can do it."

Tears ran down her cheeks, dripping from her chin onto the bloodstained floor. I tried to sound optimistic, but her eyes told me she knew the truth.

She wasn't strong enough.

Leaning forward, I examined the knife, thinking perhaps I could grab it from her hand as she stood frozen in her internal struggle. But she was still outside my circle, and I suspected that even a toe or a finger unprotected would be enough for the demon to gain a foothold inside me.

I wracked my brain for ideas, but there was nothing. Peter had left mere minutes ago, so even if he found my aunt, she would arrive too late to stop the inevitable. I was on my own.

Meg's eyes were squeezed almost completely shut in the

strain of her effort, but she still looked at me, staring into my face with desperate sorrow. I watched in horror as her hand twitched, as if to strike, then froze again.

"Meg…Meg…" I groaned, heart aching so fiercely I thought it would implode.

Maybe I could end it quickly? Force her to land a fatal blow and spare her the agony of what that demon was trying to make her do?

I inched forward, but at my movement her eyes widened and she shook her head the tiniest fraction, tears flowing even faster. Her mouth moved, so painfully slow I had a hard time following, but when I finally recognized the words, they made no sense: Thank you.

With a scream, Meg gave in and the knife descended with inhuman force, slicing through the air just in front of me as I jumped back. I didn't notice the flash of movement from below coming up to meet it.

It happened so fast I hardly understood what she'd done. But the thud of flesh hitting the floor jolted me back to reality. I saw her eyes roll back in her head as she fell backward, blood spurting from her severed left wrist as the knife tumbled from her limp fingers.

24

I screamed.

I screamed so loudly my throat felt like it was splitting in two. But I didn't hear a thing over the ringing in my ears. A wall of silence had struck me, turning me deaf.

Meg lay motionless. Unconscious, I desperately hoped, not dead. Her severed hand had rolled away, the bloody symbol on it now dark and lifeless. Her body lay half in, half out of the demon's circle. Even as I watched, the floor of rotting gore in the central circle bubbled where Meg's body touched it. Rivulets of black blood, thick and tar-like, began to flow *up*, climbing Meg's leg and fanning out in a slowly creeping web. The butcher's knife lay several feet away, and though I was tempted to make a dive for it, I knew it could do nothing to protect me against the mirage of evil watching me with malevolent eyes.

"Well. How very disappointing. Though I *do* commend her for her deviousness, depriving me of my fun. I suppose watching you suffer as she slowly bleeds to death will have to suffice as payment for all my trouble this night."

"You bastard! You monster! I'll—I'll—"

"Do what, exactly? Step outside your little ring of filth and stab me with that knife? Oh, please do, that would be exceedingly entertaining."

I stood there, quivering with rage. One look at Meg told me I didn't have long. Her skin was growing pale and the pool of blood by her severed limb was getting larger by the second. I didn't know anything about bleeding, but it was obvious you couldn't keep losing that much blood and stay alive for very long.

I had to do something. I couldn't just stand there. I had to save her.

"You know...you *can* save her."

I shot the demon a hate-filled look, wondering if he was still taunting me.

"No, I do not speak frivolously simply to torture your already deliciously dark soul. You really *can* save her. And her father. And your parents."

My body went cold, save for the heat still emanating from my right hand. "W—what do you mean?"

The demon slowly began to pace, moving back and forth like a caged lion. "There is something more valuable to me than a life taken. More valuable, even, than a departed soul: a living soul, willingly given."

My mouth was dry and my body trembled. "Explain."

"It is simple enough, Sebastian. You offer yourself. My slave in life and in death. Forever."

My heart rammed against my rib cage. I thought it might burst, so wildly did it beat in hope, and terror. But I couldn't let myself fall apart. I had to think. *Think.*

"I'll make a bargain with you," I said, fighting to keep my voice level.

Afnergu'alak raised an eyebrow, looking amused.

"If I stay put, you gain nothing. Cassius is gone, Meg c— cut you off"—I flicked a glance her way, feeling my knees go weak at the sight of her almost-lifeless body—"and you can't get to me. So if I do nothing, you lose."

The demon was silent, expression unchanging, perhaps waiting for something I said to impress him.

"So, I'll give you half my soul in return for Meg, and her father, *and* my parents. All of them, alive. Half is better than nothing. Otherwise, you lose everything."

Afnergu'alak threw back his head and laughed heartily. I had to clutch my mouth, forcing back the bile that rose in my throat at that terrible sound.

"Ah, Sebastian, Sebastian. You amuse me. Such brazenness, such presumption. It is refreshing when all I normally receive is groveling fear." He paused, eyeing me thoughtfully as he tapped his chin with a slender, black finger. Then his lips spread in a vicious smile. "I accept your offer, boy. You will keep me entertained for a time, at least, and what you ask from me is a trifling."

He extended a hand and the decaying floor where my circle touched his roiled, the putrid flesh pulling back to reveal a shard of wood, sharp on one end and just the right size to fit in a hand.

"Come now, pick it up," the demon said lazily. "You want to see your friend live, do you not?"

Eyes burning, I forced myself to look at Meg. Her leg was now completely covered in a spider web of black, the tendrils of thick blood creeping up to cover her hip as well. I had no idea if she was still alive or not. There was no discernible movement from her chest, and the pool of blood around her severed limb was big. So big.

For her. I would damn myself for her. What happened to me didn't matter, as long as she lived. Her father would come back and her mother would recover, and Meg would live a long, happy life. My parents would have a second chance, too, even if I wasn't there to enjoy it with them. I didn't know, and didn't want to know, what I'd do with only half a soul, but it didn't matter. After this, I would have to go far, far away, where my foolish mistakes and soon-to-be-corrupted soul couldn't hurt anyone.

I bent down, carefully picking up the piece of wood. "What do I have to do?"

"It is nothing very difficult, rest assured. Simply cut the symbol on your hand into the flesh, sealing our bargain in your own blood."

The hand holding the piece of wood trembled, but I hardened my resolve. I became stone, blocking myself off from what I had to do.

Faintly, I felt a nudge in my mind, and I knew it was coming from Afnergu'alak. He couldn't control me, not through the celestial symbols, but he had no compunction about hurrying things along. I let him. The nudge guided my hand, made it easier as I took the point of the wood—impossibly sharp—and cut into the back of my right hand, following the curve of the demon's name on my pale flesh.

One cut.

Blood welled in its wake.

Two cuts.

The bloody lines joined, redness starting to pool.

Three cuts, four cuts, five. The demon's name was surprisingly intricate, and with blood starting to drip, drip, drip toward the ground I was only halfway done. Yet the drops never made it to the floor. They disappeared into thin air as each one fell, as if being sucked into some other dimension.

"Good...goooood."

I could feel him watching me, his glowing, lustful eyes appearing in my mind. The rasp of his tongue echoed in my ears as he licked his lips, like he was tasting the coppery tang of my blood. And was hungry for more.

BANG!

A minor explosion rent the air and the ground beneath my feet vibrated. I paused, only half aware of what was going on outside my circle. What had happened? It felt like someone had blown a hole in a the building.

"Pay no heed, boy. Finish. Finish the symbol!"

But I heard someone shouting my name, and hurried footsteps approached in a rush.

I spun, the shard of wood dropping to the floor as I yelled to whoever was coming up the stairs, warning them that it wasn't safe. Warning them not to come in the door.

"Sebastian, my boy, are you all right? Good heavens! What has happened to Meg?" Peter's horrified voice rang out just as Aunt Barrington burst through the door, moving impossibly fast for someone her age. She seemed unsurprised at the scene that greeted her, and had come prepared. A shimmering ball of light surrounded her on all sides like a bubble that she appeared to control with her uplifted hands.

I heard a hiss behind me and turned to see Afnergu'alak, eyes narrowed, teeth bared. The demon's shadows whirled and shot forward, reaching out to engulf my aunt. I felt a moment of terrible fear. But whatever the bubble was, it stood fast and the shadows broke over it like ocean waves on a rocky shore.

Aunt Barrington stepped forward resolutely. "Sebastian, remain where you are. Do not move, and for heaven's sake do *not* promise him anything."

A sob of relief rose in my throat as I hoped for one desperate moment that Meg would be okay.

Peter's pearly form flitted over to my circle, hovering anxiously as we both watched Aunt Barrington head toward Meg's body, lying half in, half out of Afnergu'alak's circle. His tendrils of darkness foiled, the demon's eyes narrowed in displeasure, but then he raised his hands, clenching and twisting them as if he were crushing something. The floor beneath my aunt's feet crumbled, and she barely had time to jump back before it decayed to dust, leaving a jagged hole. No sooner had she regained her feet then there was a crackling rumble and the ceiling began to creak, pieces of plaster breaking off and plummeting toward her. Hands still raised, she said a word, and the chunks of ceiling glanced away as if bouncing off an invisible shield above her head.

Not giving the demon time to attack again, Aunt Barrington darted forward, zigzagging across the room as more holes appeared in the floor. But the demon's shadow coalesced suddenly in front of her, forming a black wall. Her bubble of light halted as it came into contact with the shadows, and her face tightened, a mask of concentration as she chanted and pushed forward, the demon's shadows pushing right back. Inch by terrible inch she gained ground, until she was within arm's reach of Meg. The demon screamed in fury as she stooped over, grabbed my friend's arm with one hand, and dragged the body backwards, tearing it from the web of black blood that had been trying to engulf it. Immediately, everything quieted, as if Meg's body had been a conduit of power that the demon was now deprived of.

He hissed in anger, but could do nothing.

"Is—is she alright? Is she alive?" I swallowed hard.

My aunt's expression was grave as she put two fingers to Meg's neck. "I can feel no pulse. But I am not a doctor. Perhaps—"

"She is dead, old woman," Afnergu'alak spat. "I felt her spirit leave just before you arrived. You are too late."

"Oh, shut your sniveling mouth, you foul creature," Peter said.

"He—he's lying," I said, desperate. "He's lying, isn't he?"

My aunt slowly stood, staring down at Meg's crumpled form. "I am afraid not, Sebastian."

The pure agony, the searing, crushing loss tore through

me, leaving me gasping, fighting to stay conscious. I dropped to my knees, crumpling in on myself. It was a feeling I thought I would never survive the first time, and assumed I'd never feel again, because I had nothing left that I loved.

"It is not too late." The whisper caressed my ears, and I looked up from where I knelt, broken and bleeding.

Afnergu'alak's face was barely a foot from mine, just outside my circle. His eyes were full of desperate desire. "It is not too late," he repeated. "Finish the symbol, and our bargain will be complete."

"Poppycock. Ignore him, my boy—"

"Sebastian, no! Do not listen—"

The voices of the only two people I had left in the world mingled together, pleading with me. "The dead cannot be brought back to life," Aunt Barrington continued. "What this demon has promised will only be an empty shell, knit from dust and malice, to torture you. The dead *cannot* be given new life."

I gritted my teeth, refusing to listen. If you knew a demon's name, they couldn't lie to you, right? Hadn't Meg said that? Or did it only apply to demons you had the strength to control? How could I know for sure?

"I have to try," I sobbed, fingers twitching, reaching for the piece of wood.

"No! Sebastian, your parents, this girl, they would not want this. They would not want you to damn your own soul."

"Why not!" I twisted toward her, screaming the words through my agony. "It's my fault they're dead! All of them! I killed them! I deserve this. My life for theirs!"

"Nonsense, boy—"

"Whatever do you mean, Sebastian? You have killed no one." Aunt Barrington left Meg's body, starting toward me.

"Stay back!" I warned, grabbing the shard of wood with

numb fingers and scrambling to my feet, holding it over my hand. I couldn't let her stop me. I had to pay. "I k—killed them. In the car—I was arguing, I distracted them—it's my fault." My breathing was ragged and I could barely force the confession out.

A terrible pain crossed my aunt's face, and for a moment she stood, frozen, seeming to fight a silent battle with herself.

"Ignore her. Seal the bargain!" Afnergu'alak hissed.

"Sebastian, wait," my aunt said, her voice urgent. "You did not kill your parents. Even if you did distract them, that was not the cause of the accident."

"What?" I stared at her, confused.

"No! Ethel, you cannot tell him!" Peter cried, zooming over to hover between us. "We have worked too hard—"

"What? Tell me!" I demanded, ignoring the ghost.

"We—thought it was best to keep it from you. It would help nothing, and your parents left strict instructions that you should never know—"

"What is it? What happened?"

"Ethel, no!" Peter said again.

"Your parents, Sebastian. They were murdered."

My world spun, turning upside down. I staggered. "Wha…then it…wasn't my fault?"

Aunt Barrington shook her head, eyes full of sorrow. "No, Sebastian. There was nothing you could have done to save them."

"But who? Who killed them? Where are they? I'll—I'll—"

"Who, matters not," she snapped. "Your parents wished for no retribution, no revenge, should such a thing occur. You will respect their wishes!"

I clenched my jaw, letting that matter drop for the time being as my whole outlook shifted.

Barely able to speak past my raging heart, I turned to

Afnergu'alak. "Can you, or can you not bring my parents back?"

His eyes glittered. "I am the Prince of Decay. I rule death."

"But ruling death doesn't mean you can give life. Can you bring souls back from beyond the veil?"

The demon bared his teeth, anger flashing in his eyes. "You did not ask for souls, boy. You asked for life. If I were you, I would take what you can get."

That was it, then. There would be no redemption. Not for me, not for my parents, not for Meg. All of this had been for nothing. Meg's death—I could have prevented it, if only I hadn't been so incredibly, monumentally stupid.

My mistakes crashed down around me like a rushing avalanche, sweeping away every shred of resolve I had left. My trembling legs gave out and I surrendered to despair.

Steady hands caught me. Aunt Barrington's face swam before my eyes and I wondered how one who seemed so frail could be so strong…

"Get away, woman! He belongs to me!"

A white mist appeared above me and I heard Peter's voice. "You worthless, cowardly filth. Take your hideous face and shove it up your arse! Begone, now! Shoo!"

I heard the demon's terrible laugh, then felt something cool pour over the cuts on my hand. Almost immediately, the coolness turned to stinging fire and I gasped, struggling to escape it.

"Hold still, Sebastian," my aunt murmured, massaging the stinging liquid into my skin as Peter threw insult after insult at the demon.

The laughter went on, but as I felt a cloth carefully wipe my hand dry, the sound abruptly stopped.

"What is that you are doing, woman? Get away from him! He is—no…NO! How?"

Through my bleary eyes, I saw the back of my hand. The bloody symbol connecting me to the demon was gone, and only raw, oozing cuts remained in a now meaningless semi-circle. I lifted my head and saw the image of Afnergu'alak flicker. It was fainter now, the darkness less intense.

"There now, sit here." My aunt carefully lowered me to the floor and took something silver from a pocket in her long skirt. Peter was still hollering at the demon, his white form between us and him so as to obscure Aunt Barrington's movements.

"You cannot stop me! No one can command me!" The demon prince's echoing voice, though filled with fury, was faint and fading fast. My shock-numbed mind wandered, wondering at the devious intricacies Meg had planned into our summoning. She'd arranged it so that only a shadow of Afnergu'alak could appear when we called. Had she also contrived the failsafe that banished him once his name had been erased? I knew, somehow, that I owed my life to Meg's intelligence and careful planning.

Meg…where was she?

I saw a flash of silver above me, symbols floating in the air as Aunt Barrington's hands danced back and forth.

The demon's scream, long yet fading, was the last thing I heard before I passed out.

───────

"SEBASTIAN? Sebastian, can you hear me? Wake up, boy!"

Peter's voice stirred me, and I groaned, body aching. Where was I?

A hard wall pressed against my back, and I felt dust and splinters beneath my fingers. I opened my eyes to see a dark room, lit by our flashlights and the one lamp, just as before.

Startled, I sat up. What had happened? Where was the demon? Where was Meg?

Aunt Barrington rose from a crouch in the middle of the room and came over, speaking quickly. "Can you stand? Hurry, you must go. Get as far away from this building as possible, ten blocks at least. Then call a taxi to take you home. Here." She put something hard in my hands and I recognized my cell phone. But I didn't care about that. Taking the hand she offered, I pulled myself shakily to my feet and stumbled toward the form lying in the center of the room.

"Do not touch her!" my aunt commanded, and I stopped, already on my knees, hand reaching out to caress Meg's face. It was pale, but full of peace, as if she'd simply gone to sleep.

I groaned, the pain in my chest unbearable. "No, no, Meg...I'm so sorry." My eyes burned and burned as I rocked back and forth, back bowed under the crushing guilt.

A bony hand gripped my shoulder, gently pulling me back. But I wouldn't leave. I wanted to hug Meg, to bury my face in her hair and beg for forgiveness. I'd failed her.

"Come, Sebastian. We don't have much time. I have notified the authorities and swept the room—and that car outside—clean of your presence. You were never here, and I am but a disinterested bystander who heard shouts in the night. They will arrive soon and you must be far away by then."

I barely heard her. I couldn't take my eyes off Meg's face. It was so peaceful. Why was it peaceful?

"I killed her." My body shuddered and I squeezed my eyes shut.

Skirts rustled as Aunt Barrington sank down beside me, putting a hesitant arm around my shoulders as Peter joined us on my other side. "You did nothing of the kind, Sebastian.

She made her choice long ago. Her feet were already pointed down this path before she ever met you. You did not fail her. In fact, you most likely saved her life. And her soul."

"What?" I sniffed.

"You stopped her from accepting a bargain with that demon, did you not?"

I nodded shakily. Peter must have given her a summary as he'd led her to the building. How had she gotten here so fast?

Aunt Barrington gave a weary sigh. "What the young and foolish who dabble in such things do not understand is that bargains are not as cut and dried as they may appear. A contract in blood such as your friend attempted would have bound her soul to the demon. It would have tormented her, possibly even taking over her mind, forcing her to do unspeakable things. In the end, if she had died in that state, I can only imagine what terrible place it would have imprisoned her soul to torture for eternity. When bargaining with an immortal, spiritual being, such bargains do not end in something as inconsequential as death."

Peter nodded, expression somber, and I looked at Meg's face, my heart torn and bleeding. Now, at least, I understood her expression. And her last words. What torment had it been for her to be trapped inside her own body, totally consumed by unspeakable evil? Somehow, though, her determination to save me had given her the strength to cut herself off from the demon and sever its hold. She had died free.

Gazing at the body, my aunt murmured, "And if your right hand causes you to stumble, cut it off and cast it from you, for it is better that one of your members should perish than your whole body depart into Gehenna."

Peter sighed. "Couldn't have said it better myself."

"What's that from?" I asked dazedly, unable to look away from Meg's face.

My aunt got to her feet. "A very old book. Now, enough

talk. I am sorry, Sebastian, but we must leave her. I will make sure they treat her body with respect. Go now. Run!"

"Come on, lad. I'll go with you. You'll need someone to watch your back on the streets this late at night."

I didn't respond. I wanted to be alone, to escape, to run until I dropped from exhaustion and all of this had been left behind. But my brain knew I shouldn't be alone, so I didn't tell Peter to go away. I simply left, running, stumbling, stomach heaving. I saw Meg's car in the alley behind the building and her tortured face swam into view, right before she…I could hear the wet thump of flesh on wood in my mind and I turned to dry heave over the weeds. I'd already thrown up all my stomach's contents earlier that night, but that didn't stop my guts from feeling like they had turned inside out and were squeezing themselves up and out my throat.

As soon as my stomach quit heaving, I started to run. I ran, and ran, and ran. I didn't stop. I didn't think I would ever stop running.

Not from this.

EPILOGUE

Y ou know that feeling when you are absolutely sure you've taken all the punishment life can dole out? You've reached your limit, and you just lie down and wait for death to take you? Only it doesn't. Instead, it smacks you upside the head and tells you to get your sorry butt off the floor and keep on living, because it's not your time yet. You know that feeling?

Yeah. That was me.

Twice.

This time around, though, things were different. For one, I was sitting in a chair gazing out my bedroom window, not lying on the bed staring at the ceiling. For another, instead of just skipping school, I'd been expelled from it. And that was me getting off easy.

At least one good thing did come out of that whole disaster. Though no one had actually seen me do it—which was the only reason charges weren't filed, and Bryan wasn't talking—a rumor had spread at school that I'd single-handedly trounced the whole football team's front line. Since my old soccer team had won the school championship despite my desertion, when they heard the rumor of my exploits they were more than happy to end the year on amiable terms, even Finn. Cory had been sad to see me go, but I'd assured him I wanted nothing more to do with Brookhaven Academy, or the memories attached to it. I'd thanked him for sticking by me and we promised to stay in touch.

Cory was the only bright spot in what was shaping up to be a very dark summer. DNA evidence showed that Cassius had been the only person with Meg the night she'd died, and since his fingerprints were all over the murder weapon, he was the prime suspect. It had been two weeks and they still hadn't found him, though. Using Peter and a pay phone, we'd called in an anonymous tip on Roger, his clinic, and his little basement cloister. By the time they checked it, though, everything had been cleared out and Roger was long gone. I wondered if the demon had warned him.

Meg's funeral was quiet. I kept my distance, not wanting to intrude on the family's mourning. Most of the people who came were Latinos and seemed to be family and friends of Meg's grandparents. The two older Garcias stood by the casket, hands on the shoulders of a young boy with a pale, haunted face and silent tears streaming down his cheeks. I didn't see Meg's mom.

It wasn't until much later that I found out my aunt had contacted the Garcias, introducing herself simply as the 'parent of one of Meg's closest friends,' and arranged to cover a year's fees for Meg's mom to be admitted to a private drug rehabilitation center. I never knew if the poor woman was sober enough going in to realize what had happened to her daughter. But at least she was safe from Roger and wouldn't OD in that dingy apartment.

Knowing Meg's mom would be well taken care of was only a small comfort, though a much-needed one. But it would never come close to making up for Meg's absence. I couldn't believe she was gone. There was so much I'd never get to learn about her. I'd never get to be her boyfriend, to take her out on a date, or kiss her under the stars. When I'd thought I was a dead husk, she'd shown me there was life in me still. She'd given me a reason to live. And now she was gone.

It hurt so much, I forced my mind to dwell on other things, to keep from going mad. For instance, I didn't know what to think of my aunt. At first, she'd seemed the most close-minded, insufferable prude in all of Atlanta. But when I took my mother's advice and got over myself, I could see her wisdom and compassion, even if it was expressed in her own cold, awkward sort of way.

Looking down at my right hand, bathed in the light of another day's setting sun, the cuts were clearly visible, raw, but healing. My aunt had used a mixture of alcohol and iron salts that night to wash away the symbol. Later she explained that iron, the only substance known to repel magic, was poisonous to beings like demons and fae who were made of pure magical energy. The iron had done its work to break Afnergu'alak's hold on me, and she insisted I bathe the wounds in the same mixture every day for a month as the cuts healed and formed into scars. She seemed to think, or at least hope, that time and proper care would wash the experience away, my memories of that night forgotten or buried too deep to hurt me.

What I didn't tell her was that every night I had to wrench myself awake from terrible nightmares, visions that made me sob Meg's name. My right hand would throb and I could sense…something. It waited, silent and watchful, and if I closed my eyes, sometimes I could see blood-red orbs staring at me from the underside of my eyelids. Unsurprisingly, I wasn't getting much sleep these days. I'd taken to sitting in the sunlight streaming through my window. I had no idea what good it did, but it made me feel better. Nothing bothered me during the day. But at night...I started to fear the dark for the things it brought and the memories it preserved.

I didn't tell my aunt what was going on in my head because, once she'd cleaned and patched me up, she'd warned me that if she ever caught me meddling with witchcraft again in any form, she would personally ensure that I was locked up in a mental ward to "protect" me. I absolutely believed her threat, and didn't blame her in the slightest. That's probably what I needed anyway, to be locked up. At least then I couldn't hurt anyone.

But no, I would be good. For now, at least. My aunt had saved me from a fate worse than death. She had cleaned up my mess and had shown great generosity toward Meg's mother for my sake. The least I could do was keep my nose clean until I was eighteen and no longer her problem. Then, I could finally get started finding out who murdered my parents.

No, I hadn't forgotten. It was one of the few things that kept me going, especially at night when the nightmares came. It gave me an anchor, a focus, to help ride out the crippling waves of grief I felt whenever I remembered I truly couldn't bring them back.

But I could afford to wait. I wasn't worried about police investigations or DNA evidence. None of that held answers. My parents' murder had obviously involved magic, so I knew I would only get to the bottom of it through magical means.

What a silly lot we are.

My father's words in that dream I'd had about the prince and the lion kept coming back to me. I pondered them during the long hours that I sat and stared out the window. Had it been coincidence? Or some otherworldly poke at the irony of fate and my father's doomed attempts to protect me?

And with my father's part of my dream seemingly explained, I was still trying to figure out what my mother had been telling me to wait for. Would I ever know?

"Doing all right there, young man?"

I turned to see Peter float through my closed door. "Still think knocking is for mere mortals, I see."

"I—well, pardon me. I can't exactly—"

"Relax, old man. It's called a joke. You seriously need to work on those buttons of yours. They're way too easy to push." A hint of a smile touched my lips, but it didn't last long, and I turned to look back out the window, wishing the sun would stay a little longer.

"Rough day, eh?" Peter halted beside me, staring out the window too. He had his imaginary pipe out and was puffing slowly on it.

I shrugged. "Same as every other day."

"Well, if you would leave your room once in a while, I'm sure we could change that."

Shaking my head, I got up to turn the light on. It was starting to get dark outside. "I like the quiet."

"I believe you mean you like to sulk," Peter countered.

I rolled my eyes. At least one thing was back to normal.

That reminded me of something I'd been meaning to do for days, but still hadn't worked myself up to. Well, now was as good a time as any.

"Uh…Peter?"

"Hmm?" he said, mouth full of invisible pipe.

"…Thanks…for coming back. You saved my life."

"Oh pish-tosh. It was nothing. I couldn't exactly stay away, now could I? You were—are—my task. It's rather hard to avoid the very reason for your existence, wouldn't you say?"

"I dunno." I shrugged. "I don't even *know* the reason for my existence, so how could I avoid it? How do I even know if existence has a meaning?" I stared bleakly out the window at the disappearing light, willing it to stay.

Peter's ghostly hand reached out and patted me gently on the shoulder. "Now, now. It's not as bad as all that. Everything has a meaning, my boy. Just because we lack the wisdom or cosmic sight to see it does not mean it isn't there. Be patient. Things will become more clear as time goes on. If we knew what to expect starting out, life would be rather boring, now wouldn't it?"

I snorted, but didn't argue. Maybe Peter liked stumbling around in the dark, but I wanted answers. And I knew he had some of them, too. I simply had to figure out how to worm them out of him.

For now, though, it was nice just to have company, even if it didn't fix anything. I was still lost, still walking a dark road that led to who knew where. I was still guilty of many mistakes. But at least the ache in my chest wasn't so bad. And when the faces of the dead haunted my waking thoughts and grief threatened to drown me, I could always turn to Peter and ask him if he was wearing any underwear beneath his dressing gown.

A Message to My Readers:

Thanks so much for reading *Accidental Witch*, the first install-
ment of the Dark Roads trilogy that explores the backstory of
"Professional Witch" and ne'er-do-well Sebastian Blackwell.
If you enjoyed the story and want to see more published,
please take a moment to post an honest review. Reviews are
very helpful and a great way to show support for your
favorite authors. Book two is in the works, so in the mean-
time, check out the link below to sign up for my newsletter
and get a free book to start you off on *Love, Lies, and Hocus
Pocus - The Lily Singer Adventures,* a series that co-stars Sebastian as an adult.
www.lydiasherrer.com/subscribe

(my newsletter goes out twice a month with publishing
updates, free books, and giveaways)

You can read more about the *Lily Singer Adventures* here:
www.loveliesandhocuspocus.com

Turn the page to check out a preview of Book 1 in the *Lily
Singer Adventures*

LOVE, LIES, AND HOCUS POCUS: BEGINNINGS

Now in paperback and ebook

LOVE, LIES, AND HOCUS POCUS:
BEGINNINGS

Lily Singer wished she could simply say her date was going badly and leave it at that. But such a gross understatement was against her nature. To be accurate, she would have to admit it was in the top five worst, if not in the top three. This wasn't totally unexpected. Most—actually, all—of her dates were men she'd met online who, inevitably, weren't as cute as their profile pictures suggested. Awkward and bookish, she found it much easier to start virtual, as opposed to real, conversations. Speed dating and blind dates were out of the question due to her abysmal social skills. Well, that, and the fact that she was a wizard.

No, not a witch. A wizard.

"Soo…when you said you had diet restrictions, what you meant was you could only eat burgers?" Lily asked, trying to keep the sarcasm out of her voice. Though she suspected the only way her date would notice sarcasm was if it was dressed up like a cheeseburger.

"Huh?" Jerry Slate, a good hundred pounds larger and ten years older than his profile picture suggested, looked up from his second burger to stare, confused, at her face.

"When we were setting up the date, you asked if you could pick the restaurant because you said you had diet restrictions," Lily reminded him.

"Oh, yeah. I have a sensitive stomach. I can only eat 100% pure beef burgers, and they have to be grass-fed. Free-range, you know? None of that GMO stuff. This place uses the best ingredients out there."

Lily resisted the urge to roll her eyes, consoling herself with the thought that it was better to be taken to a gourmet, environmentally friendly burger restaurant than, heaven forbid, a *normal* burger restaurant.

Looking to the side, she gazed longingly through the restaurant's front windows to the sunlit street, busy with lunchtime traffic. If only she knew how to teleport, she could escape this awkward situation with minimal embarrassment.

"So…" she tried again. "How's your gaming campaign going?"

"Oh, it's fantastic," Jerry enthused past a mouthful of half-chewed but—let's not forget—grass-fed burger. Not slowing his consumption of burger, fries, and a handmade root beer float, he launched into a detailed description of his gaming group's latest campaign against…someone. Lily couldn't remember who.

It was a topic she could safely rely on to keep him talking for a good while, though it bored her almost to tears. Boredom was preferable, however, to the awkward silence interspersed with chewing sounds she'd suffered through for the first half of their date.

Funny, she'd thought that, in person, Jerry would be more inquisitive. That was before she'd been aware of his burger obsession. As she absentmindedly separated the carrot coins from the rest of her salad and stacked them into a tiny, walled fortress between her and her droning date, she realized he hadn't asked her a single question beyond the perfunctory

"How are you?" since they'd met outside some twenty minutes before. From the time they'd entered the restaurant, his entire attention had been devoted to ordering and eating, though he had, at least, disengaged a few brain cells long enough to inform her of the best items on the menu.

Come to think of it, he hadn't been very inquisitive online, either. But Lily was good at asking questions through virtual chat. It was like doing research in a search engine. Type in a question, then browse through the resultant dump of information to find your answer.

When asked a question, especially if said question had anything to do with himself, Jerry was obligingly verbose. He went into great detail, as long as that detail involved the hundred different titles in his grunge rock music collection, or his daring feats in the latest sneak attack against his group's unsuspecting, now-no-longer allies.

It wasn't as if she'd had soaring expectations. She'd just hoped for some intelligent conversation about, oh, say, books. Or history. Or philosophy. Or anything that mattered, really.

Some people improved upon face-to-face acquaintance. Jerry was not one of them. Neither was she, come to think of it. But she, at least, didn't bore anyone with loving descriptions of each book in her expansive personal library unless she knew, for a fact, that the person was a bibliophile.

Hands nervously smoothing down the dark fabric of her pencil skirt, she cast about desperately for an excuse to prematurely end the date. She intended to block Jerry Slate from her dating profile as soon as she got home.

Ignoring the gaming babble coming from the other side of the table, Lily concentrated on the fork she held in her hand as an idea came to her. She whispered the words for a simple heat transference spell, her other hand wrapped around the power-anchor amulet she wore tied to her wrist like a bracelet. Her body heat began to seep into the piece of metal, making it grow warm as she grew cooler. When she judged it was sufficiently hot, she made a startled gesture, dropping it dramatically onto the table as she jerked back in her chair.

"Ouch!" she yelped.

"Huh?" Jerry said, stopping mid-sentence. It seemed to be his favorite word, along with *oh*.

"I wasn't paying attention and tried to pick up my fork. It's very hot. It burned my hand. They must have just washed it in an industrial washer."

Jerry reached forward to touch the fork experimentally, hand stopping short as he felt the heat emanating from the offending utensil.

"Gosh, that *is* hot. Are you okay? You don't look so good." Jerry's brow furrowed in confusion. Not even he was absentminded enough to miss the fact that their silverware had been sitting, quite cool and harmless, for a good fifteen minutes since they'd gotten there.

Lily made a show of feeling her forehead, hoping to redirect his attention. "I feel all clammy. I should probably go home. I could be getting sick. Thanks so much for the food!"

With a touch of guilt, she fled the restaurant, not looking back. If she had, she would have felt better. Jerry's momentarily stunned face quickly smoothed over as he noticed the untouched burger at her place and, not wanting to waste food, began demolishing it as well.

The warm summer air felt good on her face as Lily drove her Honda Civic down Ponce De Leon Avenue, heading back to Agnes Scott College campus. Her soft, chestnut brown hair frizzed in the humidity, despite being pulled back into a severe bun. At least it wasn't whipping around her face and getting stuck in her glasses, as it would've been had she worn it down.

Verdant foliage and colorful flowers crowded around the sidewalks, businesses, and houses lining the street. The abundant plant life was one of the things Lily loved most about Atlanta. It made the place feel less like a big city and more like a well-tended neighborhood. Plus, it reminded her of home in the Alabama backwaters.

Pulling into the college's employee parking lot, Lily gathered her things and headed across campus toward McCain Library. Though originally founded as an elementary school in 1889, Agnes Scott had become a college by the early 1900s. McCain Library, built in 1936, consisted of four main floors, a grand, vault-ceilinged reading hall, and three attached floors dedicated to the stacks. It was a beautiful example of Gothic architecture meeting utilitarian building needs and, along with the other Gothic and Victorian red brick-and-stone buildings around campus, made for a beautiful and relaxing atmosphere.

Though it was Saturday, Lily preferred to take refuge in the library and bury herself in paperwork rather than go home and risk the urge to mope about. The tall ceilings, majestic architecture, and quiet atmosphere would calm her in a way no amount of tea or chocolate could. And, of course, there was the comforting smell of books.

She passed a few groups of girls relaxing or studying on the green—it was a women's college, and non-employee males were discouraged from hanging around campus. On this sunny day, the blue sky and warm grass had lured most students outside to study, so she saw only a few scattered girls working quietly in the library's grand reading hall as she made her way to her office.

Her office was a spacious room on the first floor, with a

high ceiling and expansive windows. Tall bookshelves covered most of the other three walls, and a large, mahogany desk dominated the center of the room.

With a sigh, she dropped her purse onto one of the two visitor's chairs—both currently pushed up against her bookshelves as stepladders—and sat down at her desk. The desk's dark wood surface was polished to a shine, and each item on it was arranged neatly. Her computer, pencil holder, and file organizer were placed just so, cleaned spotless, and free of dust. Her shiny, brass nameplate was centered and aligned perfectly parallel to the edge of her desk. It read:

Lillian Singer: Administrative Coordinator/Archives Manager

It was a prestigious position for Lily's relatively young twenty-five years of age. But the fact that the previous archives manager, Madam Barrington, had taken Lily under her wing and personally groomed her for the job had made Lily the obvious choice when Madam Barrington retired a year ago. Beyond the Madam's training and endorsement, however, Lily had been well prepared for the job. With four years of undergraduate work-study in the stacks, not to mention two years as head librarian after graduation, her BA in history and minor in classics were just icing on the cake.

Of course, Lily's love of books, organized nature, and library experience weren't the only reasons behind Madam Barrington's choice. The real reason was she'd needed someone to take over as curator of the "Basement"—a secret archive beneath the McCain Library containing a private collection of occult books on magic, wizardry, and arcane science. Being a wizard herself, Madam Barrington had recognized Lily's innate ability soon after she'd begun her freshman year. The older woman had considered it her duty to keep the then-young and inexperienced girl's insatiable curiosity from getting her killed. Madam Barrington had always been frustratingly vague about exactly *who* owned the books. Her job, and now Lily's, was to care for them, study them, and act as gatekeeper to their knowledge. Only once had Lily seen Madam Barrington allow access, and that was to a very old gentleman who'd arrived late one night and whispered something in the Madam's ear. When Lily had asked how she would know to let someone in, Madam Barrington had simply smiled her mysterious smile and said, "You'll know."

Lily's worries had faded over time, as not a single person had ever appeared requesting access in the year since she'd taken over. Though the Madam was tight-lipped on the subject, Lily got the impression there weren't many wizards left in the world. Of those who did still exist, only a select few knew of the Basement's whereabouts. That was fine with Lily, as the Basement was her own personal heaven. Knowledge was the next best thing to life itself, and knowledge of the unknown and mysterious was something she'd craved ever since she could remember, long before she had found out she was a wizard and started learning the craft under Madam Barrington's tutelage.

That thirst got her into trouble on some occasions. But just as often, it resulted in exciting discoveries which added to her already encyclopedic mind. Having all of Agnes Scott's stacks, archives, and considerable online research capability at her fingertips was a dream come true, not even counting the Basement.

Now, having settled into her leather desk chair in the sunlit office, Lily relished a moment of glowing satisfaction as she surveyed her domain. Taking a deep breath, she let the disappointment and frustration of an abysmal date fade away, refocusing instead on all the good things in life. Books. Tea. Chocolate. Cats. More books. Who cared about men and dating when you had all that at your fingertips?

Speaking of men…

There was a flourishing knock on her office door and, without waiting for an answer, a tall, lanky man with mussed brown hair came swaggering through. His untucked shirt and worn pants gave him a disheveled look, though he walked as if he wore the finest Italian suit in all the world. On a leather cord around his neck hung a triangular stone with a hole in the middle. She'd always wondered what it was but wasn't one to ask personal questions.

His grand entrance was marred slightly by the absence of her visitor chairs in front of her desk, which interrupted his smooth transition from swaggering in to lounging handsomely across one of them. Instead, he had to reverse direction and pull a chair over from a bookshelf before settling his lanky form into it.

Lily hid a smile, trying to look stern instead.

"Sebastian, how many times do I have to tell you, you're not supposed to be wandering around campus. This is a *women's* college, and private property."

"Pish." Sebastian waved a hand unconcernedly. "If you're so worried about it, call security." His eyes were bright with mischief. As if to emphasize his complete lack of concern, he reached into his pocket and drew out that silly coin he was always playing with. He liked to roll it over his knuckles and perform other sleights of hand, knowing it annoyed her when he showed off.

Lily rolled her eyes. She knew that he knew that she wouldn't call security. At least, not until he'd annoyed her to the point of losing her temper, which wasn't often.

"And to what do I owe the pleasure of your visit?" Chin propped in the palm of her hand, Lily raised a skeptical eyebrow in his direction and did her best to ignore the coin. Unlike most men, he picked up on sarcasm like a child picked up candy—every time, and with great glee.

"Oh, you know. Just paying a social visit. It's been *far* too long, don't you think? How's the ol' biddy doing these days?"

Lily's eyes narrowed. Sebastian practically oozed casual nonchalance, which meant he was up to something.

"I'd like to hear you call her that to her face. And your great-aunt is just fine. The last time I visited her, she was enjoying a day in the garden."

"Still kicking, eh?" Sebastian snorted, twirling a bit of his bangs around one finger. "Far be it for the great Madam Barrington to grow old and die like the rest of us."

Lily frowned. "That's quite disrespectful. You know very well that wizards tend to live longer than everyone else. If you're going to insult my mentor, at least have the decency to do it behind my back."

Sebastian laughed, making a dismissive gesture. "Lighten up, Lily. It was just a joke. She *did* disown me, after all. I'd say that at least gives me the right to make jokes about her."

Unlike his great-aunt, Sebastian Blackwell was a witch. No, not a wizard. A witch. The difference came from the source of their power: a wizard's was innate, cultivated through discipline and study, channeled and shaped by will and word, often supplemented by a collection of arcane objects; a witch's was entirely acquired through the delicate art of give and take. Many beings—spirits, demons, and magical creatures—were happy to give aid or favors to the right person in exchange for the right thing. Others could be tricked, a few could be forced, and some were to be avoided altogether.

To drastically oversimplify, wizards were born; witches were made. Though Madam Barrington was always vague when it came to wizard culture, Lily at least knew that not all children of wizards were wizards themselves. It was genetic, like eye or hair color. The stronger the wizard and purer the blood, the better chance of passing on the gene, or whatever it was that enabled wizards to manipulate magic. So, being old, proper, and a traditionalist, Madam Barrington viewed witchcraft as disgraceful and lowly, not to mention dangerous. Only shameless fools with no true ability engaged in such activities. Sebastian's view was, since he couldn't be a wizard, he might as well be something. And anyway, he made a very good witch.

Lily happened to agree with Sebastian but never said so to her mentor. It took adept social skills, a clever nature, charisma, and force of will to live such a life and come out on top. She would make a dreadful witch, as evidenced by how terrible she was at interacting with anyone except the few friends—or annoying acquaintances in the case of Sebastian—with whom she was comfortable. The ease with which Sebastian glided around social situations made her quite jealous. He was everything she wasn't: handsome, confident, popular, and good at whatever he put his mind to, though he rarely put his mind to anything unless absolutely necessary. For, as it turned out, he was also lazy, untidy, and undisciplined. He would have made a terrible wizard.

Putting a note of briskness in her voice—she *did* have paperwork to go through, after all—Lily fixed Sebastian with a stare and asked more firmly, "What do you want, Sebastian? I know you're up to something."

"Well it sounds terrible when you put it like that," he said, grinning.

"Sebastian," she said in a warning tone.

"Okay, okay. I'll get to the point. You're no fun." Sebastian raised his hands in surrender, muttering the last part, disgruntled.

"I have plenty of fun. It's called reading books."

"Uh-huh. Right." Now it was Sebastian's turn to roll his eyes. "Anyway, I need your…consulting services."

"You mean you need my help?" Lily asked sweetly, the start of a smug grin pulling at her lips.

"No, I need you as a consultant, one professional to another." Putting his coin away, he straightened in the chair, smiling and spreading his hands wide in a disarming gesture. It was obviously meant to reassure her, but she was not impressed.

"Really? Professional? Since when are you a 'professional' witch?"

Sebastian adopted an indignant look. "Since a while. Can't you just see it? Sebastian Blackwell: Professional Witch!" he said dramatically, lifting his arm to paint an imaginary sign in the air. "I have business cards and everything." His hand dove into the back pocket of his jeans and produced a rather bent card, which he flipped onto her desk with a flick of his wrist.

"Fascinating," Lily commented, voice fairly dripping with amused sarcasm as she examined the card. The front showed a headshot of Sebastian—handsome without trying, as usual —beside his name and contact details printed in an overly curly font. The back had a stylized monogram in purple and gold.

"And what services do you offer as a 'professional' witch?" she asked, fighting the urge to laugh.

"Oh, casting out evil spirits, contacting loved ones who've passed on, consulting the fates, various potions. You know, the normal stuff superstitious rich people believe in."

"Charlatanry, you mean?" Lily asked, eyebrow raised again.

"Hey! I *can* actually do most of the stuff people ask for. When they want something impossible, like talking to their dead pet parrot or predicting the lottery, I make something up to keep them happy. Ignorance is bliss and all that. No harm done."

Lily gave him a hard stare over her glasses. She hated that saying. Ignorance was one of the least blissful things in the world, in her opinion. She believed that "the truth will make you free," a saying which was carved into the rafters of McCain Library's grand reading hall. But she reminded herself that Sebastian wasn't her problem and got back to the point. "So, what do you need my 'consulting services' for?"

"Well, I got hired for this job, see, and I've run across something more up your alley than mine."

"Is that so?" Her tone remained disinterested. She'd been pulled into too many of his wild schemes not to be hesitant. Though, to be fair, she'd egged him on in many of those schemes, whenever there was knowledge to be had or a new spell to try. Curiosity often got the better of her, and Sebastian knew it.

"Yes, it is so."

"Explain."

"I was hired to cast out this evil spirit, and it turns out the spirit isn't evil. He's actually a pretty nice guy. The real culprit is a spell put on the house almost a hundred years ago because of some jilted lover. The spirit has stayed behind to warn people away from the house ever since. So, even though he has, technically, been haunting the house, even if I get him to go away, that doesn't fix the problem, and I won't get my money."

"Let me guess: You need me to come figure out what the spell is and get rid of it, right?"

"A very astute conclusion! I'll give you an award later." Sebastian gave her a lazy smile and a wink.

Lily was not amused. "You know, you really shouldn't insult the person you're asking help from," she said, giving him a level stare. "And I still haven't heard any compelling reason why I should help you."

"Ah, yes, well." Sebastian backpedaled a bit. Lily knew his

good looks and charming ways usually got him what he needed, so she took delight in giving him as much trouble as possible. A very small part of her liked to watch him squirm. Well, maybe not so small a part. "Besides helpi—I mean consulting for the sake of our professional friendship, there's a collection of occult books in the house, which the owner has agreed to give me as part of the payment. I would, of course, hand them over to you, should you provide the afore-mentioned consultation...thingy."

Despite her better judgment, Lily's interest was piqued. New books did that to her. She could never resist learning new things. And if these were genuine books on magic, not silly mumbo jumbo written by someone who *thought* they were a wizard, they could be valuable indeed. She was always looking to add to the Basement's collection, not to mention expand her personal library.

Still mulling over the possibility of new books, she caught sight of Sebastian's smug smile. She frowned. It annoyed her to be so predictable, but sometimes it couldn't be helped. Sebastian knew her well enough to guess what was going on in her head. He knew that as soon as he mentioned books, he'd already won.

After a few more moments of silence, just to make him sweat, Lily finally nodded. "Fine, I'll help. And wipe that smug grin off your face, Mr. Blackwell. Those books had better be the real thing, or I'll have a word with your great-aunt about all this 'Professional Witch' nonsense."

Sebastian paled slightly at her threat but covered it with a shrug and a laugh. "As if the old bat could disdain my exis-tence any more than she already does."

"If I were you, I'd be more worried about what *else* she might do besides disdain it. Now, when can we look at this house? I'm not going to shuffle around my work schedule for you."

"Why not now?" Sebastian asked, rising and bowing smoothly, arm outstretched towards the door.

"Hmm…where is it?" Lily asked, considering.

"South, past Fort Benning. It's on the Chattahoochee River, a bit north of Eufaula, Alabama, before the river runs into the reservoir. About a two-and-a-half hour drive. If we leave now, we can spend a few hours poking around the house and have you back home by dinnertime."

Lily glanced at her watch. It was one o'clock. Her failed date with Jerry felt like years ago already, though it had only been an hour. Despite herself, the prospect of an unknown, malignant spell—and new books to explore—was too tempting to delay.

"Alright, let's do it," she said, standing up from her desk and moving to collect her purse. "You'll have to meet me at my apartment first, though. I need to change and get a few supplies." She was still wearing the pretty blue blouse, dark pencil skirt, and high heels she'd donned for her date.

"Sure thing, Lil." Sebastian tipped an imaginary hat and started for the door.

"How many times do I have to tell you—" Lily began, exasperated. But he was already out the door and down the hall. "—don't call me that," she finished in a subdued tone. Sighing, she gathered her things and followed him out, locking her office behind her.

Thanks for reading! Continue the adventure by subscribing to Lydia's newsletter to receive a free starter book in the Lily Singer Adventures collection. www.lydiasherrer.com/subscribe

ABOUT THE AUTHOR

Author of magic, tea, and snark-filled urban fantasy novels, with a few science fiction and dystopian stories thrown in for good measure, Lydia Sherrer believes the world is built on dreams and enjoys adding hers to the mix. She is convinced that dark chocolate and tea are legiti-  mate sources of nutrition, and one day hopes to visit every country in the world. Currently residing in Louisville, KY, she is supported by her wonderful and creative husband and their two loud, but adorable, cats.

You can connect with Lydia online!

Read all about Lydia and her books: lydiasherrer.com/about
Like her page: facebook.com/lydiasherrerauthor
Follow her on Goodreads (just search for Lydia Sherrer)
Follow on Twitter: @LydiaSherrer twitter.com/lydiasherrer
Follow on Instagram: lydiasherrer instagram.com/lydiasherrer
Listen to her ocarina music: youtube.com/c/lydiasherrer

www.ingramcontent.com/pod-product-compliance
Lightning Source LLC
Chambersburg PA
CBHW020958120726
47905CB00009B/2743